The
Lies
We
Tell

Also by Katie Zhao

The Dragon Warrior
The Fallen Hero
How We Fall Apart

The Lies We Tell

KATIE ZHAO

BLOOMSBURY

NEW YORK   LONDON   OXFORD   NEW DELHI   SYDNEY

BLOOMSBURY YA
Bloomsbury Publishing Inc., part of Bloomsbury Publishing Plc
1385 Broadway, New York, NY 10018

BLOOMSBURY and the Diana logo are trademarks of Bloomsbury Publishing Plc

First published in the United States of America in August 2022 by Bloomsbury YA

Bloomsbury books may be purchased for business or promotional use. For information on bulk purchases please contact Macmillan Corporate and Premium Sales Department at specialmarkets@macmillan.com

This is a work of fiction. Names, characters, businesses, places, events, locales, and incidents are either the products of the author's imagination or used in a fictitious manner. Any resemblance to actual persons, living or dead, or actual events is purely coincidental.

Library of Congress Cataloging-in-Publication Data
Names: Zhao, Katie, author.
Title: The lies we tell / by Katie Zhao.
Description: New York: Bloomsbury Children's Books, 2022.
Summary: During her freshman year at college, Anna Xu investigates the unsolved on-campus murder of her former babysitter, as she and an old rival have to team up to look into the hate crimes happening around campus.
Identifiers: LCCN 2021056226 (print) | LCCN 2021056227 (e-book)
ISBN 978-1-5476-0399-2 (hardcover) • ISBN 978-1-5476-0400-5 (e-book)
Subjects: CYAC: Hate crimes—Fiction. | Murder—Fiction. | Chinese Americans—Fiction. | Universities and colleges—Fiction. | LCGFT: Novels.
Classification: LCC PZ7.1.Z513 Li 2022 (print) | LCC PZ7.1.Z513 (e-book) | DDC [Fic]—dc23
LC record available at https://lccn.loc.gov/2021056226

Book design by John Candell
Typeset by Westchester Publishing Services
Printed and bound in the U.S.A.
2 4 6 8 10 9 7 5 3

To find out more about our authors and books visit www.bloomsbury.com and sign up for our newsletters.

For the Asian girls we failed

The Lies We Tell

February 14, 2015

IN HER PRECIOUS LAST MOMENTS, she felt so very isolated. There was someone there with her, and yet, she had never been more alone.

She was certain this couldn't be happening to her. Yet all the sensations were so very, very real. Until this moment, she'd never known it could be possible to exist beyond the point of terror like this.

"My sweet little doll," he said, and his breath was hot and suffocating on her skin. It was a chilly fall night, but her body was coated with sweat. The woods around her were silent and still, as though the trees themselves were simply standing by, watching the unspeakable happen to her. Help, she knew, would not be coming. Not for her.

"You'll be mine forever."

The man was hissing more words, but she couldn't register them.

Spots danced in her vision, obscuring the trees, matching the stars in the clearing above her. They say your life flashes before your eyes when you're about to die, and for her, it was the smiling faces of Mama and Baba that swam in her mind. Mama and Baba had immigrated to this country—for her. They had endured every hardship in their path—for her. Mama and Baba had given her the world. How could a stranger snatch it away? She was filled with regret not for herself, but for her family.

Her senses were dulled. She was slow, too slow to react, too slow to save herself. She was neither here nor there, suspended precariously somewhere in between. And then pain, cold—and down she spiraled into darkness.

Chapter One

I SAT INSIDE THE NOISY and busy Beijing airport, listening to the announcer state flight changes over the intercom. I held the last of my grandmother's dòu shā bāo in my hand. The egg yolk–glazed red bean bun had long since cooled from Nai Nai's oven but would still be delicious and full of flavor. Through the window I could see that my airplane had already arrived. Just half an hour left until boarding, and then departure.

Outside, the city turned grayer as evening fell until Beijing was a glittering mass of lights beyond the airport. A city that sprawled and stretched on for miles in every direction, Beijing was the place Ma and Ba had grown up, where generations of my family had been born and raised. It might have been my home, but now was my second home across the ocean. A breathtaking city in a beautiful country that I hadn't visited since I was a tiny girl.

Because *home* home was the red-bricked house surrounded by a white picket fence back in Michigan, where my parents and I lived.

This had been my last—and freest—summer vacation before I became a college student, and I'd spent it visiting relatives. Three months was over too soon, and I was headed back to the States to start my new life as a college freshman just days from now. All that remained of my whirlwind summer in Beijing were my memories, photographs, and my grandmother's red bean buns. The memories I'd made with my distant family were already beginning to fade. I desperately tried to hold on to them, but it was like cupping water in my palm. Too difficult to hold on to, too easy to slip away.

My attention shifted back to the gate attendant, who called for passengers to begin boarding. I waited for the third boarding zone and joined the line right behind a tall, lanky guy who was tapping his foot impatiently. There seemed to be some kind of holdup, and we were standing for a while—long enough for my stomach to start growling again.

I'd been planning to save this last red bean bun for the actual plane ride, but as I waited and stared, I couldn't hold off any longer. Slowly I unwrapped the plastic wrapping. I closed my eyes and opened my mouth to take a bite, preparing to savor this one.

Then something—an elbow—careened into my arm and knocked the sweet treat from my hands and onto the airport floor. My eyes popped open in shock. "No," I groaned. My last red bean bun, lying on the dirty floor. Wasted, just like that. As the daughter of two bakers, I felt as though I'd committed a sin—or maybe that the person who'd caused me to drop the bun was at fault.

The guy who'd bumped into me apologized in Mandarin, and then turned around.

The boy was around my age, maybe slightly older. He had unruly jet-black hair and dark, piercing black eyes. He was tall, even compared to me, and at five-eight I was one of the tallest people I knew. It annoyed me that he had an air of academic handsomeness about him: good looks without trying, and eyes that saw past the person in front of him, as though he spent his time worrying more what was happening between the pages of a book than in real life. I knew that expression well—it was the same one I saw every time I looked in the mirror. The guy had at least half a foot on me and a scowl on his face.

I wouldn't let myself be intimidated, though. He'd knocked my food out of my hand. I hadn't done anything wrong here. That was the last bun my grandmother had made for me, and it would be years before I'd have the chance to come visit Beijing and eat her delicious cooking again.

My annoyance grew. I longed to yell all of this at the boy, but he was just a stranger. I'd never see him again once we got off this flight. There was no point, and besides, I'd been taught to never make a scene. Plus, if I unleashed that, I'd no doubt receive a one-way ticket to getting escorted off the premises by airport security.

So instead I rolled my eyes and looked away, pointedly not accepting the guy's apology.

"Rude," I heard him mutter.

"It's ruder to cause someone to drop their last red bean bun," I said under my breath.

"What was that?"

Don't snap back, I thought. And then, a moment later, a realization struck me—he'd spoken in English, and he'd understood *my* English. Oops. Already there were a few people around us who were studying us with great interest, as though waiting for the tension to break out into a fight. Making a spectacle of myself was the last thing I wanted to do in my last moments in Beijing, so with a great effort, I turned away and pretended to be very interested in the airplanes outside the window.

Eventually the line moved us down the gangway and onto the plane. As luck would have it (eye roll) the boy took his seat just one row forward and across the aisle from me. We weren't sitting close enough for it to seriously bug me, but we were just close enough that every time I glanced in his direction, I was reminded again of my poor last red bean bun.

There was a more immediate problem, though, in the form of my seat neighbor being a preteen boy who wouldn't stop bouncing his legs up and down and cursing every few minutes as he played on his Nintendo Switch.

This was shaping up to be the longest, most torturous flight ever. I put on my headphones and scrolled through Apple Podcasts, pausing on my favorite true crime podcast, *Unsolved Murders*. I pressed play on the latest episode upload and closed my eyes. The host's soothing voice filled my ear and I drifted off to sleep.

I could have only been asleep for an hour or so when I woke up with a jolt, my neck in a painfully cramped position.

"Die, monsters!" yelled the kid next to me.

There was no way I would be going back to sleep.

Yawning and stretching, I turned my head and saw that across the aisle, the boy had picked up a book. I couldn't see the cover or even if the book was in Chinese or English, but I could tell it was a thick volume. It was a sharp reminder that I still hadn't finished all of my assigned summer reading for my first college courses. Maybe this guy was a college student, too. Not that it mattered one way or another.

I fished my copy of Homer's *The Iliad* out of my bag and buried my nose into it. It had been assigned to me for my Great Books class, a classics course that every honors student had to take as part of the program. In high school I'd been a model student, a reputation I intended to keep up at university. I'd read a handful of pages earlier in the summer, but the Wikipedia summary of the ancient Greek epic had made it sound more exciting than it was.

If other students were getting their reading done now, then I would, too. The boy likely had no idea that we were currently in competition, but I wouldn't be outdone. For the duration of the first flight, I immersed myself in *The Iliad* and the siege of the city of Troy, breaking my concentration only to eat a tasteless midflight meal. Annoying as it was, there was a one-hour stop in Toronto. By the time it was time to board my second flight, I was already sick of traveling, but at least there was only a little over an hour left of the twenty-hour travel day. The guy from the other flight was on this flight, too, but I pretended not to notice him, and he pretended not to notice me.

The rest of the way home, though, I couldn't help but wonder who that boy was.

Chapter Two

"ANNA!"

My mother's voice was sharp and loud, rising above even the din of airport chaos. That was Ma for you. Though she was a tiny woman, her presence commanded attention. Years of shouting in Asian supermarkets and yelling orders from the kitchen in the family dessert eatery, Sweetea, had trained her vocal cords more than sufficiently. In another life, she could've been one hell of a singer.

I lugged my enormous black suitcase toward them. My arms and legs ached from sitting in a cramped position for fourteen hours straight, and my eyes were strained from reading an entire Greek epic in one flight. My evidently one-sided competition with Guy Across the Aisle had exhausted me.

"Hi," I said. I hadn't seen my parents in three months, not since they'd dropped me off at the airport before my whirlwind summer in Beijing, but we didn't hug. My parents weren't exactly the hugging type.

"You've gained weight," said Ba, who stared at me, though not in disapproval.

It would've been a miracle if I hadn't gained weight, given how I'd basically eaten my way through Beijing this summer. And I had no regrets about it. The food in the States just couldn't compare. "You've gained gray hairs," I retorted.

As my parents helped me bring my luggage into the car, they launched into some gossip that they'd clearly been dying to get off their chest.

"Business at Sweetea hasn't been as good as usual lately," said Ma.

The silence that followed was pregnant with expectation. After a pause, I asked, "Why?"

"You remember the Lus, right?"

Of course I did. As my parents had told the story, their rivalry with the Lus went way back. Mr. Lu had been Ba's academic rival since they had both attended Beijing University together. Ba remained convinced to this day that Mr. Lu had been cheating the entire time in university and never got caught. In their shared classes, he consistently would outrank my father by just a few points. Eventually, in a twisted stroke of fate, our families ended up settling in the same area in the States.

Chris Lu and I had attended public school and Chinese school together up until seventh grade, when he abruptly moved back to China because of his dad's work. Last I'd heard, he was attending international school there.

But when we were in school together, we'd been locked in competition to be the top student in class. Everything from mathlete competitions to Chinese speech contests to science fairs, the winner always came down to Chris or me. Like, I *still* remembered how in third grade, Chris had taken first place in the speech contest, while I'd placed second, trailing behind by only two points. And when I'd stuck out my hand to shake his, Chris had stuck his tongue out—so quickly that only I could see it—and then shook my hand in a false display of comradery. The parents had crowed over him, though. Chris had been like that—putting on a performance for the adults while being a real snot to me.

But I hadn't seen Chris in years, so in my imagination he looked roughly the same as he had in middle school, except taller and maybe with nicer hair now. Maybe his personality had even improved, though somehow I doubted it.

"What did the Lus do now?" I asked.

"They've opened a bakery down the street from ours," Ba grumbled.

"Oh, so that's why business hasn't been doing well?"

"The quality of our food is better than ever," Ma said, rather defensively.

I resisted the urge to point out that I hadn't said anything about the quality of Sweetea's food. My parents must have wanted another outlet to vent about the Lus and had been building up to this moment for the whole summer. The best strategy now was to let them rant and get it all off their chest.

As Ba and Ma continued to bash the Lus, I sighed and wished we could've just had this conversation over WeChat earlier in the summer so I didn't have to listen to it in person now.

WeChat was the texting app that had exploded in popularity all over China, and then spread overseas. It was basically

Facebook, Instagram, Twitter, Venmo—every social media app, all rolled into one. I'd read in an article that people could even get their laundry done and buy wine over the app. So far, all I'd used it for was sending my Chinese relatives the obligatory birthday and holiday wishes and asking Ma to please stop mass-spamming me with every new sticker she discovered.

"Can we talk about this later?" I asked as the car pulled out of the airport. This wasn't the first conversation I wanted to have with my parents after a summer away from them.

Mama turned around in her seat and stuffed a water bottle and an apple into my hands. It was her way of showing affection, making sure I was fed and hydrated. "Anna, how was Beijing?"

"The food was amazing," I said, biting into the apple.

"Food, food, food. Is that all you can talk about?" said my father.

"Well, we are a family that owns a bakery," I pointed out. Food had been so central to my upbringing that before I knew it, I'd developed a deep love for it—especially the Chinese desserts my parents served at the bakery, like sweet buns and pineapple cakes. "Don't worry, I didn't spend all my time in Beijing eating. We got to see the Great Wall, and I walked around a lot," I reminisced.

"Next time, we'll all go back together," Ma promised. "This summer, your father and I had too much business to take care of at Sweetea."

"Yeah. If we'd gone away to China for the summer, imagine how the Lus would have snatched all our customers away," Ba grumped.

And we were back to the topic of the Lus already. Well, at least the break had been nice while it lasted.

"What university is Chris going to?" I asked casually. "Did his parents post on social media or something?"

"I blocked the Lus on WeChat," Ma sniffed. I waited a beat. "Brookings."

Of course, same as me. Brookings was the top public university around this area, and unless you got into Harvard or Yale or something, it was the best college to attend with the discounted price tag of in-state tuition. Heck, even students who *did* get accepted into top Ivy Leagues would sometimes choose Brookings University over those schools.

"How do you know where Chris is going if you have the Lus blocked on WeChat?" I asked.

"I have my ways," Mama said mysteriously.

That was code for the fact that her friend circle of WeChat aunties had let her know. Those ladies always knew everyone's business.

Watching the familiar Michigan scenery of trees and small suburbia pass by, I sighed. Going away to college was supposed to be a fresh start to my life. Part of me wished I'd chosen a college that was much, much farther from the small town where I'd grown up, even though I knew I was going to thank myself for saving so much on tuition down the road. It couldn't be a good sign that that my college semester hadn't even started, yet there was already drama involving the Lus.

There was another reason I'd chosen Brookings, a reason beyond the pursuit of a prestigious education.

Seven years ago, a Brookings sophomore named Melissa Hong had been found—murdered—in the arboretum. The killer had never been caught, and the case had been buried, unsolved, all too soon. I followed the case online with a morbid sort of curiosity.

In middle school I discovered someone had created a Tumblr called *What Happened to Melissa,* documenting the case through online articles and newspaper reports. Whoever was behind the Tumblr would update every week, and I followed *What Happened to Melissa* like others followed their favorite shows. But in the end, there were too few details to make sense of why Melissa was murdered, even across all the articles and reports. Plus, the Tumblr hadn't been updated since 2017. It seemed that everyone, from the police to anonymous true crime bloggers, had given up.

But Melissa Hong had been my babysitter before she went off to college. I intended to find out the truth behind Melissa's murder. I couldn't even explain to myself why I *needed* to know what had happened to Melissa, besides the fact that I'd known her, she'd been nice to me, and she didn't deserve the unfortunate fate that had befallen her. The Hongs were old family friends, and they used to come over all the time for holiday parties, when Melissa and I would play video games and stuff our faces with sweets. The Hongs had moved back to China not long after their daughter's murder when it seemed like there would be no answers.

It wasn't right, what had happened to Melissa. Not just her murder, but also the fact that the case went unsolved and that her killer was walking free somewhere.

At the very least, while I was at Brookings, I had to try to find out what had really happened to Melissa Hong.

•‖———‖•

Monday, February 16, 2015
Tragedy Strikes Brookings University Campus
Undergraduate student's body found in woods
By AMY CHANG, GEORGE WILK,
AND BRANDY SMITH, Staff Writers

On Saturday, the body of a Brookings University student was found in the woods behind Central Campus. Though a full report is not available to the public, sources close to the *Brookings Daily* indicate that evidence points to murder committed through strangulation and blunt force trauma. The murderer's whereabouts are currently unknown. Evidence collected at the scene includes a note bearing the symbol of the Order of Alpha, a society that was officially disbanded from Brookings University in the 1950s. At this time, campus police stated they are still investigating the validity of the note.

University officials said the victim is confirmed to be sophomore Melissa Hong, 18, who was last seen alive attending an evening lecture at the Center for Chinese Studies. Her body was found five hours later around 12:30 a.m. by two graduate students passing through the woods.

"The note indicated some sort of affiliation with this rumored Order of Alpha," BU Police Chief Douglas James said on Sunday. "We are currently investigating into this matter with the dean. It's possible that the murderer is using this organization as a scapegoat, as so far there's been no concrete evidence that the Order is involved."

Hong's classmates brought up concerns about her recent strange behavior. "Melissa used to be the life of the party, but ever since second semester began, she'd become noticeably more reserved," said Alice Kim, Melissa's roommate. "She was rarely around to study or go out together anymore. We'd suspected she'd been keeping a secret boyfriend, but she'd always deny it if we brought it up."

"I'm horrified and shocked," said floor mate Tim McMaster. "Melissa was always really sweet and friendly. There's no way anyone had it out for her. This was probably some random psychopath who decided to choose a victim, and it just so happened to be her. I've never seen anyone suspicious hanging around Melissa's room or in the dorm, either."

"Melissa was friendly to everyone, but it seemed like she wasn't particularly close with any of us," noted Alice Kim. "I was her roommate, but I still felt like I didn't know her that well. She was passionate about one of her classes in particular—Introduction to Chinese Studies—and spent a lot of time at office hours and extra credit lectures. I don't know if that's helpful, but I did find that curious, since she was a premed major."

Brookings Daily was able to reach Professor Gregory Wittman of the East Asian Studies department, who taught Melissa Hong in his course Sources of East Asian Civilizations. "Melissa was one of the brightest, most dedicated students in my class," said the professor. "It's tragic, what happened to her."

Investigation will continue during the winter semester for Brookings University students.

"Melissa was an incredible person, and she had so much going for her. So many people are shocked and hurt about what happened to her. I just hope that one day the murderer will be caught and brought to justice," said West Tower 4th floor Residential Advisor Selena Sharma.

Campus police added five new security guards to patrol campus, Chief James noted.

Chapter Three

IT WAS ONLY MIDAFTERNOON BY the time we were home from the airport, but I was so jet-lagged that all I wanted to do was collapse into bed and sleep for days.

"At least have a bowl of zhōu before you sleep," insisted Ma. "You haven't eaten anything yet."

There was a pot on the stove, and I watched as my mother scooped steaming rice porridge out of it and into a large bowl. My stomach growled. Even though I'd had no appetite ever since finishing those bland airplane meals, now I was suddenly starving. Rice porridge was simple but filling, and it was just what I needed at the moment.

"Are you ready for school to start soon?" Ba asked, once we were all seated at the dining table with our rice porridge.

Most families who had been apart for months would've probably spent ages catching up on every little thing, but not mine. I was grateful for it, though. There was nothing that sounded less appealing to my jet-lagged brain right now than summarizing my entire trip.

I thought back to the college packing I'd done before leaving for Beijing, and then realized I had nothing packed except blankets and sheets. "Um, my bed stuff and clothes are all ready to go, at least."

"What about everything else?" Ba asked shrewdly.

"I'm . . . gonna work on it."

"Be quick. There's not much time before move-in day," Ma said. "We did most of your college shopping before you left for Beijing, but if there's anything you still need, we can go get it tomorrow morning."

"I'll be fine." My parents' fussing over my departure for college was making me even more nervous about it, and that was the last thing I needed today. It wasn't like I was going to school on another planet; I wasn't even going to school in another state. I'd pack the necessities, and if it turned out I was lacking anything, I'd just come home. No big deal.

My mother didn't seem to notice me checking out of the conversation, though. Through a mouthful of porridge, she steamrolled on. "Let's go over the plan again. Your Ba and I have taken the day off from work tomorrow, so we're closing Sweetea for your move-in day to help you get settled in. Everyone will have to be up by at least seven in the morning to finish packing, eat breakfast, and get everything into the car for move-in."

"Seven?" said Ba, his expression crinkling as though just the thought exhausted him. *Same, Ba, same.* My father quickly averted his gaze and shoved zhōu into his mouth when Ma glared at him.

"Seven," Ma confirmed. "Anna, you heard that, right?"

"Yeah." I yawned and almost missed my mouth with my spoon. I was fighting with every last shred of my resolve not to fall asleep right there at the table.

There was a short silence, broken only by the sound of ceramic spoons clinking against glass bowls. It was a comforting and familiar silence, and tears stung my eyes as I realized how much I'd missed the comfort of home while I was away.

"What happened to your friends from Sinclair Prep? Where are they going for college?" Ba asked out of the blue.

I shrugged. "Anushka's going to Yale. Danny's attending MIT. Megan's taking a gap year. Steven's at Stanford."

"Those schools all rank higher than Brookings," my father noted.

I rolled my eyes. Maybe I preferred when my parents weren't so talkative. It certainly beat them comparing me to my high-achieving friends.

"None of your friends are going to Brookings?" Ma pursed her lips. "Well, are you still talking to those friends, at least?"

"Um . . ." Good question. I'd pretty much gone off the grid over the summer, wanting to enjoy Beijing without feeling the pressure to post pictures of my adventures on social media. Come to think of it, I hadn't even told any of my friends that I was back. It had been a fantastic decision to really live in the moment without worrying about social media. But now that I was back, I was beginning to realize how disconnected I felt from my high school friends and acquaintances.

At first my Sinclair Prep friends and I had still texted our group chat regularly, but that had fallen off over the course of the summer. There wasn't much more to say now that we'd graduated high school and would be going to different universities.

"Yeah, we talk here and there," I said finally.

Ma didn't seem satisfied with the answer, because her expression didn't change. "You've always been a loner, Anna. Try to be more open to making friends in college. Okay?"

I gave a sleepy nod, if only to keep my parents from fussing over me more. I was happy with a small circle of friends and spending most of my time alone, something that my parents, who were very social even with their customers, didn't understand. My solitude was comforting. I enjoyed my own company above all else.

"I think you should get to bed," said Ba. "You're falling asleep in your food."

I was only too eager to obey. My room upstairs was as I'd left it, though a fine layer of dust had settled over my drawer and bookshelf. I climbed under the covers, and then pulled out my phone to put up a quick Story on Instagram to let everyone know I hadn't fallen off the face of the planet.

Back from Beijing :)

Then finally I turned over and fell into a deep sleep.

•⊩———⊩•

The thought of making a last-minute escape crossed my mind as I stood underneath the sweltering August sun, my suitcases and boxes piled up around me.

I stared at the intimidatingly tall, brown-bricked building

that loomed before me, nestled between tall oak trees. A large blue sign next to the stone steps of the front entrance read West Tower. The Gothic architecture on campus was hundreds of years old. So many students had passed through this building before me, going from class to class, some of them probably breaking down into tears in between. It was a strange, unimaginable notion to think that so many footsteps had been traced on this campus, so many people had come and gone.

Including Melissa Hong, who'd ended up murdered.

Now I was moving in to the same dorm where Melissa had lived seven years ago. Taking courses in the honors program, just as she had. Walking in her footsteps. Maybe even now, Melissa's ghost haunted these halls. The thought made me tremble with fear, with anticipation.

There was no better environment, no better position, to be in to find out what had happened to Melissa. And I intended to do just that this year, no matter what.

"So what do you think of the dorm, Anna?"

The question jolted me back to the moment. It was from Elise, a blonde, talkative Brookings junior who'd introduced herself as the residential advisor of the second floor—my floor. She'd been assigned to assist with my move-in. Elise gave me an expectant look as she tossed my box of shoes into her large blue moving bin. Her voice was chirpy, but the smile she'd plastered on was slightly strained, as cracked as the sun-beaten sidewalk. I got the feeling that she'd already done this several times with new freshmen before me and would do so many times more.

"Well, it looks . . . cool," I said, and then flushed. It was a shame my brain cells had fled me. "Um, I heard West Tower is one of the oldest buildings on campus," I added in a rush to show that my head wasn't completely empty and that I had some knowledge of the dorm I was about to move in to. Beyond just the murder of Melissa Hong, I mean. "Is that, like . . . a good thing, or a bad thing?"

Elise laughed and stood up straight, wiping a sheen of sweat off her forehead. "It's not brilliant. The building certainly has history, but also the furniture in the rooms is several years too old." She caught my dubious expression and flashed a reassuring smile. "But you'll learn to manage. It's not that bad. Trust me, all the freshmen dorms are hellholes."

I let out a half-hearted laugh, unsure how I was supposed to respond to that.

"Brookings is famous for all of its ghost stories," Elise said, her expression more serious.

"Ghost stories?"

"There are rumors that the fifth floor of the Thatcher Graduate Library is haunted, which is why students try to avoid it at night. Oh, and many years ago a student jumped off the roof of North Campus—they say his ghost haunts the residence hall. And rumor has it that sometimes, late at night in the arboretum, the ghosts of past students will appear beside the river." Her eyes flashed as she spoke.

Though I tried not to show it, I was spooked by Elise's words.

"You won't have to worry about ghosts around here, though," Elise reassured me, no doubt noting the alarm on my face. She smirked. "You live so close to frat row, and all the noise the frats make is bound to scare away the ghosts."

"Great to know," I mumbled under my breath. I wasn't sure whether it was worse to be surrounded by ghosts or by frat boys.

I'd known that Greek life here was huge, having lived my whole life not far from Brookings University. Though it ranked among the top twenty universities in the nation, it was also infamous as a huge party school. Students who regularly crammed their heads full of dizzying amounts of information for a big exam could then also get trashed on the weekend.

"The frats throw the best parties, especially during Welcome Week—" Elise's face paled, as if she'd let something slip, something she couldn't say as an RA.

It only piqued my curiosity. "Welcome Week?"

She shot a nervous look back at my parents, who were listening in on the conversation with interest. Ma and Ba had been so quiet, I'd almost forgotten they were there behind us. Elise leaned in and muttered, "It starts on Thursday, and it's basically a week of back-to-back parties. Enjoy the first couple weeks and take advantage of all the free alcohol."

I nodded, as though I actually planned to attend these parties, though of course I had no such plans. Just because I'd vowed to get a fresh social start in college didn't mean I had to go about it so drastically in the first week.

Raising her voice, Elise added for my parents' benefits, "Our school consistently ranks among the most diverse and inclusive institutions, with huge communities of international students. West Tower is one of the most inclusive spaces on campus." She sounded like she was reading off a brochure. In fact, I was sure she'd directly quoted the words from the front cover of my freshman orientation packet: DIVERSE! and INCLUSIVE!

I hadn't been on Brookings campus long enough yet to judge just how diverse the incoming student body was. Coming from my almost all-white high school, though, any color in the student body would be an improvement. And already I'd spotted students of color among the early crowd for today's move-in, which was a good sign. That was one of the first things I looked for whenever I was in a new setting, and seeing that the crowd wasn't totally white was reassuring.

"What do you think of the dorm?" Elise asked politely, looking at my parents.

"There are lots of squirrels," Ba observed. We waited for him to go on, but that was it. It was a fair observation.

"There *are* typically lots of squirrels running around campus," Elise agreed. "Brookings is known for it. We even have a squirrel feeding club."

With Elise's help, we rolled the huge bin of my belongings up to the dorm, my parents lugging the rest of my stuff behind me. The blast of air-conditioning inside the dorm greeted me like a new wave of life.

"West Tower's entrance and dining hall were renovated over the summer," Elise said knowledgeably.

That explained how the building seemed to gleam from floor to ceiling. A huge glass window served as the wall to our left, and on our right were elevators and a lounge room with chic furniture.

Elise waved at a boy with brown hair and way too many piercings who was sitting at the front desk. Aside from a couple of upperclassmen who'd been assigned to help out with move-in, I didn't see many other freshmen inside the dorm yet—or any people, either. I'd had one of the earlier move-in days, so the rest of the students would slowly trickle in after me.

"Where are all the other students?" Ma asked in concern.

"They haven't moved in yet," Elise clarified politely before I had a chance to respond. We squeezed into an elevator, and she pushed on the button for the second floor. "Only the students in the honors program are moving in today."

Honors program student. That was me. My parents nodded and stared at me with pride as we exited the elevator. Elise took the lead, rolling the moving bin down the hall until she stopped in front of a brown door with the number 203 on it. "And here we are! Your room," Elise announced.

Plastered on either side of the eyehole were two cutout minions from the movie *Despicable Me*, one labeled Anna Xu, and the other, Laura Dale—my roommate.

Laura and I messaged once on Facebook when we'd gotten roommate assignments earlier in the summer but hadn't spoken since. I'd checked her profile, though, and discovered with some shock that her father was Jason Dale, a politician who was a former US senator. Brookings was an expensive and elite university that attracted students from wealthy and influential families, but I was still intimidated to find out that my own roommate was from one of those families.

On top of that, Laura looked like she was actually popular in high school, and if we'd gone to the same school, we probably would've never spoken. The odds of us becoming instant besties like in movies seemed very slim. But I was hoping that my impression of Laura from social media was dead wrong. Don't judge a book by its cover and all that.

I opened the door to find a small, bare white room with two twin-sized beds placed at either end.

"Home sweet home," Elise said brightly. "Have fun decorating! Remember my Welcome Week advice—and don't forget to keep an eye out for those ghosts." With a wink, the RA turned around and left to attend to the next freshman who was attempting to move in.

"What Welcome Week advice?" asked Ma as soon as Elise was out of earshot.

"What ghosts?" Ba said, looking alarmed.

"Um, never mind," I said quickly. If my parents got wind of the idea of me being around alcohol and parties and ghosts, they'd take me back home right this second. Ma and Ba were the definition of strict helicopter parents. "Let's—let's start unpacking."

The process was exhausting and took a miserably long time. I was basically unloading all the belongings I needed to start a whole new life on my own. There were bedsheets to be laid out on the cot-like twin bed, a small fan to set up, a writing desk to decorate.

Two hours after I'd stepped foot into the dorm, my boxes were unloaded, clothes were hung up in my closet, and books were tucked neatly in the shelf above my desk. My new room was spotless and still rather empty. I'd never been much of a decorator, but I planned to stop by one of the campus stores to buy some posters to cover up the bare walls later.

Evening had fallen, and at last, there was nothing left for my parents and me to busy ourselves with—and time, Ma and Ba realized, for them to let their precious daughter go.

"I'm not going to school on a different planet," I sighed. Ma had a viselike grip on my arm and refused to let go. "Brookings isn't that far from home. And Sweetea is just off campus. You'll still see me a lot." *Though not as much as you hope*, I added silently. I was planning to take full advantage of my newfound freedom and independence.

"But you'll be living away from home for the first time," Ba pointed out, even he getting misty-eyed.

"I'll only be a forty-five-minute drive away."

"It's just so hard. You're our only child, bǎobèi. What if something h-happens to you?" Ma sniffled, dramatically pulling a red handkerchief out of her pocket and blowing her nose on it.

"Nothing will happen to me. I'll be careful. I promise," I said. "Brookings is one of the safest universities in the world." It was a line that had been hammered into every hopeful attendee even as far back as high school.

"Oh—I almost forgot. Take this doll for good luck, at least." Ma reached into her pocket and produced a palm-sized doll with short black hair, stuffed in a red dress. The doll was familiar, but

I couldn't figure out why. Then it clicked. It was the doll I'd carried around with me religiously as a child, believing that it brought me good luck in everything from academic competitions to piano recitals.

"You kept that old doll? I haven't seen it since I was a kid."

My mother smiled and held it out toward me. "I thought it would come in handy."

I had no idea what I was supposed to do with my old lucky doll that I'd outgrown. But Ma seemed as though she needed reassurance that I'd be fine on my own, and if a lucky doll would set her at ease, then I'd keep it with me. I took it and put it in the front pocket of my backpack. "I'll keep it with me if that makes you feel better."

For a moment, my parents stood there. We all knew there wasn't anything left for them to do now except leave me, but knowing them and their overprotectiveness, we were at least another half hour's small talk away from them making any kind of attempt toward the door.

"Henry Jiang—you remember Henry, right?" Ba asked abruptly.

"Of course." Henry was three years older than me and was the son of one of my father's longtime friends. He was also a certified Chinese genius, and I'd heard enough about him growing up to last a lifetime.

"He joined the Chinese Student Association here," Ba said. "You can join with him. Then you'll have a friend."

Inwardly I rolled my eyes. But all I said was, "Sure," despite not having any intentions of joining the Chinese Student

Association, especially not to befriend Henry. Thanks to my parents continuously comparing me to him, I'd developed an aversion to all guys named Henry.

I spent another half an hour reassuring my parents that I wouldn't get murdered on campus. Though they didn't look entirely convinced, they pried themselves off me and left for home.

I was finally alone in my room, wondering how to approach this new chapter in my life.

Earlier, the idea of having so much freedom and independence had sent adrenaline shooting through me. But now that I was faced with what that actually meant—being dropped off in a new environment where I didn't know anybody—my palms grew slick with nervous sweat.

A strange, empty feeling settled over me. I'd felt perfectly fine when I reassured my parents that I wouldn't be lonely. But now that they were gone, my room felt too big. Too empty. And I was seized with sudden, paralyzing loneliness. It didn't help that Elise's talk of ghosts was still fresh in my mind.

I figured it couldn't hurt to at least put up a friendly front, keep my door open so people could come in and introduce themselves if they wanted. I dragged myself off my bed and cracked open the door just an inch to see what was going on outside.

My phone lit up with a text. Anushka had sent our group chat a picture of her standing outside her dorm at Yale.

Anushka: Officially a bulldog now!!

Anna: Omgggg so cute! I just moved in today too!
How's Yale?

Anushka: Really nice haha how's Brookings?

Anna: Idk, haven't seen all of campus yet, but the
squirrels here are huge

I waited for the others to chime in, but no one did. Maybe my friends were busy. They'd never been the best at keeping up with texting and social media, either. On some level I'd known that we weren't the type of ride-or-die friend group that would keep up with each other throughout college and after, so I'd expected this slow ghosting, but it still didn't make this any less lonely. I wished more than anything that I were still in Beijing, spending time with Nai Nai and my extended family. Every day had been packed with sightseeing or other fun activities, and I'd never had a moment to reflect on my boredom.

I decided to text Laura, my roommate.

Anna: Hey girl, when r u supposed to move in?

Laura: I'm stuck w/ my parents at a hotel :(Have to
move in tmr instead. You?

Anna: I'm already here! Just moved in today

Laura: Omg excitingggg

Anna: Haha yeah, bit lonely so far tho. Idk anyone else
in the honors program. Do you?

I waited for a reply, but it never came. Awkward. Maybe Laura's phone had died. For lack of anything better to do, I grabbed my copy of *The Iliad* off the shelf and began flipping through the pages again, as though determined to commit the book to memory. There was no such thing as being overprepared for my first college class, especially if I wanted to prove myself as a model student early on.

Just as I'd lain back down in bed, a knock sounded on my door.

"It's open," I said, getting out of bed again. The blood rushed to my head. Then I wished I hadn't responded so quickly without preparing myself to speak with a stranger. It was too late now to regret it, though. On the bright side, this was a welcome distraction from my loneliness.

A tall brown-haired boy with green eyes walked just over the threshold of the doorway. He was wearing tan khaki shorts and a black polo. He waved, giving me a wide smile. "Hey. Anna?"

I was about to ask the stranger how he knew my name, but then realized it was written on a nameplate on my door. "Yeah."

"I'm Patrick, the residential advisor for the guys on this floor. Everything going well so far?"

I forced a smile to disguise my nerves. I must've done a poor job of it, because Patrick's expression turned sympathetic.

"We're having a bonding night in the lounge. It's optional, but you should come."

"Oh, yeah, maybe," I said, though the thought of meeting a ton of new people all at once was overwhelming. I had wanted to force myself out of my comfort zone, though not this drastically. But I guess that was what getting out of the comfort zone meant, after all.

"It's a good idea to get to know your floor mates before the school year officially begins. You don't want to regret isolating yourself while everyone else is making friends. Just think about it, okay?"

I promised I would, and then Patrick left. I heard him knocking on the door across the hall.

I sighed and thudded my head against the door, sinking to my knees, wondering what was wrong with me, why I couldn't make and keep friends so easily like others could. How was I going to survive four years at this university if I couldn't even summon up the courage to venture down to the lounge?

Tomorrow, I vowed. Tomorrow I'd try again, and it would be better.

I checked my phone. No new texts. Danny, Megan, and Steven didn't even reply to the group chat. One summer apart, and my old friends' faces were already starting to fade in my mind, even though I'd seen them daily last year. How much did we have in common besides our academic suffering at Sinclair Prep? Not enough, clearly.

I hoped that in college, I'd make lifelong friends. I spent my evening watching Netflix and went to bed early with only my loneliness for company.

Chapter Four

THE NEXT MORNING, LAURA STILL hadn't arrived. I wasn't sure if it would be better when she moved in or not. On the one hand, her presence would certainly help ease my loneliness. But on the other hand, I didn't know if I could get used to the idea of sharing a room with a stranger—especially since we might not even get along well. I'd heard my fair share of college horror stories about roommates who were randomly assigned to one another and ended up hating each other and being absolutely miserable. If you asked me, this random roommate assignment system had more flaws than advantages.

Finally, around noon my growling stomach made me cave. I laced up my black Oxford boots and I braved a trip down to the dining hall. It was huge. I'd almost forgotten about the renovation down here, since the rooms and especially the showers in West Tower were so old and in need of updating. But the dining hall had clearly been updated and polished until the state-of-the-art walls and ceiling shone.

Wonder what this dorm looked like when Melissa went here.

The food was served buffet-style like every dining hall on

campus, which I already knew from orientation. There were food stations that had everything from burgers to salads to pasta, and even a make-your-own-burrito-bowl station. Desserts, too. Any kind of dessert you could dream of. Ice cream, cakes, cookies, fruit.

Forget the freshman fifteen, I was headed straight for the freshman five hundred.

I ate quickly, self-conscious about the fact that I was sitting alone whereas most of the students seemed to have found at least one person to eat lunch with already.

When I got back to my room, I stood quietly for a few moments. I could hop back into bed, or I could do something productive—like explore campus. There was the matter of investigating Melissa Hong's death. I wasn't sure what I'd find, or if I'd find anything at all, but now that I was finally here at Brookings, I had to at least take a look around.

I shoved a granola bar and a campus map into a crossbody purse and headed out the door again.

It was a warm and foggy afternoon, the air humid with the looming threat of rain. I pulled out the map and stared at the squiggles. I'd never been particularly good at reading maps, so it took me a few moments to figure out what direction to head to get across campus to the arboretum.

Fallen leaves crunched beneath my feet as I set off down the snaking brick path, which was lined by stone statues. There were a few freshmen with their families walking around, some of them hauling their belongings into giant moving bins as I'd done the day before. It took me a few wrong turns, but as I consulted the map again and again in frustration, eventually I found myself moving in the right direction toward the more natural side of campus.

The woods were dark and grew darker the deeper I wandered into them. An older woman came jogging by down the rocky road, and we nodded at each other as she passed.

My pace slowed, and I stopped for a moment, taking in the quiet nature around me. In this very arboretum, Melissa had been strangled, and then her body cast aside. Or maybe the murder had happened elsewhere, and the culprit had chosen to dump her in the arboretum. Aside from the Tumblr and a couple of other articles I'd found on Google, there was nothing else about her. It was as though Melissa Hong had been visible only briefly in death, and then buried once more.

But she'd had parents. A family. Friends. Hopes and dreams.

A lump welled in the back of my throat. I walked all around the arboretum, taking in the sights of nature, smelling the flowers. The clouds rolled overhead, and something wet fell onto my cheeks. I lifted my head up toward the sky.

"Crap," I muttered as the rain dripped down more and more steadily. I hadn't packed an umbrella, and there was nowhere to take cover. Running as fast as I could in my Oxford boots, I sprinted back toward West Tower. By the time I ran inside the front door, thunder was clapping in the distance and the downpour pelted the windows. I'd escaped the worst of it, but my clothes were uncomfortably wet.

As I headed up toward my room, I realized the door was open. At first I panicked that I'd forgotten to shut it behind me,

THE LIES WE TELL

and I could practically hear Ma and Ba yelling at me about being careless and risking my own safety. But then a blonde girl emerged from the room and stood at the doorway. She was dressed to the nines in a red skater skirt and black combat boots, tall and model-gorgeous, with a long, shiny curtain of dirty blonde hair.

I blinked. It took me a moment to recognize her from the selfie she'd set as her Facebook profile picture. In person, she was taller than I thought she'd be—the girl had at least three inches on me. "Um—Laura?"

"Yeah. You must be Anna, right?" My roommate's tone was clipped and impatient, as though she had a million tasks to attend to and I was in the way.

I nodded. "Nice to meet you."

Laura looked me up and down, and I grew instantly self-conscious of the old T-shirt and skirt I was wearing, which were now also wet. So much for giving a good first impression to my new roommate. She squinted at the window. "It's pouring out there now, huh?"

"Oh, um, yeah."

Laura flashed me a megawatt smile. I wondered if her politician father had taught her how to show her pearly whites like that. "How'd your move-in go?" The enthusiasm in her voice was almost too overwhelming to handle. Everything about her screamed extrovert, whereas I was the most introverted hermit I knew. So far, not off to a great start.

"Not bad. It didn't take too long to unpack everything, so that's good."

For a brief moment, I debated telling Laura that my parents didn't live far from here anyway and actually owned a bakery adjacent to campus, but I decided against it. Laura was attending Brookings University as an out-of-state student, which meant she probably expected her roommate to also hail from the caliber of families that could afford to pay the exorbitant price tag of an education at Brookings University. I didn't need her finding out about my solidly lower middle-class status just yet.

"Tell me about it. I'm so excited that my parents are all the way in Kentucky," Laura said. "That's, like, light-years away."

It suddenly occurred to me that Laura was all alone. "Have you met the rest of our floor mates?" Laura asked, changing the subject quickly again. It seemed to be a habit of hers, and I had a feeling I was going to struggle to keep up with her fast-paced conversation all year.

"No, just the RAs—Elise and Patrick."

"They seem nice." Then her eyes narrowed, and for the first time, she hesitated. "Have you noticed anything funny about the second floor?"

"What? Like . . . a funny smell?"

She let out a forced laugh. "No. I mean, I've only been here for a few hours, but I can already tell this place is . . . kind of weird."

My mind leapt immediately to the case of Melissa Hong. To the other ghost stories Elise had told me about the day before. My heart leapt. Could it be—was my roommate a true crime fan? Maybe she'd already scoped out the arboretum, too, or was planning on it. Laura didn't seem the type, but I'd only just met her. "What do you mean by . . . weird?" I asked cautiously.

"It seems the university's stuck all the international students in our hall."

Now *that* answer wasn't what I'd expected. I tried to ignore the disappointment that rose within me. "Yeah, they really push for diversity at Brookings," I said, not sure where Laura was going with this. "Seems like it's a pretty big deal these days."

There were many people in this state, country—hell, *world*— who were unafraid to voice their racist and homophobic thoughts, but of course that was countered by greater cries for diversity and inclusion by the other side. Brookings had obviously adopted the latter attitude, hammering the message over students' heads that it was an inclusive and forward-thinking institution.

Laura furrowed her brows, looking like she wanted to say something else. She must have decided against it, because she just shrugged. An awkward silence fell between us. Without Laura driving the conversation, I didn't know what else to say. Besides, my clothes were still wet, and if I didn't change soon, I was going to catch a cold. The idea of changing in front of a stranger unnerved me, though. I'd rather tough it out until Laura left the room.

"Um, do you want help unpacking?" I offered.

"That's fine." Laura waved me off, sending a waft of flowery-smelling perfume in my direction.

I took the hint. This conversation was over.

More to distract myself from the awkwardness of the silence than anything else, I continued organizing my desk, stacking and shuffling my multicolored notebooks. Then I browsed the week's itinerary that someone—probably one of the RAs—had slid under the door. It was full of university-approved bonding events for the freshmen students. I'd already looked it over. So far I'd missed the Midnight Social, Breakfast of Champions, and Pet the Parrot (which I wasn't too torn up about missing, to be honest). The next event was the Made in Michigan scavenger hunt, and it was supposed to take place tomorrow.

"Hey, are you attending any of these Welcome Week events?" I asked casually.

Laura paused in the middle of stringing up fairy lights on her wall. She turned around and fixed me with a sly grin, a gleam in her eye. "What, like the party at Theta Pi tonight?"

"Party?"

Laura gave me an appraising look. The corners of her lips tilted up into a small, tight smile. "I'm surprised. You didn't strike me as the partying type."

"I . . ." My mouth dried. This was where I needed to clear up the misunderstanding—clear up that I was talking about the wholesome freshman orientation events, not frat parties. Because I wasn't the partying type. Not at all. Furthest thing from it, actually.

But the words that came out of my mouth were: "Yeah, well, looks can be deceiving. I'm always down for a party."

Inwardly, my last shred of self-awareness was screaming at

me. *You've never been to a party in your life! There will be alcohol there. And trashy music. And trashy guys. What are you doing?*

"Cool. Some of my friends are going to the party. You should come," said Laura.

How had she already managed to make friends on campus when she'd been here for all of a couple hours?

I nodded and forced a smile, trying to look a lot cooler than I was. My heart pounded wildly in my chest. I wasn't sure what I'd just gotten myself into, but I knew one thing for sure: Laura was my ticket to meeting new people and making friends. Tonight was going to be an experience.

Chapter Five

AT SINCLAIR PREP, I'D NEVER broken a single rule. I'd done whatever was expected of me, and I was only known for getting high scores on exams. I'd never been to a high school party, never had wild experiences like the teens I saw on TV. My life had revolved around getting good grades, bringing home piano awards and trophies, and setting myself up to get into a top university. After I'd received my acceptance letter from Brookings University, the mark of my years of hard work finally bearing fruit, I'd found myself at a loss for what to do next. I'd even found myself at a loss for knowing who I was. Maybe that was why I'd committed myself to finding Melissa's murderer, to imagining myself in her place at this school years ago.

And honestly, I didn't really want to be me. I didn't want to be a good girl anymore. At least, not all the time.

Secretly I wanted a taste of trouble, a taste of darkness. I wanted to push the boundaries and tempt destruction but narrowly avoid being ruined.

Nobody here knew me. My parents weren't around to tell me which classes and extracurriculars to take. Nobody to tell me I wasn't allowed to party or drink. For once I was doing something wild. Something fun. Something completely and totally unlike me. College was my chance to reinvent myself, to transform the quiet, nerdy image of high school me.

And despite my pounding pulse, I knew I wanted to be someone different. I was ready to try it all, give everything a chance. So I made it item one on my list: partying and making very poor, drunken decisions.

I glued my false eyelashes into place and blinked at myself in the mirror. The girl who stared back at me was fierce and sultry, and nobody could guess that she'd grown up as the overachieving nerd. My hair was done, my lips were coated with dark red lipstick, and my low-cut black crop top and short skirt left little to the imagination. I looked completely unlike the old Anna Xu. I looked like a college freshman headed to her first frat party, maybe solving a murder mystery on the way.

Laura was getting ready, too, pulling on a slinky red dress that revealed her cleavage and accentuated her curves. She was on the phone with someone—evidently one of the people who was going to be at the party tonight, from what I could hear of the conversation.

"You ready?" my roommate asked me, after she and her friend had hung up.

"Yup." I nodded, trying to look convincing. I couldn't remember ever feeling less ready for anything in my life, including the SATs. But I'd still aced those. I'd ace my first frat party, too.

"Cool. My friends should be here any minute, and—" Laura

was interrupted by the sound of knocking on the door and giggling that followed it. She crossed the floor impressively quickly considering her lethally high heels and opened the door. "Oh, there they are. Mandy! Ellen!"

Two girls, one with short red hair and one with long brown hair, came into the room. They wore equally revealing dresses. Something about the vibe of these three girls felt the same. I was sure they could sense the odd one out—me.

But I smiled anyway, smiled big enough that my cheeks ached, hoping they'd let me fit in, even if just for this one, wild night. If there was one thing going to mostly white schools my entire life had taught me, it was how to line myself up with others even when my appearance set me apart.

After Laura did the introductions—Mandy was the redhead, and Ellen was the brunette—she grabbed her clutch and glanced at me. "You've got your key to the room, Anna? Just in case we get separated?"

"Yeah." Laura's tone was innocent enough, but I couldn't help but wonder if there was an underlying suggestion in her words—that we *would* get separated, that she was already planning to ditch me once we got to the party. Maybe I was overthinking.

"Let's get out of here," giggled Mandy.

We stepped out into the mostly empty hall. It seemed like we were the only girls on our floor who were headed out for a wild night. It was the honors program, after all, so I guess a lot of the other freshmen were probably doing wholesome things.

I'd forgone heels in favor of flats for the night, and I was really thanking myself for it as we left the dormitory and strode across the street toward frat row. It was eleven at night, which, according to Laura, was pretty early by "partying" standards. There were a lot of scantily dressed students on the streets, some of them already clearly drunk. Music thrummed on campus, coming at us from every direction.

I shivered, though not from the cold. An electrifying thrill had swept through me. My parents would be scandalized if they knew what I was doing right now. My high school classmates would never believe it. And that gave me a rush of adrenaline unlike anything I'd ever felt before.

"We're going to Theta Pi, right?" asked Ellen.

"I hear the guys are really hot," said Mandy.

"They are. I met a couple of them at orientation," Laura said smugly.

I hung back a little, trying to find an opening in the conversation with no success. I knew nothing about fraternities and sororities except that our school had a huge Greek community. The odds were slim that I'd find a fellow introvert here—not at this crowded party. Maybe I'd be a better conversationalist once I drank some alcohol.

We walked past a handful of houses. Though most of them had their lights on and college students standing on the porch holding drinks, one of them was dark and empty. Finally, we reached a huge white house on the end of frat row. There were people mingling in a line in front of a picnic table on the lawn, where it appeared that three boys—frat brothers—were checking

IDs. Lights flashed inside the house, the fast beat of a Martin Garrix song pulsing through the ground. I swear I could feel the dirt quaking beneath my feet.

"We're here," Laura announced unnecessarily.

If my parents could see me now, if they knew what I was doing, they'd kill me. Without question. Me going to this party went against every ancient Chinese proverb in the dictionary, or something.

And the fact that the idea both terrified me and thrilled me to the core made me think that there was something very, very wrong about me.

My nerves must have shown on my face, because Mandy grabbed my hand, taking me by surprise. "Relax. Is this your first party, Anna?"

"Um . . ." The mortified flush likely on my face probably gave away the answer.

"You're so cute," Ellen gushed. "Don't worry. We'll take care of you."

"We'll introduce you to the guys," added Mandy.

I let out a nervous laugh. "Oh, that's okay, I—"

"We?" interrupted Laura, though her tone was playful. "Who do you know here, Mandy?"

Mandy flipped her hair over her shoulder. "I might've met a guy at orientation."

"Wait, who?"

"Jared Hart," Mandy said smugly, as though he were a celebrity and not a frat boy and that name was supposed to mean something to us. "You know, of *those* Harts."

"*The* Harts?" Laura gasped. I still had no idea what Mandy was talking about.

"Yes, *the* Harts. His father is Jim Hart, the CEO of a Fortune 500 company. And his older sister is a model."

Ellen's jaw dropped, and Laura looked impressed in spite of herself. Even I was taken aback. I knew Brookings had famous alumni and that there were sons and daughters of celebrities and the wealthy attending the school, but I hadn't expected to bump into any of them so soon.

As the girls continued their discussion of who they knew at Theta Pi, we edged closer to the check-in table. I grew increasingly aware that I was the odd one out. Until today, I hadn't even known about Theta Pi's existence, much less that it consisted of some of society's elite.

Finally we reached the front. I tried not to stare at the boys who were checking us in, but after Mandy had mentioned Jared Hart, I couldn't help but examine them with greater interest. They were wearing tropical print short-sleeved shirts paired with salmon-colored shorts.

The frat boys hardly glanced at our IDs before nodding and gesturing toward the front door. I guess it was true what I'd heard about college parties and clubs—it was always much easier for the girls to get in than the guys.

The door flew open just as we'd reached the front step.

A shirtless guy with curly brown hair greeted us with a bunch of bananas on his head and a beer in either hand. He smelled like beer. Upon laying eyes on me, the frat guy grinned in a sort of cross-eyed way that made my skin crawl. "Hey, cutie," he slurred, stumbling into the doorframe with a stupid grin on his face.

I suppressed a shudder.

"Ew. Just let us in," said Laura, shoving past the boy.

My gut told me I was in way over my head, but before I could make up an excuse and dip, Mandy firmly yanked me by the hand and into the Theta Pi frat house.

The inside of the frat house was packed and overheated. The Martin Garrix song had changed to the Chainsmokers, and the volume had grown even louder, so much so that the girls and I had to shout to hear one another. The walls were painted a dull white color, and there were brown stains spattered on the wall here and there that were probably best left unexplained. It smelled like cheap beer and cologne. Vomiting noises came from behind me, causing Ellen to squeal. I didn't dare look back.

I swallowed and shuddered, avoiding a puddle of a mysterious brown liquid on the wooden floorboard. "Theta Pi definitely knows how to party." Not that I knew what a real party was like, considering I'd never been cool enough to score an invite in high school, but I'd seen movies. This frat party was probably as good as it got, as far as frat parties went.

"Of course they do," Laura said, as though she were an expert on the matter. "Theta Pi is consistently ranked among the top fraternities in the nation."

Well, that was just depressing to think about.

As we shuffled past people and made it farther into the heated, dirty house, the loud music thrumming in my ears, I was seriously beginning to regret the fact that I'd decided to come out and party instead of having a wholesome night in with my floor mates. I was so out of my element here, which was really the point—but now I found myself wishing I'd picked something slightly less bold as my first college experience.

"It'll be fun once we get some alcohol," said Mandy, as though she'd read my mind.

The living room of the frat house was dimly lit and spacious, all the furniture shoved to the walls to make room for the partiers. The place was crammed full with people dancing to dubstep. Drunken girls in high heels and slinky black dresses, guys in douchey tank tops and salmon shorts. Couples grinding on the dance floor. People crowding around and yelling song requests at the DJ, who was spinning in a booth in the corner.

The floor was wet and sticky. I slid on it and nearly crashed into a table where a bunch of guys were playing beer pong. I watched, transfixed, feeling as though I were watching the whole scene unfold before me like an outsider. Like I was watching a nature documentary entitled *Frat Boys in Their Natural Habitat*, or something.

Someone tapped me on the shoulder. I turned around and locked eyes with Laura, who proceeded to shove a red Solo cup under my nose. It was filled with a dark brown liquid.

"What's this?" I asked.

"It's good. Just try it," my roommate urged.

My eyes widened. Aside from nabbing the occasional disgusting sip of Baba's Chinese white wine, I'd never drunk a drop of alcohol. I took a whiff and wrinkled my nose at the pungent scent. "What's in it?"

"Vodka. It's so diluted with Dr Pepper that it's basically like pop. You have to try it. It tastes really good. Promise."

"I . . ." *No*, every sensible atom in my body screamed.

"Come on. I thought you said you like partying?" Laura shoved the drink at me. "It won't do much to you. Just loosen you up so we can enjoy this party." She took a sip, and then pressed the cup into my fingers.

I took the cup cautiously, as though it might develop fangs and bite me.

"Less talking, more drinking!" Ellen came out of nowhere, clinking her red Solo cup with mine. Some alcohol splashed over the rim onto my hand. "Oops. Sorry, Alexa!" she said to me.

"My name is Anna," I said through gritted teeth, wiping the liquid off my hand onto the wall. Guess that solved the mystery of all the brown stains.

Mandy swiped a cup from the beer pong table, downing the drink in one gulp. She wiped her mouth with the back of her hand and tossed her cup back on the table. "All right. Time to find the hottest guys at the party. I'm not going home without hooking up with someone here."

"I want to find Jared Hart," whined Laura. "Has anyone spotted him yet?"

Just take a sip, I told myself, staring into the ominous-looking contents sloshing around in my cup. *That's what you came here to do, right? To prove you can be a normal young adult. Normal and reckless. To remake yourself in college.*

I closed my eyes and tilted the cup back into my mouth. Slowly. Carefully. It really did taste like Dr Pepper. Mixed with something sharp and bitter. Before I could decide if I wanted more, Laura surprised me by tilting the cup back and nearly causing me to choke on the rest of the drink.

With one humongous swallow, I gasped for air, wiping my mouth. "What the heck?" I choked.

"Looked like you needed some help there." Laura batted her eyes innocently while Mandy and Ellen giggled.

"How much alcohol was in there?" I tried to hide my annoyance, but even I could tell I wasn't doing a good job of it. How much alcohol had I drunk in the span of thirty seconds? I didn't know a lot about alcohol, but I did know you weren't supposed to down a bunch of it in a short period of time. Panic rose inside me.

Ellen rolled her eyes. "One shot, maybe. Or two."

"Two?" I squeaked.

"Don't worry. Nothing's going to happen," Mandy said. "Well, except that you'll have the confidence boost to talk to some frat boys."

Before I could protest that I didn't want to talk to any frat boys, Laura called, "Hey, Brian!" She waved at a lone figure who was swathed in shadow in the corner. Then, before I could figure out what was going on, Laura grabbed hold of my wrist with a viselike grip, making it impossible for me to attempt to escape.

The guy named Brian looked up, his gaze locking onto mine right away. He was wearing a plain dark blue T-shirt and khakis. Laura shoved me—right into his arms.

"Hey," said Brian, his beer breath fanning out across my face. I tried not to die right on the spot. "We've met before, haven't we?" His words came out slow and slurred, and his hand strayed much too close to my butt for comfort.

"No, we definitely have not." Also, talk about the oldest pickup line in the book. I shoved Brian off me.

"Oh, come on." Brian reached for me again, pressing my body against his. He brought his mouth to my ear, his breath warming my neck and making my skin crawl. "Wanna go somewhere more private? We can check upstairs."

In the dim light, sweaty air, and pounding music, my head had grown light, and I felt a little like I was floating, but I wasn't out of it enough that I didn't know what those words meant. And that I definitely didn't want to follow Brian anywhere.

Brian wasn't even my type, but maybe normal eighteen-year-olds were supposed to be curious about sex, if they hadn't already been doing it. I knew most of my classmates, even in high school, weren't virgins. Literature glamorized romance and sex, holding it up as one of the most important aspects of human life. But I'd never felt that desire to be with a guy—or a girl, or anyone—in such an intimate way. The idea of sex flat-out scared me.

I knew I had to tell Brian no, to get as far away from him as I could. This was a mistake. But suddenly my legs felt heavy. With a rush of fear, I realized I was in his territory, surrounded by his friends, who were hooking up left and right. I was certain that even if I yelled for help, nobody would come to rescue me.

The way nobody had rescued Melissa Hong.

The thought rose in my mind, unbidden, and it unnerved

me. But it also gave me an opportunity to distract Brian. I blurted out, "Have you heard of Melissa Hong?"

His brow furrowed. "Who?"

That was a no, then.

A shadow loomed behind Brian, and a hand clapped down on his shoulder. The lighting was so dim that I couldn't see his features too well, but I could tell that he was Asian—and that he had several inches of height on Brian. "Yo. Problem here, dude?"

Brian turned around. "Huh? No. We're just talking."

"Yeah, and that's my girlfriend you're talking to," said the stranger.

"I'm no one's girlfr . . ." My socially awkward mind was slow to catch up, but after a few moments, I got there. This new person, whoever he was, was pretending that he was my boyfriend to get me away from Brian. He was throwing me a lifeline. "Hey, um . . . sweetheart," I said to the stranger, brushing past Brian as I played along.

"What the hell?" Brian grumbled. "Keep better tabs on your girlfriend, bro."

"You got it," said the other boy.

The stranger followed me, and together we weaved past the drunk partygoers to exit the house. When we were standing on the porch, I turned around to see his face, for the first time, in full lighting.

And gasped.

It was Rude Guy from the airport.

Chapter Six

I'D ALWAYS BEEN PRACTICAL. DIDN'T believe in fate. Didn't believe in coincidences. But there was something so fateful about this scenario—running into someone who I'd only seen in passing on a shared flight—that even I couldn't ignore.

"You," I spluttered. "It's you."

The boy's face scrunched in confusion. "Me, what? Have we met before?"

"You—from Beijing—" My thoughts were getting clouded, and I was slurring, but I knew this was the boy who'd knocked my last red bean bun out of my hand at the airport in Beijing. The boy who'd spent nearly the entire flight reading a book, the same as I had. Even through the buzz of alcohol, I couldn't help but feel embarrassment heat my cheeks. Maybe I was the only one who remembered our encounter. Maybe to him, it was so insignificant that he'd long forgotten it. Meanwhile, he'd been living in my head rent-free. Well, maybe not rent-free, but I certainly hadn't forgotten about him.

Then the boy's eyes widened, as though he'd just come to

the same realization. "Wait. I do recognize you. You're the girl with the scary eyes from the airport."

"Scary? You were the one who ruined my last red bean bun," I fumed. Even with my head gone all fuzzy, that detail seemed extra important to point out.

"Okay, well, I just saved your ass back there, so we can call it even." He flashed a half smile. Maybe the alcohol really was clouding my judgement, but for a moment, I thought he was flirting.

"It's not like I asked you to help me," I fired back. But it was true that he'd just gotten me out of a bad situation. Because of the guilt on my conscience, I added, "Okay, fine. Thanks for helping me escape back there. I'm Anna Xu. Nice to meet you, um—what's your name?"

"It's Chris. Chris Lu."

This was a very strange, trippy dream that I was trapped in. It had to be. Now that the alcohol had hit me full force, I wasn't sure what was real life and what was imagined anymore, but I was fairly certain that the handsome-but-annoying stranger had told me his name was Chris Lu. Which was the same name as . . .

Chris Lu was tilting his head to the side and squinting at me, as though he was trying to figure out where he'd seen me before, and that gesture was enough to confirm my suspicions.

"Wait . . . Anna? Is it really you?"

Oh, great. Now it really was apparent he was *that* Chris Lu. My parents had told me that Chris was attending Brookings, but this campus was huge. The odds that we'd run into each other at a frat party had to be minuscule. And yet.

"It's me," Chris said, when I stayed silent. "We went to school together, like, years ago. You used to race me to the bus after school, and you lost almost every time. Remember?" He frowned. "Did you forget me?"

"No, I remember you," I said faintly. "I just . . . How is this possible?"

"Excuse me?"

"You can't be Chris Lu. Chris is . . . short, and uncool, and you're . . ." I waved my hand up and down, the rest of my words dying in my throat, which was probably for the best.

"You look so . . ." Chris opened and closed his mouth. Clearly, we were both having difficulty coming up with words tonight. "So . . . different."

"It's the false lashes," I said, and winked. Oh no, that vodka was starting to hit me.

"No, I mean yeah, but also—" Chris was stammering, which was somewhat adorable, a fact that I tried to ignore. His eyes were wide with shock. "It's been, what—five years? Six?"

"Six," I said. "Not that I've been counting." Then a moment later, I realized I'd said that out loud, which caused my cheeks to heat with mortification. I had no doubt I looked like a tomato.

"Really?" Chris's mouth twitched, as though he were barely suppressing a smirk.

"So—you're back in the States."

"I am, clearly," he said. "How've you been?"

"Fantastic." It came out sarcastically, though I hadn't meant for it to.

"Yeah, I can tell." That cheek in Chris's voice was intentional. Annoying. Aside from his appearance, he hadn't changed *that* much in six years.

There was a red Solo cup in his hand, but unlike me, he didn't seem drunk or even tipsy.

I didn't know what one was supposed to say to a former rival who showed up again in their life unexpectedly, especially now that he was so much taller and cuter. It didn't help that the alcohol was making my brain fuzzy and my tongue loose, which was about the least helpful combination for carrying out this conversation.

"How many drinks have you had?" I blurted out.

Chris raised an eyebrow. "This is my third."

"What? You've had *two* others?"

"Yeah, catch up, Anna."

Much as I wanted to one-up Chris and wipe that smirk off his face, I knew it wouldn't be smart to get caught up in a drinking competition. Besides, the alcohol tasted disgusting, and I didn't want to put any more of it in my body than I already had.

"I can't believe you're still so competitive," I muttered. "Are we still kids or something?"

"Hey, you're still just as competitive as I am."

Touché.

An awkward silence fell between us. "Uh . . . I'm gonna go home," I announced, which seemed like the best option. I was probably twenty minutes away from making a fool out of myself, and that was not the tone I wanted to start college on. Even if part of me wanted to stay and talk to Chris.

"You need help getting home?"

I shook my head. "It's okay. I just live in the West Tower dorms across the street."

Chris's eyebrows raised in surprise. "So do I."

"You're in the honors program too?" I exclaimed, but I shouldn't have been surprised. Of course Chris had gotten into the honors program. "Dammit." The word slipped out without me even thinking about it.

"Well, sorry to disappoint," Chris said, rolling his eyes. "But yeah, I am. And the *honorable* thing to do would be to get back to the dorms now."

"That was terrible. Wait," I added, suddenly remembering that I'd arrived here with three other girls—my roommate and her two friends. It took me a moment to recall their names in the midst of my brain fog. Mandy and Ellen. "I was with three other girls. Where'd they go?" I cast my gaze around the living room, but there was no trace of my roommate and her friends.

"I mean, it's getting late, so they probably went upstairs. Or back to their dorms," said Chris.

Mandy had been talking about finding a hookup earlier in the night. I got the feeling that she'd succeeded. And Laura and Ellen, too.

I still had enough wits about me to compose a check-in text with Laura. Her response was thankfully swift and crisp.

Anna: Hey where did you and the others go? You good?
Laura: Yeah I'm fine. I'm with some other guys now
Anna: Ok I'm probably gonna dip too. Found someone I know here and we're gonna head back to West Tower
Laura: See ya!

I guess that was it, then. No invite to hang out with her and "some other guys." No apology for leaving me on my own to fend off Beer Breath Brian, either. Shaking my head, I looked at Chris. He might've been an old rival, but for now he was better company than the girls I'd come with, or any of the other party-goers. "Let's get out of here."

With Chris leading the way, we pushed past the crowd of people drunkenly dancing on the lawn. We left the frat, though the music still thrummed in the grass. It was a short walk back to West Tower, but the temperature had dropped in the night, and I was shivering in the cool breeze.

"Yo, you wanna get bubble tea?" Chris said randomly. "I've kinda got a craving. And there's a place right around the corner." He pointed down the street in the opposite direction of West Tower.

Now that Chris had mentioned bubble tea, even though I hadn't been thinking about it, I really wanted milk tea. It seemed like a good way to flush the buzz of alcohol out of my system. And if I was honest, I didn't want to say goodbye to Chris yet.

Six years was a long time, and much as I was annoyed at him for a multitude of reasons, I wanted to know what my former rival had been up to in the past several years. "Let's do it."

We headed down the bustling street, past drunk students and joggers, restaurants, cozy bookshops, pricey clothing stores. We arrived in front of a small, well-lit building with a purple sign that read Bubble Mania hung over it.

At Sinclair Prep, there'd been no bubble tea place. Three Starbucks, but no bubble tea in sight. I'd satisfied my craving for boba only a handful of times a year, when Ma and Ba had time to take me to Bubble Mania. Now that I had Bubble Mania within walking distance, I was planning to drink so much of the stuff that only milk tea and tapioca would flow through my veins.

We headed inside. Although it was late at night—almost one in the morning—the place was packed with college kids, freshmen and upperclassmen alike.

"Got a random question for you," Chris said as we joined the line. He gave me an unreadable expression. "Why do you pronounce your last name that way?"

I blinked. I hadn't expected that. "What do you mean?"

"Earlier, when you introduced yourself to me. Your pronunciation is off. It's Xu." Chris rolled his tongue and pushed air through it, pronouncing my last name properly. The way I did around relatives, around people who spoke and understood Mandarin. Like the sound of air blowing through blades of grass, I'd always thought of it. Around Americans, I chose to pronounce my name like "shoe." Much simpler.

Didn't raise any questions or cause mispronunciations and awkward explanations.

"Yeah, whatever. Xu, shoe, doesn't make a difference." I shrugged it off, trying to appear casual and cover up how taken aback I was. The Chinese Americans I knew had all adopted the Westernizing of the pronunciation of our last names, at least to some extent. It was part of blending in with American society. I'd never seen anyone question the practice before. *I'd* never questioned it before.

"I think it does make a difference," Chris piped up, sliding his hands into the front pockets of his black jeans. "You shouldn't have to whitewash your last name."

He was right, and I hated that I knew that deep down. "Easy for you to say. 'Xu' is pretty damn hard for people to pronounce if they don't know how to speak Mandarin. It's hard for people to mess up 'Lu.'"

"You'd be surprised."

Now that the buzz of alcohol had mostly worn off and I could somewhat hold a conversation better, I wasn't wasting a moment. "Where did you go after leaving Ponce Middle School?"

"Beijing, to live with my grandparents." And then he clarified, "I studied at an international school, so we spoke mostly English over there. Though my Mandarin improved a lot, too." There was that smirk again. "If we had a Chinese speech contest now, I'd win, hands down."

I rolled my eyes, though I couldn't exactly disagree. My Mandarin had been decent in school, but after leaving Chinese school, it had only grown rusty. My summer in Beijing had shown me the gap between my Mandarin proficiency as a kid and now. Though I hated to admit it, Chris could probably kick my ass at a Chinese speech contest. "What made you decide to come back to the States?"

"My parents opened this bakery, so we figured this was an opportunity for me to come back and study at a top university."

So that explained why we'd been on the same flight in from Beijing to Detroit. While I was coming back from a whirlwind summer of visiting my relatives in China, Chris was leaving his relatives to come study "abroad."

Before I could question Chris further, the harried-looking Bubble Mania employee behind the counter called, "Next!" and pinned us with a weary smile. As the employee served up our orders—a classic milk tea for me, and Thai milk tea for Chris— the conversation died out, and an awkward silence fell between us. I realized, with some self-consciousness, that to outsiders we must look like we were out on a late-night date. Yet the idea wasn't totally repulsive to me. I peeked at Chris, who was scanning the store for open tables. He wasn't bad-looking. Not bad-looking at all.

"Let's just head back to the dorm," Chris suggested when it was clear we weren't getting a seat any time soon. "It's late, anyway. We don't want the ghosts to get us."

I glanced over to see him smirking and rolled my eyes. "Very funny."

"I'm serious, though, it's dangerous to be out too late. Students have died on campus. Just be glad you're with me."

That seemed like a bit of a morbid turn for the conversation. My eyes narrowed as I studied Chris's side profile, and I wondered if he was referring to the unsolved case of Melissa Hong or if it was just a general comment. After a moment of silence, maybe sensing my stare, Chris turned toward me. "What?"

"I—*ugh!*"

A tall older Asian man bumped into my side, nearly causing me to drop my bubble tea. Chris caught me around the shoulders, steadying me. I was all too aware of the heat of his body against mine and immediately jumped away.

"Whoa. You good?" Chris asked.

"Um, y-yeah. Let's get out of here." My cheeks were burning, and without waiting for Chris's response, I quickly ducked out of the bubble tea shop.

The cool night air, combined with the acrid smell of smoke, met us as we headed outside. By now all the alcohol had worn off, and I grew distinctly aware of how strange this situation was—that I'd run into an old academic rival at a frat party, who also happened to be the son of my parents' rivals, and that we were now grabbing bubble tea and catching up like old pals. Chris must have sensed the awkwardness in the air, too, because he fell silent, and that made the atmosphere even more awkward.

I was struggling to come up with something to say when we passed by a shady-looking space next to Bubble Mania, the sign hanging above it with only half the letters lit up to spell Blue Jug. The inside was crowded with older adults sitting down and ordering drinks.

Two guys came out of the bar, one with his head shaved military-style, the other with a full head of brown hair. Both of them were covered in huge tattoos. They stumbled into the middle of our path while carrying a conversation at the top of their lungs.

The one nearest to me, the buff guy with buzzed blonde hair, bumped into me before I could get out of the way. The movement pushed me right into a streetlamp. My arm collided with it, and I winced as pain shot up it.

"Hey, watch it." Chris popped up right beside me, almost out of nowhere, glaring at the offender. It seemed like everyone was determined to bump into me tonight.

The drunk guy squinted at us, as if noticing our presence for the first time. "No, you watch where you're going, buddy," he slurred, poking Chris in the chest.

Bad move. I could practically feel the testosterone swirling around in the air, waiting to clash with the bad tempers. Instinctively, I knew this was a losing battle. Better to run now than to get in any heat with these guys. Better to keep my head down if I wanted to stay out of trouble.

"It's okay," I stammered to the drunk man.

"Anna, don't you dare apologize. It was not your fault," Chris snapped, glaring at the two guys.

My heart hammered, and my stomach plummeted in fear. I jerked my head to the side, sending what I hoped was a message for Chris to stop. He was going to get jumped. We were both going to get hurt. But Chris ignored me, keeping his angry gaze on the two guys.

"What're you kids doing out here at this time of night, anyway?" the other guy jeered. "Didn't expect people like you to be out drinking."

Chris threw him a withering look and raised his untouched cup of milk tea. "Sorry. Didn't realize the drinking age applied to bubble tea, too."

"Just sayin'. Rare to see you Asians outside of the library." The blonde man laughed, high-fiving his drunk friend.

My heart pumped faster in shock as I registered what he said. It was said so casually, directly to our faces. Like it was a known fact. Like they knew we wouldn't fight back. I froze. Even if I wanted to fight back, I didn't know how to.

Chris's jaw slackened, muscles tensing beneath his shirt, as if he was gearing up for a fight. He'd dropped his bubble tea onto the ground. The light brown liquid oozed out of the straw and formed a lake at his foot, but he didn't seem to notice.

Though anger pulsed in my body, turning my blood hot, I only wanted to run as far away from these people as possible. Maybe that made me a coward. I didn't care. I just didn't want the situation to escalate. Chris puffed up, quivering with visible anger, but I grabbed his sleeve.

"Please, let's just go back," I said.

His eyes flickered toward me, and some of the fight seemed to leave them as he registered the fear in my expression. Swallowing hard, Chris nodded.

I did my best to ignore the jeers and the deep shame that filled my belly as we fled the scene. When we reached West Tower, Chris turned toward me.

"I fucking forgot how racist the Midwest is," he said through gritted teeth. "You should've let me hit him, Anna. I wish you'd let me hit him. Fuck."

I stared at Chris, wondering if he was right. Wondering if I *should* have let Chris deck that guy. But then if both guys had retaliated, there was no way Chris could have taken them both on, and no way I'd be any use in a physical fight.

Then Chris's words registered. *I fucking forgot how racist the Midwest is.*

It must have been bizarre to grow up in the States as the minority, go back to China and live for six years as the majority, and then come back to the States to live as the minority again. And at the same time, I was envious of Chris. Envious that he'd spent his high school years in a place where he felt accepted without question.

The mood of the night had soured. And I was sure that my parents wouldn't be happy if they knew I was hanging out with Chris Lu, especially since he'd almost gotten into a fight just now. I mumbled something about having a headache and left Chris to go back to my room.

As I stared at Laura's empty bed, I couldn't help but think that wherever she was, she was probably having a much better time than me.

Chapter Seven

"MELISSA HUNG?"

"Melissa *Hong*," I said to the librarian sitting behind the front desk. It was midafternoon in the undergraduate library. There was a surprising number of students already studying in the library, and it made me feel guilty for not spending my time getting ahead on *my* reading. But this was important, too. I lowered my voice. "The student who was murdered seven years ago."

The elderly librarian blinked slowly behind her round lenses, her green eyes widening in surprise. "Ah. Yes, that was a very unfortunate moment of Brookings history. Well, any publicly released information would be available online," she said. "The police report is public, as well as a newspaper article written by our own students. I'm not sure how else I can be of help."

I'd already read the police report and the *Brookings Daily* article multiple times. They were vague and useless in terms of giving any actual information around Melissa's murder.

"There's nothing about this in the archives?" I asked. The university brochure boasted having one of the biggest, most impressive library systems in the nation. "I've done all the online research I can."

"Yes, I'm afraid there's nothing more to be found in the library archives. It's unfortunate, but that case was never solved, as the police never found any evidence connecting anyone to the murder."

I hadn't come to the library to turn away empty-handed. Even though I could tell the librarian was growing annoyed, her expression remained polite. Still, I pressed, "Well, is there anyone you can direct me to who might know more information surrounding Melissa Hong's death? A member of the faculty, maybe?"

The librarian narrowed her eyes and pursed her lips. "Is this for a school project, dear?"

Saying "my ongoing personal project in the pursuit of justice" sounded too corny. "Um, no, not really."

"I'm sorry, but I can't help you," she said gently. "Now, if there's anything else—"

"There is," I interrupted. "Could you help me find a book about the history of the university? Anything that might be related to a secret society called the Order of Alpha?"

"The Order of Alpha," the librarian repeated. I could tell from her weary expression that giving me information about the Order was the last thing she wanted to do, but that only further piqued my curiosity. "Another unfortunate moment of Brookings history. You aren't the first to ask about it, and you won't be the last, I imagine."

I stared at the librarian. My impatience must have been

obvious, because she sighed and said, "Wait right here." She got up from her chair and disappeared into a huge shelf of books to her left. After a few moments, she reemerged, carrying three dusty books in her arms. She set them down on the desk in front of me in a *whomp* that caused dust to fly up. I turned away, blinking. "*The Life and Legacy of Alfred Brookings, A History of Brookings University*, and *Secret Societies: Inside the Universities' Most Elite*. That should be a good place for you to start."

"Thank you," I said. After the librarian checked out the books, I put them into my backpack, just barely able to zip it shut. Then I headed downstairs to the library cafe, where I ordered myself a chocolate croissant and a small coffee. I had a lot of research to do.

•⊩⸺⊪•

Six hours and two more cups of coffee later, I wasn't anywhere closer to finding the truth behind Melissa Hong's death than I'd been before. My eyes were so dry from staring at text that when I blinked, they watered in pain.

There was nothing useful to be found in *The Life and Legacy of Alfred Brookings*, which might as well have been a biography of Alfred himself, the school's founder. *A History of Brookings University* had one chapter on secret societies, including a few called "Cross and Bones," "The Order of Sol Invictus," and "Skull Guard." There was no mention of the Order of Alpha. Finally, I managed to find a small paragraph of information in *Secret Societies: Inside the Universities' Most Elite*, in the chapter on Brookings University.

The Order of Alpha

Unlike many other university secret societies, whose
activities are only "secret" in the sense of being elitist,
hardly anything is known about the Order of Alpha.
Founded in 1902, it was the third-oldest secret society
at Brookings University. True to its name, the Order
of Alpha bears the symbol of a wolf's head. The society residence was in the Hill House on Central Campus, which later became the first female-only dorm in
the 1960s. Members would meet at Hill House and
occasionally host exclusive invitation-only parties.
However, in the 1950s, a string of crimes were connected with the Order, including the disappearance of
a student in 1958. The organization was consequently
forced to disband later that year. There has been no
known activity associated with this disbanded Order
since.

I turned to the next page, hoping to find more about the
society, but there was nothing. After consulting the glossary for
any other mentions of the Order of Alpha, I was forced to conclude that this small, vague paragraph was the only record of the
mysterious society. I had little to go on, but at least this was a
start. There were two major clues I could use—that the Order of
Alpha had congregated at Hill House, and that a student had
disappeared in 1958. I'd passed by Hill House once or twice,

and nothing had ever seemed out of the ordinary, but then again, it must have been many years since anything strange had happened there. I filed away the name to check it out later.

I sat back in my chair, closed my eyes, and let out a deep breath. In the end, though, the Order had been disbanded. I already knew that. Disappointment settled in my chest, and it was a distinctly unsatisfying feeling.

So then who had left their symbol at the scene where Melissa Hong's body had been found, and why? What was their motive? Was it to announce that the Order was back in secret, or just to thrust the blame upon something no longer in existence?

I gathered my books, threw away my empty coffee cups, and rushed back upstairs to the library, sitting at the nearest open computer. A quick Google search of "Brookings University Order of Alpha 1958 student disappearance" brought up several results. I clicked on the first one, which was a Wikipedia article, and scanned it eagerly for further clues.

According to the very short article, a student by the name of Janet Chen had disappeared in the fall of 1958 and had never been found. There wasn't much known about her background. The article briefly mentioned the Order of Alpha but made it sound like it was only rumored to have been involved with Janet's death. Nothing had ever been confirmed.

It was impossible to ignore the similarities of Janet Chen's disappearance to what had happened with Melissa Hong. The fact that the Order of Alpha seemed to be connected with both incidents couldn't be a coincidence. A knot of fear formed in my stomach. What if the Order had only given the appearance of being disbanded, but was secretly still active? Then that meant girls like Janet and Melissa—like me—could still be in danger.

I shivered. If that was true, then solving Melissa's case was no longer just about restoring justice to my former babysitter. It was about finding the perpetrators before they could turn their murderous intent toward others, toward me.

By the time I had finished reading through all the articles I could find—which didn't take that much longer, considering how little information was available—darkness had fallen outside the glass windows of the library. I hadn't even started any of my homework yet. It was only week one of college, and I'd already fallen behind on my schoolwork. That couldn't be good.

I gathered up my belongings to rush out of the library. "Get it together, Anna." I hadn't realized I'd spoken until two passing boys gave me a strange look. Oops. I hurried along, back to the safety to West Tower.

Laura wasn't in our room, and I felt guilty for the relief that surged in me at that. It wasn't that I hated my roommate, but rather that I was always performing around her. Trying to be the fun girl I'd been on the night we went to the frat party together. I couldn't relax and be myself around Laura, so it was exhausting being in the same room as her.

Laura and I seemed to have mutually agreed that we wouldn't be friends after what happened at Theta Pi, which was fine. I really didn't fit in with her and her groupies, and it didn't sit well with me that she'd basically abandoned me in a frat house.

She was spending less and less time in the room these days, so we didn't even see enough of each other to become friends.

Unfortunately, I hadn't made any other friends in my dorm. There was Chris, but I wouldn't count him a friend, really. After what had happened the night of the frat party, we hadn't spoken much except to exchange greetings when we ran into each other in the hall. The playful, almost flirty mood that had existed between us during that night had vanished. I guess Chris sensed that I wasn't super eager to forget our competitive history, and he wasn't that eager, either.

It didn't help that my parents also seemed eager to remind me of my currently friendless status.

> *Ma:* Anna, how is your first week going? Have you made friends?
> *Ba:* Have you talked to Henry Jiang yet?
> *Anna:* I don't even know who Henry is omg
> *Ma:* What about the kids in your dorm?
> *Anna:* Yeah they're fine. I'm making friends, don't worry
> *Ba:* Tell them to stop by Sweetea sometime. 10% discount for friends
> *Anna:* Omggggg

I didn't even know when I was supposed to find the time to make friends. The amount of reading I had to do for my classics, East Asian studies, writing, and even astronomy classes was astronomical—no pun intended.

Plus, there was Festifall the next day. Festifall was an event where all the student organizations preyed on innocent freshmen to get them to join their group. But at least it would give me an excuse to putting off my reading for my Astro 102 class. That was good enough for me.

·⊪————⊪·

Festifall hit me in a wave of sound, drenching me in the noises of shouting. There was even singing coming from the corner of the Quad, the center of campus, where the a cappella groups had staked their claim.

I walked behind a group of Chinese international students chattering away in rapid-fire Mandarin. I knew Laura and her friends were somewhere around here, too, but I didn't bother asking her to meet up.

As I wandered through the crowd, I felt like I was touring the inside of one of Brookings's DIVERSITY! brochures. Cultural organizations were madly recruiting freshmen. Indian Student Association to my left, shoving pamphlets at anyone who made the mistake of standing still long enough. Black Student Association to my right, chatting up a storm with a crowd of wide-eyed freshmen. The members of the Japanese Student Association, some of them dressed in kimonos, were throwing handfuls of traditional candy out into the crowd. There was even the Squirrel Feeding Club that Elise had talked about when I'd moved in.

As I ventured farther into the jungle of student organizations, I was met by a group of artsy-looking Asian kids who were wearing matching purple shirts and singing a cover of Ed Sheeran's "Shape of You."

"Hey, you're Asian!" yelled one of the guys who had his hair tied back in a man bun. He pointed right at me. "Do you like to sing?"

"No—"

"Great! You should audition. We're the Asian-interest a cappella group." The boy shoved a flyer into my hand and moved on to his next victim without even waiting for a response. "Hey, you're Asian!"

My eyes landed on the one lone white kid at the end in a sea of Asians in the a cappella group, who stuck out like a sore thumb. He nodded most enthusiastically, pointing to himself. As if to say, oh yes, Token White Boy at your service, bringing diversity to this Asian interest group since 2019.

I couldn't sing if my life depended on it. I hurried away, dodging eager faces and waving away flyers left and right. These Festifall people were scarily well-trained, professional handout-givers.

Miraculously I made it to a cluster of tables advertising for the university's more general activities. I scanned the different tables. There was a tap dance club. A robotics team. A handout reminding students about the university's mental health resources.

A pair of freshmen girls shoved past me, whispering and giggling.

"Are you thinking of rushing?" one of them asked the other.

"A sorority? Are you kidding me? I'd rather throw myself

into a lake," snorted the other. "The only society I'd consider joining is one of the secret societies here, but I don't know how to get in—they're *that* elite."

At the mention of the phrase "secret societies," I turned around in curiosity, but the girls' voices faded as they were swallowed up by the crowd.

In the corner, there was a white table with a group advertising their social media app, something called Friend Me. As I approached the Friend Me table, the blonde girl who was sitting behind the booth gave me a huge smile.

"Hey there! I'm Michelle, cofounder of Friend Me. Take a flyer." She shoved one into my hand, giving me no choice but to take it, almost giving me a paper cut in the process. "It's similar to a dating app, but specifically for making friends, not romantic connections, at Brookings University. It's especially helpful for freshmen and international students. The app was developed by a graduate student here last year, and it's still fairly new, so it's easy to meet people." She flashed a smile.

I raised an eyebrow, trying not to look too interested, even though my curiosity was piqued. Michelle gave me a sympathetic look, and I wondered if my loner status was written across my face.

"Thanks," I said quickly before moving along.

By the time I'd made it safely back to my dorm, my hands and backpack were stuffed full of flyers I didn't even remember picking up. Skimming through the piles, I didn't find anything that really caught my interest, except for the Friend Me app.

FRIEND ME: *A dating app, but for friends!*

♥

Feeling lonely in a new place? Sad that you haven't found your friend group yet? Just download Friend Me from the iTunes Store to create a profile and match with friends exclusively on campus who share your interests!

It couldn't hurt to give this app a shot. Not like there was any other way to make friends from the comfort of my dorm bed. Maybe some people would think it was weird to use apps for friendship, but at this point I was willing to give anything a shot.

I downloaded the Friend Me app and created a profile for myself, selecting my best recent selfie and answering a series of questions about my interests. That took about half an hour. For the next thirty minutes, I swiped through the profiles of different students, from freshmen to seniors and even some grad students.

It wasn't that much longer before I got my first match. My heart skipped a beat in excitement as the notification flashed on my screen, and I quickly checked out my match.

The profile showed a brown-haired, green-eyed girl. There was a fierce red streak in the middle of her hair. Her name was Jane—just Jane, no last name listed. Jane was a sophomore. Her interests included gaming, playing chess, and watching anime. I debated if I should send her an opening message. But before I could even begin to construct one—Hey, is Welcome Week going badly for you too?—my phone pinged with another notification. Jane had messaged me first.

Jane: Hey! Saw that you put "anime" in your interests so I thought I'd swipe. So happy we matched :) What's your favorite anime?

Anna: Hi :) Yeah, huge anime nerd over here lol. My favorite is probably Haikyuu! I freaking love sports anime. Hbu?

Jane: Oooh that's a good one. Hmmm such a tough choice but I gotta go with Death Note.

Anna: A classic.

Jane: So you're a freshman right?

Anna: Yup

Jane: Which dorm did they put you in? I was in West Tower last year, but now I'm stuck on North Campus lol it suuuuucks here

Anna: Oof yeah you're far away from everything. I'm living in West Tower

Jane: Luckyyyy. It's nice there, isn't it?

Anna: Yeah it's nicer than I thought it'd be

Jane: The dining hall has the BEST chocolate chip cookies. Ugh I miss them

Anna: They're god tier lol. So are you finding it kinda hard to make friends here too?

Jane: Yeah actually, which is why I'm on this app lol. Here on North Campus there's only the deer to keep me company but idk if I can call them friends

Anna: Lmaooooo. Good thing there's this app haha

Jane: Ikr? Lol have you made any friends so far?

Anna: I'd been hoping to be friends with my roommate

but we don't really vibe . . . so I haven't met anyone I'd
call a friend yet tbh
Jane: Awww . I remember being like that at first too . . .
you'll meet cool ppl, dw. We're all here at Brookings cuz
we're nerds and overachievers lol. Well, most of us
anyway
Anna: What made you choose Brookings?
Jane: I didn't get into my top choice (Columbia) so this
was the next-best place. Hbu?
Anna: I've always kinda known I'd come to Brookings
bc I'm in-state, and the tuition price is hard to beat
lol. But also . . . I feel like there's a lot of mystery
here
Jane: Yup, I heard lots of ghost stories during freshman
orientation lol

Ghost stories. Did that mean Jane knew what had happened
with Melissa Hong, or at least knew of her? My fingers typed a
question, then deleted it, then retyped it, then deleted it. Finally,
I took a deep breath and decided to take the plunge. If this Jane
person thought I was weird, I'd just ghost her. And if not, then
I'd made a new friend.

Anna: Have you heard the name Melissa Hong?

It took several minutes for Jane to reply, long enough that I
thought the message was still in the process of delivering, before
I got the notification of an answer.

Jane: The girl who was killed on campus?

Anna: Yeah, they never found out who murdered her

Jane: Are you trying to find out who murdered her?

Anna: Idk, but I just can't help feeling like . . . there's gotta be more to the story. Melissa was my babysitter when I was a kid, plus she's a family friend, so it just really sucks knowing what happened to her

Jane: Damn I'm sorry

Anna: It's ok, I don't remember her that well. But I've just always wanted to know the truth. I wish she'd gotten justice

Jane: So that's why you decided on Brookings?

Anna: One of the reasons—it'd be dumb to choose a college based on a murder case

Jane: True

Anna: Idk why I just told you all that but the fact that you haven't ghosted me is a good sign I hope LMAO

Jane: No dude I love true crime!! Trust me you could never creep me out, I've seen it all

Anna: Lmfao good to know. I dont know anyone who's into true crime like me so this is a first. Do you listen to the podcast Unsolved Murders?

Jane: No but Im adding it to my list now

Anna: Yessss I'm obsessed with it

Jane: You seem so cool, we def need to meet up sometime :) Just give me 1000 years to get from North Campus down to Central

Anna: Stoppp you're killing me omfg

I smiled to myself. Maybe this Friend Me business was cooler than I thought. Even though Jane and I had been talking for all of an hour, somehow I'd even felt comfortable enough to confide in her my private obsession with finding the truth behind Melissa Hong's murder. Already it felt like I had more in common with Jane than with my roommate or anyone else I'd met here so far.

I must've dozed off while texting Jane, because the next thing I knew the sun was shining through the curtains. The opening theme song of the *Demon Slayer* anime blasted from my phone alarm.

Groggily, I glanced over toward Laura's side of the room. She hadn't come home last night. Either that, or she'd come back while I was sleeping and had already rushed off to her first class of the day. I had no idea where she was going all day, and even at night, but it wasn't any of my business.

I checked my phone, happy to see that Jane had sent me another message while I was asleep. I quickly responded, and then I texted Laura to make sure she was okay. There was no response. Hopefully she'd reply when she woke up.

Even though my first class wasn't for another hour, I decided I should at least try for the first day of school. Sighing, I fetched my shower caddy, towel, and flip-flops. A nice, cold shower was just what I needed to clear my head. The idea of sharing a community bathroom still creeped me out—talk about a privacy invasion—but I'd mostly gotten used to it. So had the rest of my floor mates. Some a little too quickly. A girl had been popping her pimples in here unabashedly just last night.

When I returned to the room, Laura was back. She'd clearly had a wild night of partying. Her hair and outfit were disheveled, and she was frantically removing the makeup from her face. She glanced at me when I walked in but didn't even smile before turning away again.

"Had a fun night?" I said into the awkward silence.

"Yup."

I waited a beat, but it was obvious my roommate wasn't interested in disclosing further details. Okay. *Thanks for nothing, Laura.* I couldn't help the annoyance that rose within me. Maybe we didn't need to be best friends, but she could at least try to be a little more friendly, especially because I knew she could carry a conversation when she wanted to. I wasn't sure if I'd done something to offend her, but Laura was like a brick wall.

The silence stretched between us, broken only by the sounds of getting ready for our first college classes. Swinging her designer backpack over one shoulder, Laura swept out of the room, the scent of her cinnamon perfume trailing in her wake.

Something fluttered to the floor. A gold card, faintly scented like vanilla.

"Hey, you dropped something," I said, picking up the card. It was an invitation. Written in white lettering on the front were the words You're Invited . . . to the Elite of the Elite. There were a few more letters, but they were in Greek.

Laura swooped down and snatched the card out of my hand before I could examine it further. "Did you see?" she demanded.

"N-No," I said, bewildered. Laura's eyes were furious, even wild-looking. She fixed me with a long, hard stare that made me feel like I'd broken the law, or something.

"Good," my roommate said at long last. "I'll see you around." Without another word, Laura stuffed the card into the front pocket of her black leather jacket and left.

My mind raced. Given the fancy gold card and Greek lettering, it wasn't hard to guess what Laura was up to—rushing a sorority. That certainly explained her weird behavior. Explained why she was out all the time and didn't want to be friends with me. She'd already chosen her friend circle, and I wasn't part of it.

That still didn't explain why Laura had overreacted like that when she thought I'd read the whole invitation, but maybe Greek life was super secretive.

Shaking my head, I picked up my backpack, preparing to head off to my first lesson—Sources of East Asian Civilizations. It was my elective course. I'd never taken a course specifically focused on Asian books before. Back at Sinclair Prep, my teachers had taught according to the standardized curriculum, which meant only Eurocentric texts like *The Great Gatsby* and *The Odyssey*. Even in my World History course, we hadn't learned much about Asia. Call me a geek, but I was stoked to have the chance to rectify that in college.

The main reason I'd selected this elective, though, was because of who was teaching it. Professor Gregory Wittman, the

only professor mentioned in the *Brookings Daily* article in connection with Melissa. If there was a chance that he might know
something nobody else did, I intended to find out.

Not even Laura's snub could dampen my spirits. I didn't
need her, anyway. There were tens of thousands of undergrads
at Brookings. I could definitely find people who actually wanted
me around. People like Jane.

Chapter Eight

I SLID THROUGH THE FRONT doors of the Hewitt Auditorium just in time for the Sources of East Asian Civilizations professor to introduce himself.

Professor Gregory Wittman was a tiny, pale, gray-haired man who wore half-moon spectacles and a tweed jacket. I couldn't help but think that he was like a grown-up version of a boarding school student—the type of person who might age, but never quite outgrew their schoolboy selves. The professor stood awkwardly on the stage, his shoulders slightly hunched, as we filed into the auditorium. I took a seat in one of the front rows, then glanced around at my classmates.

Sources of East Asian Civilizations was an introductory course, so there were no prerequisites to take it. There were a ton of students enrolled, most of them freshmen and sophomores. They were strangers now, but maybe some of these students would be the people who would be *my* people—people who would go on coffee runs or would study with me in the library. Or maybe they just got stuck in this class because their first choices were full. Maybe they were going to drop the class as soon as possible.

Professor Wittman had the graduate teaching assistants introduce themselves.

"Cindy Tian," said the petite Asian woman next to him who looked like she could've been an undergrad student herself. "I majored in East Asian studies at UCLA, and this is my second year here as a TA."

"I'm Robert," grunted a blonde-haired, scruffy-looking man who looked like he was in his mid-twenties. "It's my first year as a TA, but I got my undergrad here at Brookings in 2018. I took a few years off to travel Asia."

Cindy had smiled and waved and appeared friendly enough, but Robert gave only the smallest of grins before he went back to looking sullen.

"All right, now that the introductions are over, let's get down to business," said Professor Wittman, clapping his hands together.

While Professor Wittman went over the course guidelines and expectations, as well as the required reading, I scanned the syllabus packet he'd set out in front of each open seat. I'd only heard of a few of the texts on the list before. *Monkey: Folk Novel of China*, written by Wu Cheng En and translated by Arthur Waley. *Dream of the Red Chamber* by Cao Xueqin. *Water Margin* by Nai'an Shi. These were Chinese classic texts, some of which I'd read in Chinese school growing up, or watched drama adaptations. Suddenly I was glad my parents had always forced me to stay connected to my Chinese culture. I might have a leg up in this class, and I needed all the help I could get for my first semester of college.

There were other texts on the list, too, ones I'd never heard of. *The Pillow Book of Sei Shonagon, The Tale of Genji, Tale of the Heike.* Just looking at the sheer amount of assigned reading for this course was enough to exhaust me. Yet at the same time, it excited me. Finally, here were a variety of texts that were challenging and completely fresh.

I wasn't alone in being intimidated by the course load, either, judging by the whispered conversations happening around me. Maybe Sources of East Asian Civilizations was one of those "weeder" courses—which, I was quickly learning, was what students called the tough introductory courses meant to "weed" out the strong from the weak. I didn't intend to be weeded out.

"I know many of you are freshmen, and this is your first college class," said Professor Wittman, who clearly hadn't missed the overwhelmed expressions on our faces. "This is a fun class, but I won't sugarcoat—it's also a lot of reading, and it's fast-paced. Those of you who decide to persevere, you'd better get used to the level of coursework expected of you. You aren't in high school any longer."

The guy next to me muttered something under his breath that I didn't catch. I gathered from the sighs going around the room that people weren't happy with the news. But the excitement of a new challenge buzzed within me. High school had been the most miserable, boring four years of my life. I'd take a boatload of reading for an elective course over drowning myself in AP classes and standardized test prep again. Now, I was ready for a challenge—ready to read something I'd enjoy for once.

Class ended half an hour early since it was syllabus week. I practically dashed out of the auditorium. To get the first-day jitters out of my system, I went back to West Tower, and then on a quick run around campus. By the time I'd gotten back and finished showering, I only had half an hour before my next class.

I quickly cobbled together a sandwich in the dining hall and scarfed it down before heading across campus to the Arthur Jameson Building for Great Books. Though I'd made sure to find all my classes before the semester actually began, it was totally different finding buildings when there was a time limit.

I made it to Great Books with one minute to spare, sweating and panting. It was a smaller class, and the seating was a bit cramped.

The course was taught by Professor Reed—or Lacey, as she told us to call her. She was a short woman who looked to be in her mid-thirties. Her blonde hair was swept back in a tight bun, and she wore glasses that magnified her light blue eyes. She would've been pretty if her features weren't screwed up in a seriously vicious glare.

"Let's get roll call and some other pesky first-day attendance business out of the way right now," she said, opening a large binder that had been sitting behind her computer. "Mason Anderson?"

"Here."

Roll call continued for about ten minutes as our professor

familiarized herself with our names and faces. ". . . and finally, Gillian Zhang."

"Here."

"Great. Almost everyone is here today. I want you to remember, students, that if you aren't here, you're wrong." Lacey shut the binder and turned toward the board. "Now that that's out of the way, I'd like to focus our first discussion on the reading I assigned over the summer—*The Iliad*. Today we'll be talking about . . ."

Already my attention was wandering. I assessed my classmates. The majority of them looked like they had spent their high school days with their faces buried in books like I had, stomping around their schools in Oxford boots and tweed jackets.

I spotted a couple other Asian kids in the class. One of them, to my surprise, was Chris Lu. I guess it shouldn't have been too surprising, since this was an introductory honors course, so pretty much everyone here was an honors freshman. Still, what were the odds that we'd be assigned to the same section of the course?

We hadn't really spoken to each other since the frat party incident, but when we locked gazes, Chris gave me a little nod. I nodded back, coolly. Old habits die hard, and I was already gearing up to outmaneuver him to become the top student in the class.

"'Rage—Goddess, sing the rage of Peleus' son Achilles . . . that cost the Achaeans countless losses . . . And the will of Zeus was moving toward its end.'" Lacey recited the opening lines of Book One, and then glanced up around at us expectantly. "Anna. Can you tell us what these first few lines foreshadow, in terms of setting and conflict?"

I jolted, my heart hammering in shock. I'd heard that professors often would cold-call in college courses, but I hadn't been prepared for it to happen so soon—and not to me. *Come on,* I urged myself. *Weren't you ready for a challenge?*

"Um," I squeaked, and then immediately wanted to kick myself. I'd studied the material the night before, yet somehow now, when the moment had come, my mind was blank. Sweat slickened my palms as Lacey leveled her gaze on me. "Well . . . the Trojan War," I blurted. "It's set during the Trojan War."

Lacey nodded, raising her eyebrows. A beat later, I realized she expected more from my answer, and a sense of panic overwhelmed me. I hadn't studied these lines thoroughly enough, though, because nothing struck me. The silence in the classroom was suffocating. I'd never wanted so badly for a hole to open up in the floor and swallow me whole.

"Oh—Chris, was it?" Lacey said, turning her attention away from me. "Go ahead."

Because of course Chris had raised his hand in the air. He wasn't looking at me, but focusing his gaze on our professor.

I willed him to mess up, even though it was petty.

"Professor, more specifically, the opening lines foreshadow the *end* of the Trojan War. Zeus declares the Achaeans to be the victor," answered Chris, as smoothly as though he were reading from an essay paper. "Then, when Homer goes on to say, 'What god drove them to fight with such a fury?' the implication is that the gods were directly involved with the war and conflict."

"Well-put," said Lacey. "Now this is an example of a college-level response. Whatever standard you all were held to in high school, it no longer applies. I expect more thoughtful answers from each of you. Got it?"

Chris sat up taller in his seat, while others exchanged nervous looks around the classroom. I bit my lip. Even if Lacey hadn't directed the words exactly at me, I still couldn't help but feel as though they were a personal dig. And why did it have to be Chris, of all people, who showed me up in our first Great Books lecture?

The tips of my ears burned. This was going to be a long semester.

For the next hour, Lacey rambled on and on about the Trojan War. Luckily, I had something to entertain me.

Anna: It's only my first day and I can't wait to graduate already
Jane: Looool you're hilarious
Anna: Long shot, but have you taken Great Books with Lacey Reed?
Jane: Yeah actually, I took it last year. She's the only Great Books prof lmao
Anna: is she always this . . . strict? She cold-called me and it didn't go well

Jane: Ouchhhh. Yeah that's Prof Reed for ya

Anna: Maybe I should just drop this class :(

Jane: Aw chin up. I'm pretty sure I still have all my homework and quizzes from last year. I can just lend it to you lol

Anna: You'd do that?

Jane: Yeah ofc. That's what friends are for

Anna: skfjaslkdfajsklfa you're literally the nicest person I've met here. Thanks :)

Jane: Np. I find it hard to believe you haven't met nicer ppl here tho lol you seem super nice yourself

Anna: Ahaha thanks, it's just rare for me to vibe with anyone cuz I don't like most ppl lol. So friends are hard to come by

Jane: That's why you're on Friend Me huh?

Anna: Yup. Tbh I don't even talk to my high school friends much anymore lol

Jane: Omg really? Did something happen?

Anna: Nah we just don't have much to talk about. We were like . . . academic friends

Jane: Ohhhhh I know what you mean. Like you study together but you wouldn't hang out at the mall or something right?

Anna: Exactly. Like I couldn't tell them that I'm trying to investigate a murder on my own lmao. They'd think it was weird

Jane: We rly are a lot alike cuz I'm pretty much the same

Jane and I messaged throughout the entirety of Great Books whenever I dared to pull out my phone as Lacey looked the other way. We texted through my final class of the day, too— Astronomy 102.

I learned that Jane hadn't chosen her major yet, but she was leaning toward a concentration in math with a minor in Japanese language. She'd been in the honors program last year, just like me, but ended up dropping the program because there were too many requirements, which she called "annoying."

Anna: Wdym annoying?
Jane: Like you can just take easier classes outside of the program and still make honors status if your GPA is high enough lol. So might as well save yourself the trouble of all the honors classes
Anna: Oh wtf then why would anyone do the honors program?
Jane: That's what I'm saying LOL. The university won't tell you, but it's way more trouble than it's worth. I'd just drop the program if I were you
Anna: Wow I had no clue . . . tbh tho I think I'll continue w the program.
Jane: Rly? Why?

I couldn't exactly tell Jane the truth—that I was basically retracing Melissa Hong's footsteps, even trying to get to know one of her former professors. Jane would definitely think I had screws loose.

Anna: My parents want me to do it haha
Jane: Lol good luck then

By the time Astro 102 had finished—a whole forty-five minutes ahead of the normal scheduled end time—it was time for me to make good to my promise to my parents and check in on them at the bakery.

I headed across campus, crossing the Quad, where students were relaxing and enjoying the freedom of syllabus week. It was a crisp, cool fall afternoon. The leaves turned shades of gold as they fell from the campus trees, scattering across the sidewalk. There was nothing as beautiful as autumn in the Midwest. I hugged my jacket closer to me, bristling against a sudden cool breeze that rustled the trees and leaves.

Jane: What're you up to tonight?
Anna: Gonna go check in on my parents' bakery first and then do homework lol
Jane: Whoa your parents own a bakery? Do I know of it?
Anna: Probably? It's really close to campus. It's called Sweetea
Jane: Oh I haven't been there yet, but I've heard of it. I'll have to check it out
Anna: Yeah come thru sometime! I can make sure you get a discount on our baked goods :)
Jane: You're the bestttt. Ok won't keep you lol have fun at the bakery!

I walked down State Street, where Sweetea was tucked in a corner of the town not far off campus. But before I came in view of the familiar location, my eyes landed on Sunny's Bakery. It was shiny and chic, with an edgy, modern look to it, all off-white walls and golden hues. I could see how even in just a few months since its opening, Sunny's Bakery had edged us out for the competition, bringing the appeal of Chinese cuisine with a more modern, aesthetic Western spin. Located just this much closer to the college campus, it had to draw crowds of students at all hours of the day and night. Our bakery tended to draw an older crowd and had a comforting family-style feeling to it.

Sweetea's vibe, and my parents', was focused on staying traditionally Chinese without so much Western influence.

It wasn't Chris's fault that Sunny's was here, was cool . . . but I couldn't help but feel annoyed at him anyway. We'd been here first before the Lus moved in and upstaged us. Plus, I was already irritated enough with him for showing me up, even if he hadn't meant to, in Great Books. If he *had* meant to show me up, that was even worse.

"I'm here," I called as I stepped into Sweetea. It was empty except for some regulars: an old Cantonese couple who didn't understand a word of English, and a new face I didn't recognize—a college-age, athletic-looking Asian guy who was wearing a hood that obscured his features. Gave off the vibes of a typical frat boy. There was also an older female worker I didn't recognize—new hire, I guessed—who smiled at me in some confusion from the counter as I headed to the back of the kitchen to grab my uniform, an apron and hat. Ba was back there along with two other pastry chefs, hard at work kneading some dough.

"Anna. How was your first couple of days on campus?" Ba asked.

I shrugged, tying my hair back into a ponytail. "Okay, I guess."

"Making friends?"

"Um . . . yeah," I lied. I'd made *friend*. As in singular. As in Jane, only.

The smell of dough and Chinese sweets wafted toward me, and I inhaled the familiar scent, feeling much more at ease than I'd been since moving into my dorm. Not that I'd admit that to either of my parents. If they knew how lonely I'd been feeling, they'd immediately try to convince me to move back in. Despite my loneliness, that was the last thing I wanted to do. I was a college student now. I was determined to sort my problems out on my own. Besides, Ma and Ba had their hands full trying to deal with Sweetea's plummeting revenues.

"Go watch the register," Ba said, making a shooing motion at me.

"Yeah, yeah." I headed out toward the counter. After about fifteen minutes passed with no new customers, I said, "Hey, Ba, have you considered . . . you know . . . redecorating this place?" I waved a hand toward the gray-white walls, the five sets of sad-looking wooden tables and chairs that sorely needed to be updated.

"We don't have that kind of money in the budget," my father said.

Money had always been tight for my family, but I was sure Brookings was putting a bit of extra strain on them. I gritted my teeth. I didn't care if Chris had saved me from that Theta Pi Neanderthal the other day. We had to edge out Sunny's Bakery for business.

Bored with the slowness of the shift, I started texting Jane again. But then the door opened, signaling a customer coming in. Finally.

"Welcome to Sweetea!" I said, wincing a little at my own overdone enthusiasm. My smile fell when I saw who'd come through the door. It was a short, stocky Asian man wearing a Sunny's Bakery shirt. He had a saran-wrapped pan of food raised in one hand.

"Um, what can I do for you?" I asked. I had no idea why the enemy had wandered into Sweetea territory, but it had made my afternoon infinitely more awkward.

"Can I speak to the manager?" asked the man.

"Sure." I turned around toward the kitchen and bellowed, "Ba!"

There was the sound of someone tripping and banging into something hard. Cardboard boxes tumbling over, followed by muffled swearing. "Don't yell, Anna!"

My father emerged from the depths of the kitchen, his top hat knocked sideways, his expression in a grumpy frown. "Lao Lu," he said, after he and the stranger sized each other up for a moment. "It's been a long time."

The tension in the air was so thick, you could've cut it with one of the bakery's knives.

"Hǎo jiǔ bù jiàn," Mr. Lu finally said. Then, switching to a slightly accented but otherwise fluid English, "I, ahem, wanted to properly come by to say hello from Sunny's Bakery." His mouth curled up in a forced smile. "We opened just across the street from you. You may have noticed."

"Yes," Ba said through his teeth, and I found it remarkable that he was still keeping his cool.

Mr. Lu reached out his free hand to grip Ba's slack hand in a firm handshake. He switched quickly to speaking Mandarin. "I would have said hello earlier, but customers swarmed us almost as soon as we opened. It's been quite wild." Mr. Lu laughed.

Whether the humble brag was intentional or not, it was possibly the worst thing he could have said. Mr. Lu was digging his own grave with every word. Ba had forced a cold smile that didn't reach his eyes. "That's very . . . fortunate for you," Ba said after a painful silence.

"I brought over some samples of our desserts if you would like to try them," Mr. Lu offered, holding out the tray in his hand. It contained an assortment of Chinese sweets: some that I'd tried already, like pineapple cakes, and some that I'd never seen in my life, like a strange purple soupy substance.

"How—thoughtful," Ba replied in a robotic voice. He accepted the tray of food with equally robotic outstretched hands. Then he added in a slightly less frosty tone, "Would you like to try some of our bread? It's all fresh baked. Just came out of the oven."

"No, that's okay," Mr. Lu said, not unkindly. "I've just eaten."

Ba's shoulders stiffened at the rejection. "Ah, I see," he said, his voice once again as frosty as the arctic tundra. In Chinese households, turning down food was as good as an insult, and both men, of course, knew that. Mr. Lu's "greeting" wasn't a greeting so much as it was an open snub.

Mr. Lu's smile had changed, too, sharpening into something coldly triumphant. We all knew that between the two of them, Mr. Lu had won this strange battle of politeness.

"I have to get back to work," he said, and then excused himself. Ba and I watched him in silence as he headed back across the street to Sunny's Bakery.

"He got you there," I said, turning back to face my father.

Ba glared at me, as though this whole exchange had been my fault.

"What?" I protested.

"Go restock the napkin holders," he ordered.

"But I just did that."

"Check them again anyway!"

I sighed as Ba marched back into the kitchen. I'd hoped that Sweetea would finally get busy again now that students were back on campus, but no such luck.

Anna: Lol the guy who owns Sunny's Bakery came by and basically snubbed Sweetea today 🙃
Jane: Aw, I'm sorry. That's rude af

Anna: It's ok lol not like it's your fault. Really wish my
Ba and the Sunny's Bakery owner could get along tho.
They'd make a killing if they could collab
Jane: Or if the other place just went out of business
Anna: omfg 😵

⊷———⊶

The night before my first college quiz in Great Books, I was stress cleaning my room and doing anything I could to keep myself from panicking. I'd already studied *The Iliad* from back to front. Jane had even emailed me her old quiz to study. We used our personal emails so it wouldn't be traceable to the university. There was nothing more to be done than trust that I knew the material, and that I'd ace the quiz the next day.

Still, I couldn't help but worry that I'd blank on the quiz the next day. In high school I'd been at the top of my class, but university was a different ball game. Sometimes star high school students ended up flunking their college courses because they underestimated the material, and I didn't want that to be me. I couldn't let that be me.

I rummaged through my drawer, searching for my favorite sweater, a black crewneck with a picture of Light Yagami, the protagonist of the anime *Death Note*. It was my go-to lounging-around-home sweater. It wasn't in any of the drawers I checked, nor could I find it hanging in the closet with the rest of my clothes. But I could've sworn I'd just tucked it into the drawer with the rest of my sweaters last night.

Maybe it was the exam fog getting to me, making me

misremember things. The alternative explanation was that someone—well, really only Laura—had gone through my drawer and taken my sweater.

Laura wasn't exactly the best roommate, but the idea of her stealing my clothes still seemed far-fetched. Especially given the fact that she didn't seem to have any interest in anime. I shook my head. The fact that my brain had even suggested that conclusion was ridiculous. I'd probably misplaced that sweater, lost in the laundry somehow.

"I'm losing my mind," I muttered. That had to be it. Those long hours of studying were messing with my memory now. Not to mention, when I wasn't studying, I was preoccupied with thoughts of mysterious societies and the murder of my former babysitter. That was enough to make anyone scare easily. But there had to be a perfectly reasonable explanation for this. Maybe Laura accidentally took my sweater. Maybe I accidentally put it in with her laundry.

Anna: Hey!! Quick random question haha . . . did I put my sweater in w ur laundry by accident? Or did you take it maybe? It's black and has a picture of an anime character on it, and it says "Death Note"

Laura: No I haven't seen it

Anna: Ur sure you didn't take it by accident? I can't find it anywhere

Laura: Yeah ofc . . . I'd give it back to u immediately if there was a mix-up. I don't wear stuff like that and I wouldn't take ur clothes. That's just weird

Anna: Oh I didn't mean to imply that you'd take it.
Sorry!!

No response. Laura was being as sweet and understanding as usual. I shook my head, wondering why I'd even bothered texting her about this. Of course she wouldn't be taking anime sweaters, on purpose or on accident. Rereading my texts, it dawned on me that in Laura's shoes, she might have misread my tone and thought I was accusing her of theft—especially since she and I didn't have much of a relationship in the first place. Great. Laura was probably telling her friends all about her rude anime-obsessed roommate now.

I switched off the light and headed for my bed. Sleep didn't immediately overtake me. I lay awake for a while, still trying to figure out where I'd put my favorite sweater.

Chapter Nine

THANKS TO JANE'S HELP, I passed my first Great Books quiz with flying colors. She was right—Lacey didn't even bother creating new tests each year, just switched up the question order and threw in a new one here and there, so studying Jane's old quiz had been enough to get me through.

Lacey strolled by our desks, handing out our graded quizzes facedown. Heart pounding, I snatched mine up and turned it over. A solid A was marked in the top right corner. I'd only gotten one of the questions wrong.

I let out a sigh of relief. Maybe I could sail through college like I'd done in high school. If nothing else, at least I'd still have my grades.

I wondered if Chris had scored an A, too. As soon as the thought entered my head, I slid a quick peek over at his seat in the next row over. He'd left the right half of his paper practically hanging off his desk, and I could see the A+ scrawled at the top of his page clear as day.

The sight put a considerable damper on my high spirits.

Jane: I stopped by your Chinese bakery for breakfast today. Sunny's Bakery right? Got a red bean bun, it was pretty good!

Anna: Oooh yum, that's my favorite. But actually my family's bakery is Sweetea. Sunny's Bakery is kind of like our rival bakery lol

Jane: Oooooof. Shit, did I just fraternize with the enemy?

Anna: It's cool. Just don't mess up next time, or else.

Jane: Wait fr?????

Anna: I'm jk LOL

Jane: Omfg

Anna: 😂

Even though Chris Lu wasn't too bad—I mean, he had saved me at that frat party, after all—that didn't change the fact that the Lus' bakery was still a rival to my family's. Nor did it change the fact that he hadn't lost his academic edge at all while he was in China. That gave me two solid reasons to hate him.

So there was nothing wrong with me not being suddenly friendly with Chris. Even though a teeny, tiny part of me did feel guilty for giving him the cold shoulder. In my defense, though, it seemed we'd come to the mutual silent agreement to act as though that night at Theta Pi hadn't happened, and even though we kept bumping into each other on this huge campus somehow, it was best to each pretend the other didn't exist.

First Laura, now Chris. Apparently my newfound talent was

mutually deciding with people that we weren't going to acknowledge each other.

At least I had Jane, who was such a great friend that it didn't matter that I wasn't rushing a sorority or befriending everyone in my dorm. Jane was open and accepting, and she'd never judge me like others might. I had the feeling that I could share anything with her. She didn't hold back when sharing with me, either. We talked about everything from the most underrated anime to ranking each dining hall by food quality.

Jane was the only friend I needed on campus. There was no time for me to seek out other friendships, anyway, not while Sweetea and Sunny's Bakery were currently caught up in a heated Battle of the Bakeries. Everything else on my plate, including trying to find out more about the Order of Alpha and Melissa Hong's murder, would have to wait.

⊶————⊷

Friday afternoon, after all my classes for the first week had concluded, I decided to take matters into my own hands. I tied my long black hair up into a high bun and placed my largest sunglasses over my eyes in preparation to swing by Sunny's Bakery for a little spying. I doubted the Lus would recognize me—aside from Mr. Lu's awkward visit to Sweatea, I hadn't ever met them before—but I wanted to be sure nobody would be able to link me to Sweetea.

Sunny's Bakery was packed and the line to order snaked out the door and down the street. I stood in line for about fifteen minutes before I could even get inside the establishment. Once I was through the doors, I immediately put my supersleuth skills to the test.

My gaze zoomed past the cozy-looking couches that lined the pale, baby-blue walls, latching onto the employees standing behind the front counter.

"I heard there's another Chinese bakery just down the street," the man in front of me said offhandedly to the woman with him. "Want to check it out after this one?"

"Maybe another time," said the woman. "People say that place isn't very . . . aesthetic."

I had to resist the urge to inform her that Sweetea was very aesthetic. And I filed away a mental note to talk to my parents about that later. The upholstery was due for an upgrade, admittedly. We needed to go for a trendy off-white color, like Sunny's Bakery.

Eventually I found myself at the head of the line. I'd spent my time waiting coming up with a list of menu items that sounded the best. There were Asian sweets listed on the menu, but there was also a huge section of the menu dedicated to Western sweets like chocolate Vienna cake, tiramisu, and lemon cake. No wonder Sunny's was so popular with the locals. They were drawing in two crowds—those who wanted Asian desserts, and those who wanted Western ones. Sweetea only served Chinese sweets. Maybe I'd have to talk to my parents about changing that if they wanted to attract more customers.

"I'll have the rice pudding, grass jelly drink, and pineapple cake," I told the young guy who was working behind the counter.

The worker looked up at me, and then jabbed away at the cash register. "Is that all?"

"Oh, and I'll throw in a strawberry milk tea. Since you asked."

"Your total is twenty dollars and twenty-two cents."

When my order arrived, I sat down at the last empty stool in front of the window and spread out my food in front of me. Hopefully their food would be rank so I'd have something to actually complain about when I reported back to my parents.

Unfortunately, all of it was amazing. I took a few bites of everything, and then I dumped the rest of it into the trash, not caring that I was attracting stares and grumbles of "What a waste."

The situation was even more dire than I'd thought.

Anna: OMG. You're right and I hate it
Jane: ?????
Anna: The food at Sunny's Bakery is good :/
Jane: Well, taking them down wouldn't be fun if they weren't a worthy opponent. Like a shonen anime lol

As I snorted at Jane's comparison of my situation to shonen anime—and admittedly, I could see similarities—I ducked into Sweetea. Though there were a few groups of students hanging around, the crowd was noticeably smaller than at Sunny's Bakery.

Ba gave me a surprised look when I headed toward him. "Anna. You didn't mention you were coming."

"Ba, can I talk to you for a second?"

My father narrowed his eyes. "Just for a second. It's quite busy today."

It wasn't that busy at all, at least not compared to Sunny's, but I wouldn't be the one to burst his bubble. We headed to the back of the kitchen, where the warm and comforting scent of bread overwhelmed me.

"Have you ever thought of expanding the menu?" I asked.

"We just added taro rolls to the menu last month—"

"I mean, expanding the *style* of the menu. Like adding Western desserts," I interrupted. "Chocolate cake or tiramisu. Stuff like that." *Stuff that'll make this bakery more appealing to Western customers*, I thought but didn't say.

Ba raised an eyebrow. "Chocolate cake? Why, are you suddenly craving chocolate cake? I can make you one."

"No, I'm not craving chocolate cake. I just . . . I went to Sunny's Bakery just now," I admitted. "They're doing really well combining Asian and Western desserts. I think if Sweetea tried something like that—"

My father raised a hand and waved it dismissively. "No."

"You didn't even let me finish."

"Sunny's Bakery has their own style, and we have ours," Ba said firmly. "We won't be copying them."

"It's not *copying*, more like taking inspiration—"

"I said no, Anna."

I blinked at the harsh tone of Ba's voice. My father's expression softened.

"Your Ma and I have been brainstorming new recipes to

attract new customers to Sweetea," Ba said. "We'll be upgrading our menu soon with new Chinese desserts, and we'll be sticking to our unique brand. Don't worry. We might not have a huge customer base, but the customers we do have are loyal and love what we offer."

Though I longed to say more, I bit back my words and nodded. There was no use arguing with my father. He was one of the most stubborn people I knew.

"Now, you should get back to studying," Ba said. "Have a red bean bun before you go."

I grabbed a fresh red bean bun off a rack as I left. I had some spare time. I could go back to my dorm now and hit the books—or I could scope out Hill House, the old headquarters of the Order of Alpha, which was just on the next street over.

It wasn't even a debate. Holding the warm bun in my hand, I quickly headed in the direction of Hill House. As I drew closer to the building, I tried to imagine how this campus must have appeared decades ago, when the Order of Alpha was active. How many secret society members had trekked down this same path? Had they been plotting against students like Melissa Hong and Janet Chen? Or had those deaths truly been a coincidence, and the Order of Alpha innocent of anything terrible?

I walked up to the towering brick building behind the sign that read Hill House. The curtains were drawn. I couldn't tell if anyone was inside the all-girls dorm right now. I had walked up the steps and was right in front of the door, my knuckles raised to knock, before I even realized what I was doing. If somebody *did* answer the door, what would I say? "Oh, hello, I was just wondering if you could let me snoop around your rooms so I can gather clues for a decades-old murder case?" That would earn me a slammed door right in the face.

Before I could decide whether to knock, the decision was made for me, and the door swung open. I leapt back down a step in surprise as a girl with red glasses and curly black hair came out of the dorm.

"Oh, sorry," she said, eyes widening in alarm at the sight of me.

"It's okay."

The girl gave me the once-over, and now her eyes narrowed. "Wait. You don't live here, do you?"

"Um . . . no." The door was open wide enough that I could peek inside. Oil paintings. Flower vases. Cushy armchairs. The dorm appeared modern and ordinary at first glance. I tried not to blink, as though that might help me form a memory of this place.

"Are you here to visit someone?" the girl asked sharply, frowning as she followed my gaze behind her.

"Y-Yeah," I lied, glad that she'd supplied an excuse for me.

"Who is it? We're not supposed to let just anyone into the dorm." The girl pressed her lips together firmly, and after a beat, I realized she was waiting for an answer—a name. The name of the person I was supposedly visiting.

"Um . . . I'm here to see Betty?" Betty seemed like someone who would be in an all-girls dorm. I held my breath, hoping for the best.

"There's no Betty here." Now the girl looked really suspicious.

"Oh, s-sorry. Wrong dorm," I muttered, backing away. "Um, have a nice day." Then I turned around and fast walked away from the dorm, wanting to kick myself the whole way. If there was a reward for Worst Sleuth Ever, I was surely in the lead.

Maybe my trip to Hill House hadn't been completely useless, though. Now I knew that they had strict rules, and I'd been able to glance inside, however briefly. Whatever Hill House was now, it really was an all-girls dorm—a very exclusive one. That was good information to know.

I boarded one of the blue campus shuttles. I could've walked back to West Tower, but I was feeling lazy, and it was unseasonably cold out today. The brisk autumn wind whipped against my face.

Though the bus was almost packed and a bit malodorous, I managed to find an empty seat and squeeze into it. After two bumpy stops, the bus pulled to a stop in front of West Tower. I stood up to get off, eager for fresh air and space outside, when the sensation of a hand brushing against the back of my neck caused me to jump a little in surprise. When I turned around, there were so many students crowding to get toward the front of the bus, I couldn't tell who'd bumped into me.

I turned away, shaking my head. I was getting used to strangers bumping in to me without offering any attempt at an apology. It was rude, but with a student body of this size, it was pretty much unavoidable.

Maybe it was the chill of the late afternoon turning into evening, but the skin on the back of my neck tensed with the lingering sensation of fingers. Every story I'd heard about girls who were assaulted while walking around late at night on campus suddenly came back to me. My heart thudded wildly, and I couldn't shake the feeling that someone was watching me as I rushed back to West Tower.

When I turned around, though, there was no one.

Chapter Ten

I WAS SITTING IN A study room in my dorm. It was early into the morning hours at that point, and nobody else was around. My textbooks were stacked in a pile in front of me.

As I reached for the top book, a whisper came from behind me. Somebody was saying my name.

I whirled around, and the sharp blade of a knife flashed in the darkness, aimed at my throat. I screamed.

"Anna! What the fuck!"

I jolted awake in my bed, still screaming. It took a moment for me to register where I was, which was decidedly not in the study room. Nor was there a knife at my throat, nor was I in imminent danger of anything besides seriously pissing off my roommate. Though judging by the murderous expression on Laura's face, I already had.

"Sorry," I murmured. "Nightmare."

Laura rolled her eyes, and then muttered something under her breath that I couldn't hear. It was probably for the best, as I doubted it was anything particularly nice. Then she turned over onto her side and flung her blanket over herself. I checked my phone, which was on the nightstand next to my bed. It was three in the morning.

I needed to get back to sleep or else I would seriously regret it in a few hours, yet my mind wouldn't stop racing. I'd clearly been too stressed out between schoolwork and my interest in Melissa's case lately. Because in that nightmare, the person with the knife hadn't uttered my name—they had muttered Melissa's.

Try as I might, I couldn't fall back asleep. Nor could I keep the cold case of Melissa Hong out of my head. Internet searches for the Order of Alpha had led me nowhere, though, so if they *were* still active—illegally—they were keeping their activities well hidden.

The nightmare was probably a warning from my subconscious to stop digging into the case before I uncovered something dangerous and got myself into trouble. I would ignore it, of course. I was making progress. If I turned back now, the time I'd spent on this case would be wasted.

No, I wouldn't be giving up. In fact, I planned to do the opposite. It was time to visit the one person I knew who might be able to give me a hint about what had happened to Melissa.

⋅⊩⎯⎯⎯⫞⋅

Later that afternoon, I found myself standing outside the mahogany door of Professor Wittman's office. I raised my hand to knock on the slightly ajar door, hesitating. Though I'd summoned the courage to speak up several times in Sources of East Asian Civilizations discussions, speaking one-on-one with a professor felt nerve-racking on a different level. Of course I knew that he would welcome students during his posted office hours, but how would he feel about being asked about his dead former student? If Professor Wittman reacted poorly, that wouldn't bode well for me. Though, it was too late to turn back now.

A voice said, "Come in," before I could bring my knuckle to the door.

Taking a deep breath, I opened the door and entered Professor Wittman's office. There was a slight odor in the air, familiar, though I couldn't quite put my finger on why. There was, predictably, a large desk, along with a cushy-looking black armchair, which the professor currently occupied. His desk was covered with stacks of papers and books and a couple of potted green plants. Along the walls were calligraphy scrolls covered in Chinese characters. Across from the door, there was a giant white bookshelf with five levels stuffed full of textbooks. The ones I could see had Chinese titles on the spines. The books that didn't fit had been stacked in a neat pile beside the bookshelf.

For a white man, Professor Wittman was *really* into East Asian culture.

My professor wasn't alone. One of the TAs, Robert, was sitting in one of the chairs across from the professor's desk, and he watched with interest as I walked into the room.

"Oh, Anna," said Professor Wittman with a look of pleasant surprise on his face. "What brings you in today?"

If I started off asking questions about Melissa, I'd probably scare him off. Better to ease into the conversation first. "I had a few questions about this week's reading," I said instead.

"Ah, yes. *The Tale of the Heike*. One of the most celebrated classics in Japanese literature. It's a tough text to assign as one of the first readings, but nevertheless enjoyable, I hope, to read about the bloody history and decline of the Heike family." Professor Wittman fixed me a sharp look over his spectacles, and I for some reason got the sense that I was being tested. If this was a test, I was determined to pass it with flying colors, as I did with all my tests. A model student did nothing less.

"Yes, definitely enjoyable," I said. It wasn't a total lie. *The Tale of the Heike* was an older text, but the translated version we were reading for class was easy enough to understand, even though the Buddhist themes and the Japanese history were unfamiliar to me. The reading was long and tedious and had kept me up until the early hours of the morning on more than one occasion, but I was used to pulling long hours to finish schoolwork. Plus, the complicated plot was fairly fascinating once I was able to get into it—it was basically Japan's *Iliad*, and the epic story followed the power struggle between the Minamoto clan and the Taira clan in the Genpei War.

"It is my belief that a man's good or evil deeds are inherited by his descendants. It is also said that the accumulation of good deeds brings happiness, while sorrow waits at the gate of him who commits evil." Professor Wittman closed his eyes, bringing the tips of his fingers together, and leaned back in his chair. "Indeed, a Buddhist principle that we'd all do well to adapt to our modern lives, no?"

"It's a noble notion, but I feel like the text is too idealistic," I blurted out. "The characters' violent decisions lead to vengeance and ultimately their downfall, but in real life we don't always see consequences for arrogance and rashness."

"Well, *The Tale of the Heike* is a very old text, after all," piped up Robert, reminding me that he was there. "And Japan is different from the States. Quite a bit better." His eyes took on a dreamy look, as though he wished more than anything that he were in Japan and not here.

Robert was studying the professor and me, and I suddenly felt self-conscious. For the first time it occurred to me that I might have interrupted something between Professor Wittman and his graduate student instructor. "If you're in the middle of something, Professor, I can always come at another time—"

"Ah, don't mind Robert," said Professor Wittman. "We're just planning the next lesson together. He's helping me choose the movie we'll be watching next week—not for your class, sorry," clarified the professor with a rueful smile. "One of the other classes I teach."

"A movie?"

"I'm trying to convince the professor to let us watch my favorite movie—*The Wolverine*," said Robert. I thought he was joking, but maybe not, because neither he nor the professor cracked smiles.

Professor Wittman said, "Well, maybe nothing *that* fun, but certainly something entertaining."

I let out a weak laugh, swallowing back my true thoughts—that watching *The Wolverine* seemed like a bad idea. I'd watched it a few years back, and though I didn't care to recall many of the details now, I did remember that it was about a man who went to Japan and continuously "saved" a helpless Japanese damsel-in-distress from the evil Japanese men in her life. Because it was a superhero movie, there were plenty of action sequences, all starring the white guy ripping through Japanese characters. The movie had made me uncomfortable, though it was a hit with American audiences.

"You don't have to stand there, Anna," said Professor Wittman, and his voice brought me back from my thoughts. "Please, have a seat." He gestured toward the open chair next to Robert.

Robert gave me a half smile, which I returned after a pause. He continued to stare.

"Oh—okay." I took off my backpack and sat down, then pulled my textbook out. When I asked Professor Wittman about the authorship of *The Tale of the Heike*, he launched into a lecture about the blind monks credited with compiling the book in the mid-thirteenth century. By the time he was finished, I was overloaded with information and rather more confused than I'd been before, but I reassured him that he'd answered my question.

Besides, my main goal in coming to office hours wasn't to ask about the authors of the text—it was to find out any clues I could about Melissa.

"Is there anything else I can answer today, Anna?" Professor Wittman asked.

I glanced down at the notebook I'd brought with me. "I . . . do have one more question."

"Ask away."

"Did you know Melissa Hong?"

A sharp intake of breath, followed by silence that was thick with tension. After a long moment, I dared to glance up. Professor Wittman was frozen in his seat, staring at me as though he'd never seen me before. Robert's gaze traveled from Professor Wittman to me back to Professor Wittman, his expression unreadable.

"May I ask, why are you asking about Melissa Hong?" the professor said, a slight tremor in his voice. His face had drained of color.

"I read an article about her. You were quoted in it."

Professor Wittman closed his eyes, his forehead scrunching together, as though he were being forced to remember something unpleasant. "Yes, she was a student of mine," he finally said, opening his eyes. "What happened to her . . . it was terrible."

"Yeah, it was." I knew I was pushing my luck, but now that I was here, I might as well go all in. "Can you tell me more about that—about what happened to Melissa?"

"I don't know," Professor Wittman said harshly. "How would I know? I was in no way involved."

"Oh, no, I didn't mean to imply you were involved with any of it, Professor." I tried to backtrack, but the damage had been done. Or maybe the professor had never intended to open up to me in the first place.

"I'm afraid I can't help you, Anna."

"I just—I want to know what she was like," I blurted. My heart hammered with adrenaline. I was so close. I couldn't be turned away now. "Can you tell me—"

"Everything I could possibly know was already in that article," snapped Professor Wittman. "As I said, I can't help you, Anna, and I would greatly appreciate if you didn't pursue the matter. Now, do you have any further *academic* questions?"

Shame flooded through me as the adrenaline ebbed. "N-No, that's all. Thank you, Professor."

"Feel free to shoot me an email if you think of any other questions later."

Defeated, I stood up, swinging my backpack around behind me. Out of the corner of my eye, I saw something shiny and bronze. It was the glimmer of a plaque sitting next to a potted plant near the bookshelves, and there was the emblem of a wolf's head on the plaque.

"What is it, Anna?" The professor's sharp gaze followed mine, and then he shifted his body ever so slightly, blocking the plaque from my view.

Aware that Professor Wittman and Robert were both giving me intense stares, I gulped and shook my head. My heart thumped. I'd only glimpsed it, though I thought I knew what it was. Maybe I'd seen wrong.

Whatever the case, I wasn't going to say anything further. I'd already annoyed Professor Wittman enough, and I couldn't risk getting into his bad books.

"Nothing. See you in class," I muttered, still trying to figure out what I might have just seen.

"Anna," called the professor.

I turned back around. "Yes?"

"Don't look further into the matter of Melissa Hong's

death." His eyes were cold and serious, filled with warning. The sight of them sent chills down my back. "It's for your own good."

·II———II·

If Professor Wittman hoped that he could intimidate me into dropping my investigation, he was very, very wrong. Maybe I hadn't gotten any further leads by speaking to him, but by the time I'd walked all the way back to my dorm, another idea had occurred to me.

Alice Kim and Tim McMaster, the two students quoted in the *Brookings Daily* article, had to be recent graduates. There was a chance that they were still using their university emails. That was probably my best chance of contacting them, since searching for them on social media had proved to be a fruitless effort—there were multiple Alice Kims and Tim McMasters, apparently.

After consulting the university student contact page in our school's portal, I managed to find their email addresses and drafted an email.

BCC: akim@brookings.web; tmcmaster@brookings.web
From: axu@brookings.web
Subject: Melissa Hong Information

Hi,

My name is Anna Xu, and I'm a freshman at Brookings University. I came across your names in an article about

Melissa Hong. I'm trying to find out what happened to her, and I was wondering if you could let me know any important information about her—any details that you might remember, no matter how big or small. Anything would be helpful.

Thanks for your time!

Anna

At the same moment I pressed send, my dorm room banged open, and my roommate came in.

"Oh my God. Do you want to go shopping before Game Day? I don't have anything cute to wear," Laura was saying, not bothering to lower her voice as she spoke on the phone. "Why do our school colors have to be so musty? Ugh."

I tried my best to tune out Laura's voice. Now that I'd sent off that email, all I could do was wait for Alice or Tim to reply. In the meantime, I had to focus on the paper I was currently writing, but it wasn't nearly exciting enough to draw me in. It was much more interesting to eavesdrop on Laura's gossip.

"It's not about the football, Mandy," Laura huffed. "Nobody gives a shit about football besides the meatheads of this school. Game Day is all about the tailgating. We're going to look hot and get so wasted that we won't even remember the details of the game. Then there are after parties, and . . . yeah, I've been invited to, like, five, so we should try to at least stop by them all . . ."

The way Laura talked, you'd think she'd come to Brookings for the parties and not the education. There was no sign of her conversation ending soon, either. If I stayed in my room, I'd spend the whole evening eavesdropping on my roommate's conversation rather than make any actual headway on my work.

Letting out a passive-aggressive sigh, I shoved my laptop and textbooks into my backpack and headed downstairs to the study lounge to finish my work. Laura glanced over at me as I passed by her bed but otherwise didn't acknowledge me leaving.

The dining hall had closed for the night, and stressed students had flocked to the lounge instead. The last study room was occupied by Chris. We made eye contact through the glass wall, and I jolted with the feeling that I'd been caught doing something wrong, even though I hadn't.

I had half a mind to turn around and leave as though I hadn't seen him. I didn't have the energy to banter with him, and if I was being honest, when I *wasn't* bantering with him, being around him made me nervous. Before I could leave, Chris got up from the table and opened the door. I could still flee, but it would make things rather awkward the next time we saw each other in class.

"You need a place to study?" Chris asked. He was wearing a light blue dress shirt, as though he'd come from a semiformal event, but it had gotten crinkled—possibly a sign of how hard he'd been studying.

"Um . . ." Well, there was no use in lying; clearly I'd come down here to study, with my backpack full of my books. "Yeah. Everywhere else is full, so do you mind if I . . . ?"

"Join me? Sure."

This wasn't very academic rivals of us, but I was fine setting that aside for the moment if it meant I had a quiet space to finish my work. Judging by the dark circles under Chris's eyes, he was as exhausted as I was.

"What're you working on?" Chris asked as I pulled out my laptop and books.

"I have to finish up my *The Tale of the Heike* analysis for Wittman," I said.

"Oh, yeah." He whistled. "That paper took me forever."

So he'd already finished, then. Of course. Well, now I was really determined to finish this paper tonight. "What're you working on?" I nodded over at the thick book in his hands.

"I'm getting ahead in the reading." Chris turned over the book to show me the title.

"*The Analects of Confucius*? We're not supposed to start that for another couple of weeks."

"That's what 'getting ahead' means," said Chris.

I yearned to throw a barb at him, to defend myself and tell him that I'd been getting ahead, too—at least, before my current workload began crushing me. Chris wasn't human. This was the proof. There was no way he was managing to keep up with a full honors course load while having free time to read Confucius.

Rolling my eyes, I turned my attention back to my paper. Spite was a great motivator, and by ten o'clock, I'd typed the final period on my essay. "Done," I said, the word slipping out of my mouth in relief.

"Do you want me to look over your essay?" Chris offered. His expression seemed sincere, but maybe he was making fun of me on the inside. Besides, I'd sooner ask a random stranger for help than Chris.

"No, that's okay. I'm going to bed," I said, shoving my belongings back into my bag. "Have fun with Confucius."

"I will." The way Chris said it cheerfully, he'd clearly missed the sarcasm in my voice.

I shook my head as I left the room. *What a weirdo.*

When I got back to my room, Laura was gone, which was more of a relief than anything. The halls were empty as I headed back out to take a late-night shower. It seemed most people had already gone to bed or were out for the night—either studying or partying. At Brookings, it seemed there was no in-between.

In the shower, I let the hot water run on my back and stood under it for several minutes, trying not to stress too much about all the work I still had ahead of me. I twirled a lock of my wet black hair, which had grown out just past my shoulder.

Strange. My fingers pressed at the nape of my neck, where there was a small clump of hair missing at the back. I looked down, expecting to see hair in the drain, but there wasn't any. Which meant that the hair must've fallen out *before* I got into the shower, somehow.

Maybe a ghost pulled out your hair.

That didn't even make sense. Ghosts weren't supposed to be able to touch people, and in any case, what use would a ghost have with my hair?

Maybe the stress of schoolwork and thinking about a dead girl had really gotten to me, and I was losing it.

I checked my towel, the shower caddy . . . and couldn't find the hair anywhere, which meant it must've been torn out earlier that day or even that week.

When I got back to my dorm room, Laura was, predictably, not there. I Googled "stress causing hair loss," which showed tons of articles that linked stress and hair fallout. So that was my answer, then. My coursework was making me go bald.

Anna: Hey I've got a weird question for you

Jane: Lol shoot

Anna: Have you ever been so stressed by schoolwork that your . . . hair starts falling out?

Jane: Damn wtf is that happening to you??

Anna: . . . yeah LMAO

Jane: Can't say that I have but I'm pretty sure it's happened to one of my friends before

Anna: This school is taking all my money and now my hair too lmaooo I hate it here

Jane: You've just gotta take better care of yourself! Go relax and watch some Netflix or something. Maybe consider switching the shampoo you use

Anna: Ok

I wasn't sure if I was satisfied or saddened by the confirmation that stress could indeed cause a person's hair to fall out when they were combing it or showering. The school year had only just started, which meant my workload would only continue to grow and stress me out even further. At this rate, I was going to be bald by the end of freshman year. But if that was the trade-off for acing my first year at university, then so be it.

Chapter Eleven

THE STRESS FROM SCHOOL SPILLED over into my personal life, to the point where I found myself in a bad mood more often than not.

My lack of enthusiasm must have been obvious at my next Sweetea shift, because Ba shooed me away from the cash register fifteen minutes into the shift.

"Your frown is scaring away all the customers," was my father's explanation. "Go stand in the back and help the kitchen staff."

"It's not like we had customers in the first place," I muttered.

"What was that?"

"Nothing," I said. I slunk into the back, where a young new hire, a fellow student by the looks of her, was washing dishes. "Do you need help with that?" She nodded and handed me a dirty dish.

There was something nice about the monotony of washing dishes, the mind-numbingness of it all. Minutes turned into hours as I scrubbed the dishes clean, Ba popping in to check in on us every once in a while.

Then the sound of a familiar voice floated into the kitchen from the front. ". . . have a medium jasmine milk tea boba, please?"

Chris. I nearly dropped the plate I'd been cleaning.

"Careful," said the girl, grabbing the plate from me.

I turned away from the sink and walked slowly toward the front until I could make out the figure standing in front of the cash register. It *was* him. Chris. What was he doing here? A mixture of emotions warred inside me—annoyance, embarrassment, curiosity, and maybe just a tiny dash of pleasant surprise. But mostly annoyance and embarrassment. Had Chris come to see how poorly Sweetea was doing compared to Sunny's Bakery?

Without thinking, I marched toward the front until I was standing right next to my father behind the cash register. Chris's eyes snapped to mine, and he gave a half smile.

"What are you doing here?" I asked.

"Getting bubble tea," he said in a "duh" tone of voice.

"No, I mean, what are you doing *here*?" Maybe I was too quick to jump on the defensive, but I had to be if there was even the slightest chance that Chris had come here just to confirm how much more successful his family's bakery was.

"Do you know him?" Ba asked, staring between the two of us. A crease was forming between his eyebrows.

"I was looking for—" Chris started, but then stopped, his cheeks coloring.

"Looking for . . . ?" I prompted.

"Never mind."

I narrowed my eyes. Chris was acting weird. Maybe the stress of college life was getting to him, too, like it was getting to me. Or maybe he was acting weird because I'd caught him scoping out the rival business to Sunny's Bakery.

"If you're thinking of stealing our secret family recipes or something, don't even try," I told Chris, only half joking.

He snorted. "Why would I do that? I'd be more worried about you trying to figure out *my* family's secrets."

"Yeah, right," I fired back, as if I hadn't totally already tried to scope out Sunny's Bakery.

"Your order," Ba interrupted. He handed over a medium-sized bubble tea to Chris. "Who are you?" he asked bluntly. "You seem familiar with my daughter."

"Um . . ." Chris darted an uncertain look at me.

"This is Chris," I said. "Chris Lu. You don't recognize him, Ba?"

"Chris?" My father blinked, and then his eyes popped wide open in shock. "Jiahao Lu's son? I didn't recognize you. How many years has it been? You've gotten so tall now. I remember you used to be tiny . . ."

Chris gave a polite smile and nod, and I stifled a grin at how uncomfortable he looked as Ba continued reminiscing. I shrugged at him. If there was one thing I knew, it was that when parents started taking a trip down memory lane, it was best to stay quiet and let them finish. It was only when a family came into Sweetea that Ba came back to the present, cutting off his reminiscing rather abruptly to take their order.

"Phew. I thought I was never going to escape," Chris

muttered under his breath. I laughed before I could catch myself.

"Oh, you can go, Anna," Ba called from the cash register. "Go study."

I didn't need to be told twice. Quickly I took my hat and uniform off in the back, and when I returned to the front, I was surprised to see Chris still there, evidently waiting for me. I tried to smoothly hide my surprise, and we stepped out of Sweetea together, into the bright afternoon.

"Was that your first time at Sweetea?" I asked.

"Yeah, it was."

Though I knew I probably shouldn't ask, curiosity was getting the better of me. "What did you think?"

"Um . . . what did I think?" Chris took a sip of his bubble tea and shook the container. "The boba's pretty good. Not too sweet."

"Yeah, it is. Everyone likes the boba."

"Service was a little slow, though," Chris remarked.

"Really? I think the speed was okay," I said defensively.

Chris said nothing, which was distinctly unsatisfying. Maybe he was thinking about how much quicker the service was at Sunny's Bakery. For several moments, we walked in silence.

"Why are you so determined to turn everything into a competition, Anna?" Chris finally asked. "You always think I'm just trying to one-up you."

"Me? W-Well, I . . . ," I blustered. Though I hated to admit it, Chris had a point, and it bothered me. Maybe I didn't know how to act around Chris if we didn't keep up this competitive relationship. This was what I knew, and it was most comfortable to fall back into old habits. Otherwise maybe I'd have to come to terms with the fact that Chris and I had more in common than I cared to admit. "I could say the same about you. Remember when we were kids and you'd always come brag to me about your grades?"

"Yeah, but that was when we were kids."

"But you're still like that. Isn't that why you came to Sweetea today?"

"God, no. Is that really what you think of me?" Chris sighed. "I just wanted to check it out. I don't have an ulterior motive. At least, not like what you're thinking."

"Really? Then what *is* your ulterior motive?"

He stared up at the sky, heaving out a long breath. "You're so dense."

"What?"

Without explaining, Chris tossed his empty cup into a nearby trash can, and then waved toward me. "Use your head and figure it out on your own time. I'll see you around." Then, before I could respond, he sped up and blended in with the crowd of students making their way down the sidewalk.

I didn't understand Chris sometimes. If he hadn't gone to Sweetea to compare it to Sunny's Bakery, then why had he come? The question kept me occupied as I headed to the library to finish up homework. Even by the time I'd finished my work, I still wasn't able to figure out what Chris had meant.

Or maybe, deep down, I just didn't *want* to know what he had meant.

Chapter Twelve

"WELL, STUDENTS, CONGRATULATIONS ON MAKING it beyond the add/drop deadline," said Professor Wittman. "You've outlasted your peers, who seem to have dropped like flies."

I glanced around at the noticeably emptier room. Where the seats had been full just a week ago, about a third of the students had clearly dropped Sources of East Asian Civilizations from their schedule, judging by the abandoned seats.

This didn't seem to concern Professor Wittman, who had a little half smile on his face as he rolled up his sleeves. "This course isn't for the casual student," said the professor with the air of someone who considered his work to be very important. "So look around at the classroom. These are your *real* peers for the next several months."

My gaze traveled around the room again, and I accidentally made eye contact with Chris. I quickly turned my attention back to Professor Wittman. No doubt Chris would continue giving his best effort, which meant I couldn't let my guard down either. I was bent on keeping up, even if it meant averaging three hours of sleep a night and coming to class with bloodshot eyes. Even if it meant the stress caused more hair loss.

"I've graded your essays on *The Tale of the Heike*," announced the professor brightly. His eyes lit up as though he were giving us a treat, and he pointed to a tall stack of papers at the corner of his desk. Professor Wittman liked to do his grading the old-fashioned way. "These essays will be weekly, and while a good . . . effort . . . was made last week, I expect higher quality writing moving forward."

Nervous looks rose onto my classmates' faces. Sweat slicked my palms, and I rubbed them on the dry fabric of my leggings. I'd written my essay arguing for the shifting depiction of warriors in Japanese history as a parallel for the change in alliances by the emperors and social dynamics over time. I thought I did a solid job. The work would've scored me an A back in high school.

The professor went around the room passing out our essays. When he placed mine in front of me, I could only meet his gaze briefly to nod, and then I quickly looked away again. My stomach dropped when I saw that big red B stamped on top of my paper, even though I'd mentally prepared myself for tougher grading at university. So much blood, sweat, tears—and, apparently, hair— had gone into researching and writing this essay. I'd even gone to office hours, and it still hadn't been enough to get an A.

Could the professor have purposely marked me lower because of my questions about Melissa Hong that day? But that had nothing to do with my essay. He wouldn't be that petty. Would he?

I was pretty sure Professor Wittman was grading tough just for the sake of grading tough. Probably he hadn't let any of us ace this essay. That only made me more determined than ever to get an A. Maybe I'd stay up later, spend more time at office hours. Whatever it took.

Despite the professor's harsh grading, I found myself fascinated by the material. Soon we were moving on to meatier textbooks, the first being *The Analects of Confucius*. It was possibly the most confusing text I'd ever read, and was split into twenty books that were a series of conversational exchanges between the characters.

Though I'd finished the week's assigned reading—ten chapters in the book—I'd been so busy cramming for an Astronomy quiz and finishing up the reading for Great Books that I hadn't had time to really make head or tail of Confucius's ramblings. I'd stayed up almost all night just to finish skimming through the ten assigned sections.

Luckily, my face wasn't the only perplexed, exhausted one in Thursday's lecture.

"Though we're moving on from *The Tale of the Heike* to learning about Confucius's teachings, I've made the transition easy for you all thanks to the thematic crossover in these two texts. Can anyone tell me what that common theme is?"

Professor Wittman's question was met with blank stares. I could almost see the confusion in the air, and more than one student wore an expression that suggested they were one more difficult question from standing up and leaving.

If the professor minded, he didn't show it. Possibly he was

used to blank gazes in his lectures, or even took joy in befuddling his students by throwing them headfirst into ancient Chinese texts. Without further explanation, Professor Wittman split the class into ten discussion groups, to be led by him and his two graduate students.

I joined a small circle of three other students, and there was a quick round of introductions. There was Matthew, a brown-haired sophomore boy with blue eyes that were glazed over with boredom. Jessica, a pale sophomore with short pink-and-purple hair and heavy eyeliner. Kathy, a freshman Chinese international student with long black hair that hung like a curtain down to her waist, who told us she was also living in West Tower.

"Which floor?" I asked. "I'm in West Tower, too."

"No way." She grinned. "I'm on the fifth floor."

"Ah, I'm on the second. I think I might've seen you in the dining hall before, though."

"Probably. I spend more time in there than my actual room," Kathy said with a straight face. I studied her for a moment. She didn't seem to be kidding.

"The West Tower dining hall is the best one on campus," Jessica piped up. "I lived there last year. Take full advantage of it while you're there."

I was suddenly aware that we'd left Matthew out of the conversation entirely, not that he was making any effort to participate. But one of the TAs—Robert—was watching us and walking over to our circle, so I quickly dropped my gaze back down to my weathered secondhand copy of *The Analects*.

"So, um, what did you think Confucius meant by 'Observe what a man has in mind to do when his father is living, and then observe what he does when his father is dead'?" I said quickly, glancing over one of the quotes I'd sleepily jotted down in my notebook the night before.

"He was talking about filial piety there, wasn't he?" said Kathy. "Loving and taking care of our parents, and all that."

"Very good," came the sound of Robert's gruff voice. The TA hovered over us and fidgeted with his hands, as though unsure what to do with himself, and then sank into an awkward squat. A wave of his overpowering cologne swept over us. Robert placed his hand on my desk, and I leaned away without thinking. "What do you think, um—sorry, your name?" The TA glanced expectantly toward Matthew.

"Matthew."

"Matthew, what did you think of this week's reading?"

The boy blinked, as though he'd never heard such a question before. "You mean in general?"

"Yes."

It could not have been more obvious that Matthew hadn't done the reading or paid attention in lecture. The boy stuttered out a vague response, but Robert appeared to have lost interest even as Matthew was still cobbling together his botched overview of *The Analects*.

Robert's watery eyes met Jessica's, Kathy's, and then mine. "What are your thoughts on the reading, Anna?"

I startled. I hadn't realized he'd remembered my name, since we hadn't interacted outside of that one office hours encounter.

But then, I guess I had been one of the most active students in class, answering Professor Wittman's questions. I couldn't help it. The course reading fascinated me far more than any Greek or Victorian classics I'd been assigned to read in high school, and it was my favorite out of my classes so far. Besides, I couldn't stand the horrible, stomach-clenching classroom silence that often followed the professor's questions—the moment before he began cold-calling on students. Better to answer Professor Wittman of my own free will than be startled and forced into doing it.

"Well, I think it's clear that Confucius values the equalizing of education, which wasn't available to the lower ranks during the Zhou dynasty," I said. "He's also strict about morals and politeness, and about people satisfying their basic needs without wanting more. He's basically the father of Asian fathers."

The last part slipped out almost without me meaning to, and Kathy let out a snort. To my surprise, so did Robert.

"Don't write that on the exam," said the TA, but to my relief, his eyes were crinkling at the corners. Then he walked away, but that overpowering cologne scent lingered in his wake.

"I gotta be honest," Matthew said once Robert was out of earshot. He tapped his dog-eared copy of *The Analects*. "I think Confucius was high as fuck when he wrote this. I have no clue what he's talking about."

⊷⊷———⊷⊷

I hadn't given up on trying to solve Melissa's murder, but with Professor Wittman refusing to talk and no response from Alice and Tim, I had no choice but to pause my investigation.

Besides, my schedule was filling up quickly. When I wasn't occupied with schoolwork, I was trying to come up with ways to reinvent Sweetea and snatch business back from Sunny's Bakery. If only karma worked in real life as was suggested by *The Tale of the Heike*. My parents had always put nothing but good karma into the universe, and I wished more than anything that the universe would return that by blessing them with fortune. But it was far more likely that I'd end up having to take matters into my own hands.

Jane: Still stressing over the Sunny's Bakery stuff?

Anna: Yeah :/ They're really costing us a lot of business

Jane: Just sabotage them lol

Anna: Wtf noooo

Jane: I'm jk 😂

On Saturday I woke up to the sound of music blaring from outside. It took me a moment to remember that it was Game Day. I'd grown up around this area and knew that the football scene was huge, but I'd never been part of it. Even though I wasn't a sports fan, my veins buzzed with excitement.

For Brookings, football was one of the most crucial components—especially our football rivalry with Richland University, another top school in our state. It was more important than small concentrations, like astrobiology. And to some, it was more important than academic success. Students who would skip their nine a.m. lectures because those classes were "too early" would get up at six-thirty to start pregaming for the football match.

Laura's bed was empty, as usual. I only saw her on weekday nights now. I had no idea what she was up to, except that it involved secrecy and probably sororities. Though I didn't plan to get involved in Greek life, I wasn't completely out of the loop, so I at least knew that it was Hell Week—aka the week when all the Greek life hopefuls were rushing their top choice fraternities and sororities.

A couple of nights ago, Laura had wandered back into our room completely drunk, and one of her girlfriends had had to tuck her into bed. She'd made such a fuss moaning and vomiting into a bucket that I'd had to leave to do my studying at the undergraduate library, affectionately nicknamed the UgLi by students. I didn't dare come back until almost four in the morning, by which time Laura had fallen fast asleep. Even then, the room had still smelled faintly of alcohol and vomit.

Oh, well. I hadn't seen Laura since then. I basically had the room to myself now, and that was pretty nice, even if it did get lonely sometimes.

When I checked my phone, rubbing the sleep out of my eyes, I found a new text from Jane waiting for me. And quickly, my sleepiness vanished.

Jane: Looks like you don't have to worry about Sunny's Bakery any longer . . . www.brookingsdaily.com /chinese-bakery-vandalized

As I read through the *Brookings Daily* article Jane had linked, my horror grew.

Late Friday Night, Hate Crime Strikes Chinese Bakery On Campus

Brookings University campus police have reported that on Friday, September 29th, at approximately eleven p.m., Sunny's Bakery was vandalized. The owner stated that a figure wearing all black smashed the windows and painted the words "GO BACK TO YOUR COUNTRY, CHINK" on the wall, along with a drawing of a wolf's head. The damages for the broken windows are approximately $2,000, and a GoFundMe has already been created in Sunny's Bakery's name. At this time, no further information has been received about the identity of the culprit.

News traveled at the speed of light. The dorm came alive with the sounds of murmuring and slamming doors. I read and reread and reread the article over and over again, my horror growing as the words sunk in.

Go back to your country, chink.

There were already several comments under the article.

JACOB LIU: This is so racist. Are they gonna catch whoever did it??

ALYSSA KANE: They drew a wolf's head . . . is this the work of the Order of Alpha?

SEAN NAKAGAWA: @Alyssa Kane It's definitely the Order behind this

NIKHIL PRAKASH: @Sean Nakagawa The Order isn't real, this is the work of some racist POS

RACHEL MADDOX: This is so heartbreaking :(Everyone pls donate if you can!!

The Order of Alpha. My heart hammered, and my blood turned to ice in my veins. Just as I'd thought my trail had gone cold and that I'd never live to see another reappearance of that symbol, here it was again, attached to yet another crime.

"Goddamn you," I cursed.

The people in the comments section of this article didn't know much more than that either, judging by the heated debate they were having over whether the secret organization existed, and if it did, why they'd so boldly put their symbol on an act of hate.

And now, someone—either the real Order or a fake organization using its name—was carrying out hate crimes.

In my panic, I texted my parents over WeChat. If Sunny's Bakery had been targeted, then chances were Sweetea could be next.

Anna: Did you guys see what happened to Sunny's Bakery??

Ma: Yes, the attack. It's awful.

Ba: We're contacting the Lus to help them through this

Anna: And is Sweetea ok?

Ma: We're closing the bakery for now just to be safe
Ba: We would prefer if you come home too. You can commute to class. It's not so far

I bit my lip, briefly considering the idea. No doubt I'd feel safer with my parents, my family, around me. Home wasn't too far from campus. Still, it was enough of a hassle to move out of the dorms I'd just moved into that it didn't seem worth it. I'd finally begun enjoying my independence, and I didn't want to move back in with them unless it was an emergency.

Anna: It's ok, I'm safe here in my dorm. We have RAs and campus police to protect us
Ma: Are you sure?
Ba: Let us know if you change your mind and want to come home
Ma: It's not safe, Anna. You should come home

After I reassured them multiple times that I'd be fine, Ma and Ba finally signed off. I cracked open my copy of *Frankenstein* and realized just how much I'd been assigned to read for my Great Books course. I tried to focus on the words in the book and not the ominous words that had been etched into my mind: *Go back to your country, chink.*

It wasn't the first time I'd seen or heard similar words, sometimes even directly to my face. And I knew it wouldn't be the last. The local law enforcement's flexibility with white supremacists had allowed many racists to feel more confident about attacking people of color.

I made it a few pages into my reading before shutting the book and giving up. I was too on edge to do homework. There was no point in keeping up this facade of normalcy when there was nothing normal about what had just happened. Maybe I didn't know how to solve this problem exactly, but I did know I had to do something.

I left my room and headed down the hall toward Chris's. I hesitated, feeling awkward. We hadn't interacted much. Maybe he'd find it weird that I was speaking to him now. I forced the doubts from my mind and knocked on the door before I could stop myself.

The door swung open after a moment. Chris's roommate, a brown-haired boy wearing a purple Brookings hoodie, stood in the doorway, blinking at me. I vaguely remembered his name to be Devon—and it was on the door, too. "Oh, hey," Devon said. "You're . . ."

"Anna," I said. We'd met a couple of weeks ago, but back then we'd all been meeting so many people so quickly that it was almost impossible to remember anyone's names.

"Can I help you?" Devon asked.

"Oh, I'm . . . I'm looking for Chris."

At that, Devon's expression turned pained. "Chris took off for home earlier this morning. You know, his family's bakery was—"

"Vandalized." The word had come out too loud, and I cleared my throat awkwardly. "I know." A thick, gloomy silence fell between us. "Um, do you know when he'll be back on campus?"

Devon shrugged. I waited, but he didn't add anything.

"Okay. Thanks anyway." I headed back down the hall, feeling a bit dumb. Of course Chris wouldn't be on campus now. Of course he would've gone back home to be with his family. If Sweetea had been vandalized, I would've done the same.

I wasn't even sure why I'd gone to try to find him just now. It wasn't like we were friends. Sure, we lived on the same floor and had a couple of classes together, but he was supposed to be my academic rival.

Jane: Heyyyyy sleepyhead

Anna: What's up? I'm not sleeping

Jane: Oh I thought you were still asleep lol. You didn't reply to me. Did you see the article about Sunny's Bakery?

Anna: Yeah

Jane: Looks like you didn't have to sabotage them after all lol

Anna: That's not funny . . .

Jane: Umm lighten up lol

Anna: Wtf?

Jane: Didn't you want that place to go out of business anyway?

Anna: No of course not. I just wanted Sweetea to get some business. I didn't want any racist sickos to vandalize Sunny's Bakery.

Jane: I'm just trying to look on the bright side for you.
Sheesh. No need to get your panties in a twist.

I stared down at my phone in disbelief. It was hard to tell tone over text, but still, Jane's last text oozed with snarkiness.

It was true that I had complained about Sunny's Bakery to Jane. And yeah, maybe it would benefit my family if the rival bakery went out of business. But there was nothing about this that was funny. A hate crime wasn't something to joke about. And that wasn't something I could—or should have to—explain to another person.

My phone was shaking. After a moment, I realized it was because my hands were shaking. Suddenly, I realized that though Jane and I had been texting for weeks now, we still hadn't coordinated our busy schedules to meet up.

And maybe meeting Jane in person wouldn't be such a great idea after all.

Chapter Thirteen

JANE TEXTED AGAIN LATER THAT morning as though her last message hadn't happened.

> *Jane:* So what're you up to today? Wanna set a date to finally meet in person soon?

I left her on read. Even seeing Jane's name flash on my phone screen made me feel queasy. Maybe she hadn't actually lifted a finger against me or anyone else, but the fact that she thought what happened to Sunny's Bakery was a joke horrified and unsettled me in a way I couldn't explain.

Though my workload was towering, I decided to head down to Sunny's Bakery. A morbid curiosity had risen inside me. I needed to see for myself what was going on there, to witness the vandalization and the symbol of the Order. Needed to see with my own eyes the damage that had been done.

It was a sunny morning, the light hitting the tops of statues and filtering through the enormous trees. There was a decent amount of people out and about, jogging along the road, but the closer I got to Sunny's Bakery, the fewer people there were. It seemed most had been warned away from the area.

A handful of onlookers—mostly students, from the looks of their backpacks—were ogling the scene of the vandalization. Sunny's Bakery had been roped off. Shattered glass littered the ground, though it seemed someone had done their best to sweep it out of the way of passersby, keeping it inside the ropes.

There were those horrible words—*Go back to your country, chink*—painted on the wall. Next to it was that symbol that had been found where Melissa Hong's body was discovered seven years ago. The Order of Alpha's wolf head.

I needed to take a picture. Grabbing my phone out of my pocket, I raised my arm and realized I was shaking again. *Keep it together, Anna*, I urged myself, which was something I was doing often these days. Taking a deep breath, I steadied my arm long enough to snap a few photos. Maybe once I examined these, I'd find a clue that the police had somehow overlooked—a clue that could point toward the culprit behind this, and if they were linked to Melissa's murder at all. It couldn't be a coincidence that they were both linked to this symbol of a secret society that had supposedly been disbanded seventy years ago.

⊪————⊩

Campus life and Game Day continued as though nothing had happened. Pretty much nothing had the power to stop football around here. By late afternoon, Chris still hadn't returned. Feeling helpless, I threw myself into my studies to avoid having to listen to my own thoughts and fears.

In the evening, I ignored the ruckus of post-football parties in favor of shutting myself inside the Thatcher Graduate Library. I had some serious work to do for class.

The stone steps led up to a high Gothic revival building with rose windows and decorative panels that gave it the appearance of a Victorian castle. I recalled from my orientation tour that it was one of the oldest buildings on campus.

The inside was designed as a cathedral nave, giving it a church-like appearance. Speaking any louder than a whisper would cause echoes and earn death glares from the librarians, so the graduate library wasn't the ideal meeting spot for group homework. It was the perfect place to cut off distractions, though.

I headed straight up to the tenth floor where there were fewer students and tucked myself up in a corner behind stacks of old books to finish my reading, losing myself in the words of scholars from centuries ago. Before I knew it, my whole Saturday had passed in a blur of Homer's *The Odyssey* and Wu Cheng En's *Monkey: Folk Novel of China*. I'd read both before—*The Odyssey* my junior year of high school, and *Monkey* in Chinese school. They were vastly different texts in terms of themes, settings, and characters, but both featured journeys. *The Odyssey* was about Odysseus's back home, whereas *Monkey* was about the monk Xuan Zang's journey out West to seek out the Buddhist scriptures.

I was so lost in the stories that, for a brief moment in time, I forgot everything else that was going on in my life.

When I finally finished my reading, darkness had fallen outside the glass windows. I wrapped my windbreaker around me more tightly and picked up my pace as I headed for the library exit. The sound of raised voices caused me to turn toward a crowd of people exiting the library. One of the brown-haired girls at the back of the crowd bent down to tie her shoes, and I realized that the brilliant red streak in her hair looked very familiar. It only took me a few seconds to pinpoint why.

"Jane!" I blurted out without thinking. I hadn't expected to run into Jane at all. Didn't she say she lived super far from Central Campus?

Jane continued tying her shoes as I walked up to her, not giving any indication that she'd heard me. My footsteps faltered. Maybe I'd been wrong. But, no—this girl looked exactly like Jane, though her hair was longer than in her Friend Me photos, which made sense given that some time must've passed since she'd had those photos done.

"Jane?"

She finally glanced up at me, but her expression was blank. Her green eyes, though, gave me the confirmation I needed. This was Jane, no doubt about it. "Are you talking to me?"

"You're Jane, right? It's Anna. From Friend Me?" With my every word, Jane's eyebrows rose further, and my heart dropped lower. There was no way I had the wrong girl—she looked exactly like her photos. "We've . . . we've been texting?"

Jane's eyes darted to the crowd of people, which was moving along without her, and she quickly stood up straight. She gave me a freaked-out look, as though I were some random creep. "I'm sorry, but I don't use Friend Me. And I don't know any Anna."

This wasn't happening. My cheeks heated with mortification. Maybe I *did* have the wrong girl. "Do you have, like, a twin? Or a sibling? I just—I've been talking to someone who looks exactly like you."

Jane shot panicked looks around at the crowd, as though she thought I might suddenly run at her or something. Slowly, she backed away. "I'm an only child. Listen, sorry, but I can't help you. My group is leaving, so . . ." Without finishing her sentence or waiting for me to say anything, Jane—or whoever she was—ducked her head and scurried off.

Leaving me watching her, stunned and in disbelief. That girl had been Jane. I was so sure of it. And yet, she hadn't recognized me at all. Which meant one of two things was true: either Jane had put on this huge act to pretend she didn't know me . . . or "Jane" was a totally different person who'd been catfishing me using this random girl's photo.

My hands shook. I desperately hoped my hunch was wrong, but my instincts were screaming that I was right—about the latter.

Jane didn't exist. Someone had been catfishing me on Friend Me all along.

⊷————⊶

Anna: Hey um random question . . . have you been to Thatcher lately?
Jane: No lol it's far from me
Anna: Then do you happen to have an identical twin?

Jane: No lmao and what's with all these questions? You haven't been talking to me at all and now it's 99 questions out of the blue.

Anna: I've just been busy

Jane: Are you mad at me for some reason?

Anna: I'm not mad

Jane: Then why aren't you talking to me anymore?

Anna: I told you I've been really busy

Jane: Are you about to ghost me lol?

Anna: I just don't wanna talk to you

Jane: Like, ever? That's the definition of ghosting.

Anna: Ok fine then. You know what? I AM mad. I'm mad that you took this hate crime as a joke. It's really, really not funny.

Jane: I already apologized for that

Anna: Ok, and? Just bc you apologized doesn't mean we can go back to the way we were before

Jane: Jesus . . . you're so ungrateful. You said it yourself—I'm the nicest friend you've made here. And the only friend, right? Is this how you treat your only friend?

Anna: Yeah well . . . that was before I knew your true colors.

Jane: So that's it? You're ending everything just like that?

Anna: What do you want me to say?

Jane: I won't let you, Anna. I'll make you realize. You'll see.

Anna: Make me realize what??

Jane: That I'm the only friend you need at Brookings, and it's a mistake to end our friendship.

Anna: You're creeping me out.

Jane: You're offending ME

Anna: Stop messaging me, and lose my number. I'm so serious right now.

Jane: You'll regret tossing me aside. Fucking bitch

Anna: No, I really don't think I will. If you want to know the real reason why I was asking you questions earlier, it's bc I ran into a girl at Thatcher who looked exactly like you, only she didn't recognize me at all. You've been using her photos to catfish, and that's fucking disgusting and creepy. I'm blocking you now. Don't ever try to contact me again.

Jane: You'll go the same way Melissa Hong did

I couldn't believe this bitch was bringing up Melissa Hong as a way to threaten me. And that the threat was actually working. Because maybe that was what my investigation was truly about. Maybe that was my greatest fear—that I, someone who looked like Melissa Hong, someone who had known Melissa Hong, would be killed and tossed aside in cold blood, my murderer never caught and apprehended. Perhaps it would be my parents who'd be so devastated that they'd return to China, their dreams dashed and broken.

You'll go the same way Melissa Hong did. It was the most frightening thing Jane could've said to me at this moment.

My heart racing, I quickly blocked Jane's profile, and then deleted the Friend Me app from my phone for good measure. My hands shook with adrenaline, and there was cold sweat lining my palms.

There. I'd never given Jane my last name, and we'd never added each other on any other social media. That meant she couldn't track me, and I couldn't track her, so there was no way she could make me regret anything. No way she could carry out her threats.

Jane and I were through.

Chapter Fourteen

THE SUN BEAT DOWN ON me from high above. Though we were well into autumn now, it was an unusually warm Saturday, the temperature in the high seventies, and I wished I'd worn something lighter than a sweater to go outside.

I blinked at the chaotic surroundings, surprised that so many people had turned out for the march. Someone from the Asian Student Union had gotten a GoFundMe up and running on Twitter and Instagram within a few hours after news had spread about Sunny's Bakery and had managed to raise $20,000 in only one week.

Now, groups of ASU members were gathered around outside on the Quad, some of them leaning against cardboard signs. A makeshift stage had been set up in front of the steps of the undergraduate library.

I wasn't supposed to be here. My parents didn't know, and they'd even gone out of their way to forbid me from involving myself in this ASU march, or anything that might link me to hate crime protests. I stared at the family group chat on my phone.

Ma: There's a march happening on campus. Don't go, ok Anna? Keep yourself safe
Ba: You don't know what might happen to you out there. It's very dangerous
Anna: I won't
Ma: Ok, stay safe. You can always come home if you want

If they knew I'd gone against their wishes and come out to today's protest anyway, they would've been furious. I'd brought a pair of sunglasses to disguise myself just in case any pictures were taken and uploaded to social media.

Sorry, Ma and Ba. My parents had done their best to shelter me my whole life, but I didn't want to be sheltered. Not anymore.

I scanned the crowd gathered for the ASU's march against hate crimes. There were a few familiar-looking faces, but the only person I could recognize by name was Kathy from my Sources of East Asian Civilizations class. She was holding a cardboard sign that read Hate is a Virus.

"Anna. I didn't expect to see you here," Kathy said as I approached her.

"I didn't expect to see *you*. You're part of the Asian Student Union?"

She smiled and puffed out her chest with pride. "I'm the freshman representative. It's cool that you showed up for the march. We didn't know if we'd get any turnout." There were rings of exhaustion under her eyes that suggested she'd been up late last night.

"Do you really think this will work?"

The girl next to Kathy threw me a disgruntled look. "Well, at least we're doing something," she sniffed. "What else can we do?"

I didn't have a response to that question.

The longer the ASU was gathered, the more people stopped to watch us. An older girl was standing with the other board members on the makeshift stage, and she waved Kathy over. Kathy took a microphone from her hand and took center stage.

"As your ASU freshman representative, first I want to acknowledge the Black Lives Matter movement that has opened doors for other people of color to speak up about our own experiences of discrimination. Thank you to our Black brothers and sisters for speaking up against discrimination and racism and being the change our country needs." Her opening statement was met by cheers from the crowd.

"I'm honored to lead today's march for our Asian community. Today we're showing them that our voices matter. It's clear that on the Brookings campus, there are whole groups of people who feel like they don't belong here, that they aren't safe on this campus. That because of their gender, sexuality, the color of their skin—they have to sit through every class period in fear of discrimination, in fear that they'll be ridiculed, attacked, or even kidnapped." Nods and shouts of agreement greeted Kathy's words. "Times are changing, and it's clear that a lot of people aren't as progressive as we'd always thought they were. Many who hid their racism are now crawling out of the woodwork, unafraid to brandish it. That's why now, more than ever, we need to be vocal about reporting hate crimes. We need to speak up and speak out. That we are people, and that we reject their hate." At this, more cheers. Kathy raised her voice. "We'll be walking from here all the way down State Street to the football stadium, and then back again. And if anyone else has ideas to promote harmony on our campus—besides those diversity and inclusion workshops—I'd love to hear them after."

I glanced around at the crowd and was surprised to see Chris there, standing beside an oak tree. His eyes were shining bright when they met mine.

"That's all. Now march, people!" shouted Kathy.

Leading the audience in an uproar of hollering, Kathy hopped off the stage. The crowd parted for her as she walked toward Madison Street. The rest of the ASU board members followed, and after another beat, so did I.

Behind me, the rest of the crowd fell in line, feet stamping as we marched. Marching for the hope of a safer campus, a place where discrimination and hatred and fear could not be welcome. We marched for well over an hour. Many stopped to watch us, and some even joined in on the protest after they'd learned what it was all about.

I had no idea if what we were marching for was even possible. But the marchers' confidence made me want to believe that in this cold, cruel world, love and understanding still stood a chance.

———•││————││•———

That night, I found a surprise waiting for me when I checked my email inbox.

To: axu@brookings.web
From: akim@brookings.web
Subject: RE: Melissa Hong Information

Hi Anna,

Thanks for your email, and sorry for replying late—I don't
check this email much anymore. I hope your freshman year
is going well.

Honestly I don't know how much more helpful info I could
give you beyond what I said in the Brookings Daily interview
about Melissa. But one thing I really did think was odd was
how much time she spent at office hours for one of her
East Asian studies classes—I forget the name. My wild
theory is that she had a secret boyfriend or girlfriend there,
and one day they got into a big argument, and then they
decided to get rid of her. Idk, Melissa just didn't seem quite
like herself toward the end—super emotional and
defensive, like the way people get when they're in toxic
relationships. Or maybe she was just stressed about grades,
but somehow I don't think that's it . . .

I don't know if this is helpful, but you should know that
around the time Melissa disappeared, some strange, spooky
things began happening in our dorm. We never reported
them, but looking back we totally should have. Melissa
started noticing that her hair was thinning/missing in weird

places. And sometimes when I was walking back to the dorm with her, we got the sense we were being followed. I know people like to share West Tower ghost stories, but I don't believe in that stuff . . . and I always suspected Melissa had a stalker that we didn't know about.

P.S. If you haven't already, you should try to find out all you can about the Order of Alpha. I think discovering their link to Melissa is the key to solving what happened. I hope you're able to get to the bottom of this. Melissa deserves justice, and I'm just sorry I was never able to get it for her.

P.P.S. Professor Gregory Wittman used to be pretty close to Melissa. He should still be teaching in the East Asian Studies department. I'd go talk to him . . . honestly, I always thought he was kind of suspicious.

Thanks for everything,
Alice

Chapter Fifteen

WITH EXTRA CAMPUS POLICE GUARDING the area around Sunny's Bakery, there were no further incidents. There also weren't any arrests. The police were on the case, but nobody had been caught and punished, and already the news cycle had moved on to the next big story. The way it dropped reminded me of what had happened with the Melissa Hong murder seven years ago. I remembered seeing her death reported on the news, the articles that circulated on WeChat. And I remembered how after a few days, everyone stopped talking about Melissa's murder. I wondered how long it would take before everyone here forgot what had happened at Sunny's Bakery.

Midterm exams were fast approaching, and soon everyone had shifted their focus to more immediate concerns—like cramming for exams. Alice's email was on my mind every day, but I hadn't figured out what to do yet. I knew for sure that I needed to talk to Professor Wittman again, but I'd been hesitant to repeat my visit to his office hours just yet. What if he straight up refused to talk to me about Melissa like last time? In fact, he'd told me to stop asking.

There was also the matter of the "strange, spooky" things that Alice had mentioned in her email. Missing hair, being followed . . . from the sound of it, somebody had been messing with Melissa back then. The same way I suspected somebody was messing with me now. The thought was terrifying. What if somebody *had* done away with Melissa, and they were planning to do something to me next?

No, I had to be overthinking. There was no way somebody was actually out to get me. That was like something out of a horror movie.

Later that night, I found Chris sitting alone in the dining hall, having a late dinner. I was surprised—I'd been deep in my thoughts. For a moment, I debated whether I should go over to him but made the decision before I could overthink it.

"Hey, Chris," I said, sliding into the seat across him in the booth. I hoped my expression didn't reveal the frightening thoughts that were currently occupying my mind.

He looked up from his stir-fry noodles. There were huge bags under his eyes, indicating stress from midterm season, or stress from his family's bakery—likely a bit of both.

"Oh. Hey."

"Mind if I sit here?" The instant the words tumbled out of my mouth, I blushed in embarrassment. "Oh, I mean, I'm already sitting here, I guess."

"Nah, go ahead."

The silence stretched between us. I picked at my burger and fries. I didn't have much of an appetite. Neither of us were eating. Finally, I felt like I had to say something. "Um, so, how's your family holding up after . . . everything that happened?"

"They're . . . managing." Chris let out a sigh. "The bakery is undergoing repairs. It'll probably be close to winter when we can reopen. But we will reopen." He set his jaw in determination. Then he shook his head. "So how's studying going, anyway? We've got that huge Great Books exam in a week."

"Ugh. Don't remind me," I groaned, though secretly I was thinking that the talk of studying was a welcome distraction from the much darker thoughts I'd been entertaining. Without Jane's help with old exam materials, I was going to have to study everything on my own. I'd already blocked out the entire weekend for a last-minute cramming session, and I'd be lucky to get two hours of sleep between now and Monday.

As Chris and I vented about Great Books, we finished up dinner, and then headed back toward the dorms together.

"Yeah, and I wish our professor would be more specific about what the exam will cover," Chris grumbled. "We've done a shitload of reading. No way am I gonna be able to remember everything for the exam."

"Professor Wittman won't let up with the readings, either." Just thinking about the amount of unfinished reading I had to do for Sources of East Asian Civilizations was enough to give me a headache.

"Don't get me started on that guy," Chris said. "Not that the texts aren't interesting, but how are we supposed to become experts on classic East Asian texts in one semester? It's not like Great Books. Like, I read Mary Shelley and Homer in high school. I've never even heard of most of the books on our Sources of East Asian Civilizations syllabus."

Even if I hadn't read most of the texts on our Great Books syllabus, I'd heard of them all. *The Iliad, The Odyssey, Frankenstein.* Back in high school, English teachers had practically shoved those titles down our throats. It made me almost not want to read them.

Chris and I rounded the corner, only to come to a halt at the sound of a familiar female voice shouting, "Out of the way!"

Elise was clomping down the opposite end of the hall in high heels, dressed in a skimpy black romper that clung to her curves and left little to the imagination. I immediately averted my eyes. It took Chris a noticeably longer time to tear his gaze away from the sight of our disheveled RA, who was clearly dressed for a night out.

"What? Don't look at me like that. I'm not on duty," Elise snapped defensively, barely glancing at her residents as she sauntered past us and ducked into the girl's bathroom.

"Put your eyeballs back in," I hissed at Chris.

"I wasn't—they *are*—"

"You were totally staring."

Before Chris could retort, Elise's scream pierced the air. Chris and I took one look at each other, and then raced down the hall.

A few doors swung open, curious, sleep-deprived faces appearing behind them. "Did someone just scream?" Devon poked his head out of his room, rubbing his eyes, having just rolled out of bed with his *Teenage Mutant Ninja Turtles* pajamas still on.

Chris and I rounded the corner and nearly collided with Elise, who was stumbling away from the bathroom. She turned around, and I saw that her heavily lined eyes were now not only bloodshot from lack of sleep, but also popping with shock. "Ew, who left this creepy thing in there?"

"What is it?" I asked, while Chris gazed on in concern.

"Some weird . . . doll."

At the word "doll," my mind immediately flickered to the thought of my own lucky doll. I hadn't thought much about it since Ma had given it to me, though a few days ago I had noticed that it had disappeared from my backpack. I'd assumed it had fallen out in my room somewhere and hadn't made time to look for it yet.

"Whoever did this prank, it's not funny," Elise yelled out toward the hall. "Some of us really get creeped out by dolls!"

Privately I agreed with her. Horror movies in general I could handle, but horror movies with dolls—I didn't mess with those.

"You good with checking it out?" Chris nodded toward the bathroom. "I wouldn't let you go alone normally, but since it's . . . you know . . ." An uncomfortable expression crossed his face. "The ladies' room," he mumbled.

"Yeah, I've got it. Just wait out here with Elise. I'll go scope out the scene." Leaving the irritated Elise beside Chris, I pressed my hand to the ice-cold door and pushed it open. I stepped through the doorway and scanned the empty bathroom.

As I approached the shower curtains, I spotted something

unusual out of the corner of my eye. What appeared to be a small, travel-sized object was sitting on the shelf meant for holding shampoo and conditioner. At first I thought it was a large hairball, but a closer look showed me it was a doll that was covered in black human hair.

A small, familiar-looking doll with long black hair, stuffed in a small red dress. My doll. The one I'd lost. There was no way I'd brought it into this bathroom.

I opened the shower curtain and spotted red words that had been written on the wall next to the doll.

Nice try, but you can't un-Friend Me.

I swallowed the urge to scream. Shivers racked my body. Slowly I raised my hand to the back of my head, where the clump of hair had gone missing weeks ago. That hair was now, inexplicably, around the neck of my missing doll.

Someone had planned this in advance. They had cut off a chunk of my hair without me noticing, had stolen my doll while I wasn't paying attention. This was not just a display to say "gotcha"—this was a threat, and I knew exactly what they meant to say.

Nice try, but you can't un-Friend Me . . . because I have access to you whenever I want.

"Jane," I hissed under my breath. The realization was terrifying, and also, if I was honest with myself, electrifying.

I would be lying if I said I'd ever been more alive.

Chapter Sixteen

I HAD JUST ENOUGH SENSE left in me to realize that I shouldn't touch anything at the scene. I snapped a couple of pictures with my phone, and then I all but ran out of the bathroom, chest constricted with a horrible, sick-to-my-stomach feeling. Yet at the same time, the adrenaline pumping through my body gave me a rush like nothing I'd felt before. Exhilaration and fear went hand in hand, it seemed.

Chris's eyes met mine, concern written all across his face. "What did you see?"

"It's . . ." I couldn't find the words. I shook my head and handed over my phone to show him the photos. Chris examined the screen, thumb swiping from picture to picture, his expression morphing from one of concern to pure disgust. Outrage.

"What is this?" he hissed, holding my phone back out to me like it had mortally offended him. My trembling fingers brushed against his, his hand closing over mine for a little longer than necessary as I took my phone back.

Chris's breathing was coming out rapid and heavy. "Someone's threatening another student in West Tower?"

Someone was threatening me. But I couldn't force myself to say the words out loud. Admitting that would make the threat become that much more real. I didn't want to see the horror that would dawn in Chris's eyes if he knew how deeply I was in trouble.

Jane had gotten my doll somehow from my backpack. Jane had gotten a hold of my hair from my head.

West Tower wasn't safe. My room wasn't safe. Nowhere was safe.

You'll go the same way Melissa Hong did.

A warning. A warning of what was to come. Maybe the reason I'd been obsessed with Melissa's case was because deep down, I had an inkling that I might one day meet the same fate.

"... Anna?"

The hall was spinning around me, and Chris uttering my name brought me back. He gazed at me with concern. I forced a smile at him, trying not to let my fear show on my face.

"I need to report this to the dean," Elise said, finally coming back to life. Her expression was glassy and dazed, but her eyes were growing sharper with clarity by the second. Mumbling to herself, the RA pushed past us and a crowd of people who'd gathered behind without our notice. She walked as fast as she could with her four-inch heels clicking down the hall.

Devon and a few other confused floor mates stood gaping at us with expectant looks on their faces. "What did you see in there?" Devon demanded.

"Let me through—I'm your RA. What's going on?" Patrick pushed his way to the head of the pack, his feet tucked in his bunny slippers, shower caddy in hand. "Has something happened?"

"An . . . incident . . . occurred," Chris said, jaw working hard to pronounce the words, a grave look on his face. "Someone left a creepy doll and message in the girls' bathroom. Elise just went to report it."

After Patrick caught onto the tension in the air and the grim expressions on his residents' faces, his annoyance faded away into concern. "A threat? Was somebody hurt?"

Chris and I exchanged looks, neither of us wanting to be the bearer of bad news.

"Uh," I finally said, "you should see what we found in the girls' bathroom." I held up my phone. Patrick plucked it from my trembling fingers. He squinted at the screen, his face slowly morphing again, from confusion to fear.

Devon craned his neck to try to see the image, but Patrick blocked it from his view just in time. "Everyone back to their dorm rooms," the RA ordered, in a more authoritative voice than I'd ever heard him use. His eyes were burning bright, lips set in a thin line. "Now!"

We obeyed. Gladly. Scattered back into our dorms, confused and scared.

As usual, Laura's bed was empty. I spent the night tossing and turning, unable to sleep even a wink. When I closed my eyes, all I could see was that doll, my hair falling out in clumps—and swimming beyond that, the shadow of a face, of an unknown stranger. An invisible enemy who might be out to ruin me. A stranger who clearly had been following me, who knew me.

And then a frightening idea struck me. Slowly, as though in a nightmare, I reached for my phone. I redownloaded the Friend Me app. I'd gotten a lot of new matches, but as I scrolled down the list, I couldn't find Jane's name. I double- and triple-checked but eventually was forced to conclude that Jane had deleted her account.

There was no way for me to reach her now. Furthermore, Jane had deleted the proof of her existence. I hadn't thought to screenshot any of our conversations before her account had vanished. If I went to the authorities, I'd have nothing to back up my claim that Jane had existed and was stalking me.

And now, I realized with a horrible sinking sensation, I knew nothing about Jane, whereas Jane knew all too much about me.

◦⊩————⊩◦

The next evening, Patrick called an emergency meeting for all the residents on the second floor of West Tower, forcing us to cozy up together in the downstairs lounge.

"I am very disappointed in all of you." Patrick paced back and forth in front of us, lifting his head every few steps to pin us with a glare. "West Tower is above bullying. I suggest whoever wrote that threat in the girls' bathroom come clean now."

Elise nodded, a tight, fierce expression on her face. "Otherwise, there will be consequences."

Nobody moved. We all stared around at one another, at the odd divide between us. The international students were huddled on one sofa. On the opposite side of the room, everyone else had taken their spots on the couch and surrounding chairs. Laura, for once, was around. She had perched herself onto the one and only stool. Her ever-growing posse of girlfriends had taken their spots next to her.

So much for DIVERSITY. So much for INCLUSIVE.

Chris and I sat on the floor in the middle of no-man's-land, with Devon sitting right beside us.

Patrick and Elise had called this meeting because they suspected someone in our dorm had done it. And now, I couldn't help but see my dorm mates in a different light. Any one of them could have been pretending to be a girl named Jane.

I'd spent hours and hours recalling the information Jane had told me. She lived on North Campus, but maybe that was a lie. Maybe she'd lied about her major, too. She could have fed me nothing but lies, and I'd been dumb enough to trust her with the truth about me. A Facebook search of the name "Jane" brought up too many profiles, but none of them resembled Jane's profile picture, nor did they match the description she'd given me.

More and more now, I was certain "Jane" didn't exist. Certain that "Jane" was an identity constructed so that somebody could stalk other students—like me. Now I was kicking myself for telling this person so much.

My skin prickled. I didn't feel safe here. I didn't feel safe being me any longer, and I wondered if I would feel comfortable in my own skin ever again.

The meeting the RAs had called ended up being a big fail. Nobody came forward. Of course not. And as soon as Patrick and Elise were finished grilling everyone, the students dispersed back to their busy lives.

"You know, you guys are welcome to chill with me if you want to talk through some things," Patrick called toward our retreating backs. "Or report anything you've seen or heard. My door is open. Always."

The invitation made me feel guilty that I was hiding information from everyone else. My omissions were a lie. But I knew, in my gut, that this was between Jane and me. Besides, I didn't have any proof or evidence to start an investigation against Jane. I didn't even know Jane's real name.

No, this was something I had to do on my own. As much as it terrified me, this Jane person was someone I had to find—and take down—on my own. Jane, I realized, was hunting me, threatening me, the way somebody had seemingly been stalking Melissa. Was this how Melissa had felt—terrified, electrified?

I ran through our conversations again in my mind, kicking myself for being so open with a stranger before. It hadn't occurred to me until now that though Jane knew a lot about me, I didn't know much about her beyond the fact that she was a sophomore living on North Campus—or so she'd claimed. Maybe even that had been lies.

"You know something. Don't you?"

I froze on my way back to my room, my heart slamming to a stop. Chris had stopped in the hall. He was staring at me with narrowed eyes, as though he could see right through me. He probably could. Guy was too smart for his own good. "Know something about what?" I said as innocently as I could.

"The threat," Chris said. "You've been acting strange ever since."

I weighed my options. I could continue acting like a fool and lying my way out of this situation, insulting Chris's intelligence in the same breath. Or I could let Chris in—and just Chris—on what had happened with Jane.

I squeezed my eyes shut. I'd always done everything on my own. Maybe having another person, someone who'd been similarly ostracized by this university, would help. "I'll tell you, but in private," I said. "Come to my room?"

He nodded. In front of my door, I swiped my card through the slot, and then opened it. After making sure it was shut tight behind Chris and me, I flung myself on my bed.

Chris stood awkwardly for a moment, and then mussed up the hair on the back of his head, causing it to stick up even more. "So what exactly do you know, Anna?"

I sighed and pointed toward the seat behind my desk. "Sit down. This is going to take a while."

Chapter Seventeen

BY THE TIME I'D FINISHED giving him the basic rundown of events, everything from the way I'd been following Melissa Hong's case to Jane's laughing about the attack at Sunny's, to Jane's threat, Chris's eyes were huge, saucerlike. It would've been funny if anything about the situation were funny at all.

"You're in danger, serious danger. *Shit*, Anna. I get why you'd be frustrated about what happened to Melissa, but why would you try to solve the case yourself? The police couldn't even do it."

"Melissa was the daughter of family friends," I explained. "I . . . I *knew* her. And . . . I don't know, I just . . . I just want everyone to have closure." How could I put it into the words, this feeling that if Melissa didn't get justice, then I couldn't rest easy, either? This feeling that the people who looked like me were worth nothing to the majority of this country's population, and that we could only count on each other. "It's not right, how Melissa's killer was never caught."

"I get that. And I get that you have a strong sense of justice. I just can't believe you've been trying to handle all of this on your own. Why haven't you told anyone else before now?"

"It's a bit weird, isn't it, to tell people that you're trying to Sherlock Holmes a cold murder case. The only person I've confided in since coming to Brookings was Jane, and look how that turned out." This was exactly why I never told anyone anything. Even letting Chris in on what happened was a risk, and it was one I was only willing to take because he was also a victim in this situation, so I was ninety-nine point nine-nine percent sure he wasn't the culprit.

Chris bit his lip, frustration creasing his brows. "Well, you need to at least tell Patrick and Elise," he said firmly.

"I can't."

"This person—this Jane—they're targeting you. They clearly know too much about you already. It's not safe, Anna. If they were willing to catfish to get close to you, they clearly won't stop at anything to get what they want."

Just thinking about how I'd been catfished made me want to puke. "I don't have any proof to show Patrick and Elise. And even if they do believe me, I'll probably be pulled in for questioning and all this other stuff. It'll interfere with my classes."

"You getting attacked by this catfishing person would also interfere with your classes," Chris pointed out.

"Not if I catch them first."

"You're not making any sense," he said bluntly. I winced, because it was true. "You know that? You're not Sherlock Holmes or Nancy Drew or any other protagonist in a mystery novel. You're in real danger if this stranger is after you."

Part of me knew that Chris was right, but the bigger part of me didn't want to give Jane the satisfaction of knowing that I'd had to go to the authorities. Didn't want to give them that power over my life.

"What if I do go to the authorities, and they do nothing?" I met Chris's stare unflinchingly. "You know how they're pretty much all talk and no action when it comes to people like us."

Chris opened his mouth, then closed it. I could tell that as much as we both wished it weren't true, he knew I was right. Until I had some solid proof that someone was targeting me, going to the authorities would be a waste of time.

"So what's your plan, then, if you're not going to clue in our RAs on what's going on? You're not stupid enough to go after this person all on your own." When I said nothing, Chris groaned. "You are that stupid. Jesus, Anna."

"It's not stupid. It's the only option."

"No, the other, sensible option is to report this to—"

"I won't do it, Chris. They wouldn't even believe me. Like I said, there's no proof."

He sighed and buried his head in his hands. "As if midterm season weren't already stressful enough. Now you're adding all this to your plate, too."

"Midterms are the least of my concerns now." I let out a hollow laugh.

Chris didn't crack a smile. "Okay. So you won't tell the RAs. What now? Do you have any clues about this Jane person?"

"It's got to be someone who I've been in contact with," I said. "They—they've been following me. That's how they got the doll. That's how they know I live in this hall." I shuddered. "Chris, I . . . I think it's someone in this hall."

He didn't say anything at first. "That's a possibility," he said finally.

I swallowed, and then blurted out a thought that had been percolating in the back of my mind, growing ever stronger. "It might be my roommate. Laura. Or maybe one of her sorority sisters. Though it's not like they're around all that much, so I don't know when they would've had time to cut off my hair and steal my shit."

"Laura's got the easiest access to you," Chris muttered, looking deep in thought. "But that's the worst-case scenario if it's true. I mean, does she even have a motive for doing something like this?"

I opened my mouth but realized I couldn't think of anything specific or concrete. "We're not exactly friends, but I haven't done anything to her."

"Which sorority is she in?" Chris asked.

Again, my brain stumbled trying to formulate an answer. Now that I thought about it, I hadn't seen any specific Greek letters on Laura's clothing, nor anywhere in our room. None of her Instagram updates had announced her joining any specific sorority, either. "I—I dunno, now that you mention it. Maybe she's not in a sorority after all. I just saw one of those fancy invitations, and assumed . . ." I trailed off, and I flushed, hoping Chris didn't think I was dumb for not double-checking. There was a short, slightly awkward silence. I cleared my throat. There was one more idea that I'd been toying with, but I had no idea if it had any merit. "I was also thinking . . . maybe . . . this is linked to what happened to your bakery. The graffiti that people are saying has to do with the Order of Alpha."

His eyebrows rose. Disbelief flitted across his features. "The police haven't dug up anything about that Order, though. There's no evidence of them being active."

"We don't know that for sure, do we? I've done some research on my own, and there is evidence that the Order existed at one point—it was founded in 1902 and disbanded in 1958. There's not much more on it anywhere, though."

"Of course not." Chris sighed, rubbing his forehead as though he had a throbbing headache.

"If the Order of Alpha were real, and Laura got herself into it somehow . . . well, it'd explain a lot, wouldn't it? It would mean they're involved in the hate crime at Sunny's Bakery, and what happened with my doll." It was also looking likelier that Laura was involved in some kind of secret organization, since it didn't appear as though she were in a sorority after all. But I also couldn't wrap my head around the idea of Laura going through so much effort to scare me. We weren't on good terms, but there was no way she could hate me that much—right?

"Speaking of—what's happening with Sunny's Bakery?" I asked.

Chris let out a long, exhausted sigh. "The bakery will be okay. My parents are planning for a grand reopening. They're shaken, but they're determined to keep running the business."

"It's good that they didn't shut down." Looking back on the rivalry that existed between Sunny's Bakery and Sweetea, I

realized it seemed so silly. Now there were much bigger problems to tackle.

"Yeah, but the culprit behind it got away." Chris's expression
morphed into one of barely restrained anger. "And I'm going to
get to the bottom of it. No matter if the Order of Alpha is fake
or whatever. I'll expose whoever is behind this."

There was only one way I could see right now to find out
whether these incidents were connected, and to try to bring justice to the criminals. I took a deep breath. "Next time I see Laura
leaving this room, I'll tail her. She usually comes back on Thursday nights—which is tonight. So I'll see where she goes and
what she's up to."

Chris nodded. "I'm coming with you."

"No, Chris, I don't want to involve y—"

"Too late," he said firmly. The tone of his voice left no room
for argument, and my words faltered in my throat. "I'm involved
now. Deal with it."

Even though part of me was worried, another part of me
couldn't help but feel relief knowing that Chris was going to
be helping me out. I felt better knowing someone was on my
side. Knowing someone was watching my back when I couldn't.

"Thanks. I'll—I'll message you to come over when Laura
leaves again."

Chris nodded and stood up. "I'll be in my room. Gotta do
at least some studying, right?" He cracked a wan smile, and then
loped out of the room.

I watched him go. There had been warmth when Chris was
present. And now, with him out of the room, the air had turned

cold again, and I imagined invisible eyes watching me. I shuddered and huddled my limbs together.

We had a plan, somewhat. Now all that there was left to do was wait.

•||———||•

I didn't have to wait long, only an hour or so, before Laura came back from the dining hall. She barely looked at me. I ignored her in kind, too disturbed by the idea that she might have something to do with Jane to want to talk to her or even breathe in the same air as her.

Not that I had to worry about that for long, because Laura had made it quite clear by now that she shared the sentiment. As quickly as she'd rushed in, she hurried out of the room, her heels clacking behind her. Once the door shut behind her, I texted Chris.

> *Anna:* Ok we need to go now.
> *Chris:* Omw

I met Chris halfway down the hall, and I pointed toward the elevators, which were closing, Laura's curtain of hair vanishing behind the doors.

"The stairs," I said.

We raced down the staircase. By the time we got down to the ground floor, Laura had gotten out of the elevator and was striding across the floor. Her eyes were glued to her phone, and she didn't even spare us a glance.

We tailed Laura out of the building and into the cool late

October air. She turned left, and then right, and then walked to a large, red-bricked building. The sign outside read Hill House.

My heart skipped a beat. *Hill House.* This was the all-girls dorm that had once hosted the meetings for the Order of Alpha when it still existed. That couldn't be a coincidence.

"You think that's the meeting place?" asked Chris.

"Yeah. Hill House. This is where the Order of Alpha used to host their meetings." I'd been half expecting Laura to lead us to a secret underground tunnel or a hidden wall in a building, or something. Yet she'd strode into Hill House so openly, as though she were doing something as casual as visiting a friend. In this scenario, Chris and I came off like the creeps who were stalking.

Chris ducked and crouched down into the bushes below one of the large front windows. He waved me over, and after a moment I followed him, maneuvering around the leaves and branches that scratched against my body. Together we peered into Hill House.

The living room area was packed with people, and with pink decorations, like lights and streamers, clearly meant to celebrate something—someone's birthday, judging by the Happy Birthday balloons in the center.

Chris and I pressed our ears to the window, as close as we dared while hiding in the shadows. I could barely make out snatches of dialogue here and there.

"—glad you could make it," said one girl, who was dressed in a white power suit that gave her the air of a young politician.

A voice—Laura's voice, I was certain—responded, ". . . wouldn't miss it . . . since our fathers are good friends . . ."

"It's just a birthday party," I sighed. Disappointment settled over me. Maybe Chris and I were both overthinking, and Laura was never in our dorm because she was too busy being a college socialite. Being in a sorority or a secret society wasn't the only way of staying well-connected at Brookings. Laura was the type to have been popular in high school, and that popularity translated well to university.

The girls started cheering about something, and one of them brought out a huge cake.

"Okay, I've seen enough," Chris grumbled.

"Yeah, let's not crash this party." The last thing we needed was for a partygoer to spot us peeking in at them and freak out that we were stalking them.

We headed back toward the dorm in somewhat dejected silence. Though, I wasn't crossing Laura off my list of suspects just yet. She was pretty much the only potential suspect I had, after all.

When we reached our floor in West Tower, we parted ways in the hall. There wasn't much more to say. Chris and I hadn't come any closer to finding Jane, and there was still the matter of our midterms to study for.

"Good night," Chris said when we reached his room.

"See you."

I headed for my room, and then I was finally free to collapse into my bed after another long day. I didn't even attempt to do any of my homework. Just curled up into a ball of exhaustion, closed my eyes, and slipped into an uneasy sleep.

Chapter Eighteen

THE NEXT MORNING, I WOKE up to a text from Chris. Seeing the notification brought a smile to my face—until I actually read the message.

> *Chris:* Yo, have you seen this??? You don't have to watch. Just read the comments . . . it's so fucked up

I clicked the link, which sent me to a Twitter video that already had over a hundred thousand likes and thousands of comments. It showed an elderly Asian woman walking down a street in New York City, and then getting beat up by a much larger man. I paused the video. I didn't want to keep watching. I couldn't bring myself to read the comments.

My hands shook. Tears formed in my eyes, turning my vision blurry. I didn't know the woman in the video, but my mind immediately jumped to Ma and Nai Nai. The woman in the video could've been either of them.

Anna: This is so sick. Is she ok?

Chris: She's in the hospital, but the police haven't caught the guy yet

Anna: :(

Chris: Sorry I didnt mean to put a damper on your morning

Anna: It's ok. I prob would've seen it as soon as I checked Twitter anyway

I'd just woken up, and I was already tired. All I wanted to do was go back to sleep. But even the comfort of sleep evaded me. It was impossible to empty my mind when that consistent fear plagued my thoughts.

Always, always there was that feeling of being watched—by Jane, by anyone who had it out for students who looked different. That feeling followed me from building to building, from class to class. Even at night, though Laura hardly ever returned to our room these days and I was constantly alone, I couldn't quite shake this bone-deep feeling of fear. Of dread.

Maybe it would be my friends next. My family next. Me next.

Immersing myself in schoolwork had always been my sanctuary away from real-world problems. But I couldn't do that now that those problems had bled into my school life. There was no escape, no means of distraction.

It felt like I was living in a bad dystopian novel. Except this wasn't fiction. This was reality. A reality in which hatred was crawling out of the woodwork. Like worms. Like silent, deadly snakes. Staking their claim on what was supposed to be an inclusive campus.

Laura was still at the top of my list of suspects, but it was hard trying to get any proof when she was barely around. We didn't share any classes. I rarely saw her in the dining halls, and every time I did happen to see her, she was surrounded by a loud group of friends—none of whom I recognized.

Eventually, I remembered that I had the contact information for two of her friends, and I initiated a group text to do some digging.

Anna: Hi, hope you guys are good :) I have a quick question . . . have you been hanging out with Laura a lot lately?
Mandy: Hey girl omgggg it's been a while. Um I haven't seen Laura since Game Day tbh
Ellen: Yeah same
Anna: Really? I thought she was going out with you guys, bc I never see her in the room anymore
Mandy: Nope she's not with us. Actually I've been meaning to ask you what's going on with her cuz she basically ditched us after we tailgated on Game Day and hasn't been replying to my texts
Ellen: I think Laura's been hanging around a lot of sophomores and other upperclassmen . . . but idk who they are

Anna: That's so weird . . .
Mandy: Yeah ikr? Rude too
Ellen: Social climber 😐

Talking to Mandy and Ellen didn't necessarily help me gather any solid proof on Laura, but it did tell me at least one thing—I wasn't the only one Laura had ditched for her new crowd. Maybe that was all there was to the story, and Laura was just a social climber.

Or maybe there was something more sinister going on beneath the surface.

•╟──────╢•

Midterms passed in a haze of late-night study sessions fueled by coffee. I knew I hadn't aced any of my exams, but hopefully I'd scraped at least a B on most of them. And right now, while my mind was occupied with concerns for basic safety, I couldn't bring myself to worry about schoolwork, too. Homer and Confucius would have to forgive me.

I bought a can of pepper spray along with a small pocket-knife that fit inside the seams of my jeans and made it a habit to carry both around with me everywhere. I didn't know when and where I might be attacked, and I wasn't taking any chances.

Ma: Anna will you be coming back home for fall
break?
Anna: I don't think so cuz I have a lot of homework to do
Ba: You aren't finished yet for break?

Anna: I'm trying to get ahead
Ma: Ok, work hard. Come by the bakery sometime if
you want a treat
Anna: 👍

As long as I gave my parents the excuse that I was studying, they'd be fine with me doing pretty much anything. It didn't feel right lying to them, but there was no way I could tell the truth. They'd rush me home if they knew what I was really up to. Right now, I needed to keep digging around to find out what was going on.

Without the distraction of classes over fall break, Chris and I trekked across campus one evening for an extra credit Center for Chinese Studies lecture, our steps scattering brown leaves underfoot. I'd told my parents I wasn't coming home for this break because I had too much homework to get a head start on, though the truth was that I wanted to stay to enjoy my freedom and continue the investigation into Jane.

A gloom hung over us. If it could take shape, it would be a gray cloud, sucking the sunlight out of the sky. The only good thing about the day was that the weather was nice for once. November was just around the corner, so this would likely be the nicest weather we'd have for a while. The leaves were clumping on the ground in multicolored piles. The view was almost too beautiful. It was hard to believe that such horrible things could happen on such a breathtaking campus.

As we walked, I kept thinking about Laura, though I was growing less convinced that she had any connection to Jane. Just because I didn't like the girl and she didn't like me wasn't proof that she was capable of doing anything horrible like this. Of course, I couldn't cross her off the list completely, but so far there was nothing pointing toward her as the culprit—unless I counted the fact that she was my roommate and technically had the easiest access to my belongings.

"... listening to me at all, Anna?"

I jolted out of my thoughts and noticed with guilt that Chris had been talking to me while I'd been zoned out. "Sorry. What?"

He rolled his eyes but didn't seem that annoyed. The fall breeze had given his messy black hair a windswept look that made him appear devilishly mischievous—and handsomely so. My heart skipped a beat. I had to glance away, my neck and cheeks burning. Yeah, I'd always known Chris was a good-looking guy, but it hadn't really sunk in before.

"Never mind. We're already here anyway."

Chris held the door open for me, and we stepped inside the auditorium at the Center for Chinese Studies. This center, I remembered from the *Brookings Daily* article, was the last place Melissa Hong was seen alive. It was a modern, ordinary building, and from what I could see, there was one main auditorium and several much smaller rooms that were classrooms.

There was a solid turnout for the event, more than I'd expected for an evening lecture on Chinese tradition at the beginning of fall break. Possibly this was because there were Asian snacks and drinks being served, like choco pies, haw flakes, and even aloe vera juice.

The lecturer was a graduate student who introduced herself

as Weining Chen, and then went to discuss Chinese intellectuals and traditions. I glanced around the room and noticed a few familiar faces from Sources of East Asian Civilizations. There was Robert, our TA, who was staring at Weining with intense focus. Sitting together on the opposite end of the auditorium from him were Jessica and Kathy from our class. They both seemed totally enraptured by Weining's lecture.

"There's so many people here," muttered Chris.

"Are there not usually this many?"

"I've been to every lecture in this series so far, and this is definitely the biggest turnout."

"You've been to every lecture?" Somehow that didn't surprise me, and somehow, annoyingly, it made me like Chris even more. I wasn't supposed to like him. He was supposed to be my rival. Yet I couldn't help but feel like Chris was the only true ally I'd made at school so far.

At the end of the lecture, Weining plugged a couple of upcoming events being hosted by the Chinese and Japanese departments—including the organization of an anime convention at the university, called Animagination, that was to be held the next weekend.

Once the lecture had concluded, there was time for the attendees to mingle or queue up to ask the graduate student presenter questions.

Jessica and Kathy came over to us, smiling. There was a pen tucked behind Jessica's ear. "Hey. Didn't expect to see you guys here. Did you come together?" A sneaky expression stole over her face, and she raised her eyebrows suggestively.

"Um . . ." Suddenly, the room seemed about twenty degrees hotter, and I could not look at Chris. Kathy giggled but quickly covered it up with a pretend cough.

"Yeah, we were hanging out together anyway," Chris answered easily. He'd probably missed all the subtext of Jessica's words. Boys. "You guys come to these lectures often, don't you? Pretty sure I've seen you both a few times."

"I have to come to at least two every month," said Jessica. "It's a course requirement for the Asian studies major."

"Oh." I hadn't known that Jessica was actually majoring in Asian studies, but in hindsight, the pink-and-purple hair might have been a giveaway.

"I just come for the free food," said Kathy with a cheeky grin, waving a pouch of rice crackers in the air.

"I'd still come even if it weren't a requirement," Jessica continued. "I just love Asian history and politics and culture. You know?"

"Well, I am Asian, so I guess I can't say no," I joked, causing Kathy to laugh.

Jessica's smile widened. "Hey, are you guys around next weekend to check out the anime con? Kathy and I are part of the anime club, and we're hosting it." Her words came out a bit jumbled and awkward, as though she were nervous about asking us. That, more than anything, made me want to say yes. I knew exactly how nerve-racking and impossible it felt to try to make friends in college.

Besides, I needed something fun, something happy to keep my mind off what was going on. Even if just for one day, I wanted to be able to pretend I was just a freshman in college having the time of her life. And in any case, there was no way anyone would dare attack me or anyone else at a convention with tons of people.

"It won't be, like, anything huge like Comic Con or anything," Kathy added. "It's low-key. The idea is that you can come and go as you'd like, and it's free unless you want to buy something from the vendors."

"That'll be a good study break," said Chris.

"Definitely." We exchanged numbers, and then Chris and I headed back to West Tower, spirits higher than they had been in weeks.

Chapter Nineteen

"ORDER OF ALPHA?" ELISE BLINKED at the sight of me standing outside her room on Friday morning. She yawned, clearly exhausted from having being on RA duty all night. "I haven't a clue, but I doubt it exists—not since it was disbanded. If it does, it's operating illegally, not to mention it's the most well-kept secret of the decade. Why are you worrying about the Order on a Friday morning? Is it because of what happened weeks ago at Sunny's Bakery?" Her eyes filled with concern.

"Never mind," I mumbled. I didn't like the direction I sensed the conversation was going in. Maybe it was better to consult an older staff member—somebody who might have known more about the Order of Alpha in their active years. Somebody who, last time I'd been to their office, had a plaque bearing their symbol on it.

Ever since I'd first visited Professor Wittman's office hours and spotted that plaque of a wolf's head, since he'd told me to stop asking about Melissa Hong, I'd sensed that this day would come. That I'd have to confront him about what he might know, and what he might be hiding, without taking no for an answer. Now, it seemed, the moment had arrived.

My heart hammered, and my hands shook as I fired off a text to Chris.

> *Anna:* Hey, are you free rn?
>
> *Chris:* Yeah what's up?
>
> *Anna:* Come to Wittman's office hours with me, I think he knows something about the Order
>
> *Chris:* Really? How do you know???
>
> *Anna:* I saw a plaque of a wolf's head in his office that I'm like 97% sure is related to it, but I never said anything cuz I'm not 100% sure, but rn I'm sure that he can at least tell us SOMETHING
>
> *Chris:* That's fair. Ok gimme 5 min and I'll meet you down in the lobby

I headed down to the lobby first, and a few minutes later, Chris showed up, wearing a black polo, khakis, and a slightly nervous expression. My first thought was that he looked cute, but I smacked that thought away almost instantly.

Together we headed across the Quad to Professor Wittman's office.

"So, in the event that our professor *does* know something about the Order and tries to silence us—this outfit I chose isn't too bad to be buried in, is it?" Chris asked.

"Oh my God, Chris."

"What?"

"Please don't joke, I feel like I'm going to puke." My stomach was rolling with nerves. Professor Wittman appeared like he couldn't hurt a fly, but what did I know about him, really? The man could be much more capable than what I gave him credit for.

"Oh. Sorry."

There was a long pause as we headed inside the cool, air-conditioned building. "You do look nice today, though."

Out of the corner of my eye, I saw Chris's expression crack into a smile. "You look good, too."

Ignoring the fresh butterflies that entered my stomach, I led the way up the staircase, past a few students who were going the opposite direction, and stopped in front of Professor Wittman's slightly ajar door. I knocked.

"Come in," said the professor. As Chris and I entered, he glanced up from the book he was reading at his desk, his expression registering some surprise. "Anna. Chris. Didn't expect to see you both together. Have a seat." Professor Wittman pointed at the two chairs in front of him, and we sat down. "Now, what brings you in today?"

I exchanged a nervous look with Chris, who gave me a nod. Taking a deep breath, I turned back to Professor Wittman. "Professor—I know this isn't related to class, but we were wondering . . . wondering if you knew anything about . . . the Order of Alpha."

If the professor was shocked by my words, he did a good job of hiding it. He gave me a long, lingering look that was filled with disappointment. "I warned you, Anna," he said quietly. "I told you to stop inquiring about Melissa."

I averted my gaze and focused instead on the calligraphy scroll hanging from his wall. Pressing Professor Wittman further was a risk. I wanted to stay in his good books. But I'd already come so far, and besides, this matter was more important than my standing in the professor's eyes.

"What is your connection to the Order?" I asked. "And what's the connection between Melissa and the Order?"

"Why do you want to know?"

"We were curious about the history behind it," I said. "It was disbanded many years ago, but the symbol has popped up again twice in connection with recent crimes—the murder of Melissa Hong in 2015, and now, with the vandalization of Sunny's Bakery. We want to know what they are about, and what the connection is to the recent events."

"I'm very sorry about what happened at your family's establishment," the professor said hurriedly, a somber look on his face.

"Thank you. It's not your fault," said Chris.

"But if you continue to withhold important information from us, it might be at least partially your fault," I added.

Professor Wittman blinked, looking stricken. "My fault . . . ," he murmured. He leaned back, and several emotions crossed his face—sadness, confusion, frustration. Finally he turned his gaze back to Chris, and then me. "Fine. If you think it'll help stop these crimes, I'll tell you what I know about the Order. The potential existence of secret societies has always been a point of fascination to students at Brookings," he said, reclining in his chair thoughtfully. He examined me, and once again I got the impression that he was able to see the thoughts churning in my mind. "You aren't the first students, nor do I suspect you will be the last, who have come to me asking about secret societies—this one in particular. Do you think it's likely that the Order of Alpha is still secretly operating right now, Anna?"

I have no idea; that's why I came here to ask you, was what I wanted to say. Professors, I'd learned, had mastered the art of spinning your own questions back at you rather than responding to them head-on. "I . . . think it's not entirely unlikely." There. As a student, I'd learned how to spin professors' own cryptic answers back at them.

Professor Wittman nodded as though I'd said something wise. "You're right. But I also think that the only people who could tell any of us for sure would never speak up for obvious reasons, and there's no use in dwelling on such matters. Unless the two of you have an important reason for doing so?"

"I . . . well . . ." Without a shred of evidence for the existence of the Order—or any order—it didn't make sense for me to keep pressing the professor. To explain why I was sitting in his office, why I feared my life was in danger at this moment, I'd have to start from the beginning with my unusual interest in Melissa Hong's unsolved murder. And though Professor Wittman didn't look like he could harm anyone, I didn't trust him enough to tell him all this information—I couldn't. It had been a risk, and a waste of time, coming here. "Never mind. Thanks for your time, Professor Wittman."

"Wait." The professor held up his hand. I'd started to get up, but now I sank back down into the seat.

Professor Wittman sighed, reached under his desk, and, after a few moments, pulled out the plaque I'd glimpsed weeks ago in this same office.

Chris said, "Professor, that's . . ."

"It's the mark of the Order of Alpha. My grandfather was a member of the last class, right before the university disbanded them."

Professor Wittman passed the plaque over the table, and I found myself staring down at a wolf's head with a fierce coat of black hair around it, its jaws opened wide to reveal sharp, gleaming teeth.

My heart hammered in my chest. I stared down at the plaque, scared that it would disappear at any moment. Maybe this wasn't definitive proof, but it was something—a step in the right direction, a confirmation that I wasn't completely off base with my speculations. A confirmation that whatever was happening, the Order—or someone determined to attach their symbol to the crimes—was behind it.

"Why'd you keep this plaque?" was all I could think to ask.

Professor Wittman stared at the plaque with what could only be described as a mixture of disgust and fear. "It didn't feel right to throw it away. I'd rather carry it around to preserve it, remember the vile history of the Order. After all, those who fail to learn from history are doomed to repeat it." He heaved a long, deep sigh, as though he'd wanted to get this off his chest for years. "The school has done its best to scrub itself free of the taint of this secret society, so you won't find anything much about the Order online or elsewhere." Professor Wittman's eyes darkened. "The Order of Alpha was banished for a reason. They had a history of being racist, misogynistic, and homophobic. Several crimes committed between 1902 to 1958 on campus were traced back to them, but they boasted a roster of some of the most powerful and well-connected members, so no real punishment fell upon them. They managed to get away with these heinous activities for a long time, until finally enough students spoke out against them. If the Order has been revived, then they've done so by evading campus authorities."

"You think that's what they're doing, then? You think the Order of Alpha has secretly revived itself?" Chris pressed, his eyes wide with disbelief.

Professor Wittman pressed his lips together in a thin line. "I find it far more likely that someone who knows about the Order is using it as an emblem for their own terrible actions and crimes."

That was more or less my own theory, and hearing something similar from the professor's mouth only confirmed my strong gut feeling.

"You said earlier that other students have come to you asking about the Order. Who?" I asked.

Guilt entered his eyes, confirming the answer before he even spoke. "I've taught here for nearly three decades now. Many have come to me over the years. Brookings has always drawn the best and the brightest, and it's inevitable that some will get caught up in conspiracy theories and solving mysteries that past students were never able to solve."

Like Melissa Hong's murder.

"Anyone who might be going around committing crimes and attaching the Order's symbol to them?" Chris asked sharply.

Professor Wittman let out a laugh, though there was nothing funny about the situation, and his laughter soon died. "No, no. Absolutely not. I'd never tell a student who I'd think might use the information for evil." He shook his head, as though he were trying to convince himself as much as us. "No, definitely not."

I couldn't help the note of desperation that entered my voice. Couldn't shake the feeling that we were so close, but yet so far, from finally getting a breakthrough. "Professor, please—if there's anyone you can think of who might even be *slightly* likely to commit any crimes in the name of the Order—"

"I think that's enough, the both of you. If I knew any potential leads for suspects, I'd report them to the police myself," Professor Wittman said sharply. I shrunk back at his tone, and he must've regretted how harshly he'd spoken, because his eyes softened. He pulled the plaque back across the desk and placed it on the floor. "I'm sorry that I can't be of more help. Now, do you have any questions related to class?"

Chris shook his head at me, as though indicating that we'd better go. He was right. It would be useless to probe Professor Wittman any further. We'd already learned a good amount by coming here.

"No, that's all. Thank you, Professor." I stood up and turned toward the door.

"Anna, Chris—I can't stop you, but I implore you to do your-selves a favor. Don't go snooping around in too much dangerous business." Professor Wittman's eyes pierced mine, and harsh warning lines formed in his face. "I see very bright futures for the two of you, and I don't want you to get into any trouble."

We nodded. But I was planning to do nothing of the sort. No matter what, I was going to get to the bottom of what was going on.

Before I knew it, Saturday had arrived, and I'd made no further headway into the investigation. In the dining hall at breakfast, Chris and I met up and tossed around ideas.

"Well, at the very least, we can confirm that was the Order of Alpha's symbol," said Chris as he carefully cut his pancake in half. "Should we start just walking all around campus, then?"

It wasn't exactly a brilliant plan, but I couldn't come up with anything better on the spot. We spent the day walking all around Central Campus but found nothing that matched the symbol on or in the buildings. It was the worst feeling, knowing that we'd finally gotten a lead by speaking to Professor Wittman, but that that lead wasn't enough to get us a true breakthrough. It was the most frustrating feeling in the world.

As evening fell, Kathy texted us, reminding me of something important I'd nearly forgotten about.

Kathy: Hey! You guys still planning to stop by Animagination?

Anna: Omg yes of course!! Will stop by around dinnertime!
Chris: On our way
Jessica: No worries, take your time :)

"Shit, I totally forgot about the convention," Chris groaned. "We should give this a break and go check it out."

I rubbed my forehead. Even though I didn't want to stop thinking about the Order, even I had to admit that we were going around in circles and wasting time like this. "Good idea."

We grabbed sandwiches in the dining hall before heading out to meet Jessica and Kathy across campus, at a building called Mason Hall.

We'd arrived half an hour before the convention was supposed to end, so most of the vendors were starting to take their booths down. I'd only ever attended a small local anime convention before, and the atmosphere felt similar. There wasn't an overwhelming number of booths with anime merch, nor were there that many people left still hanging around the convention.

I spotted Jessica and Kathy at the end of the hall, talking to someone at a booth with anime posters plastered behind it. Kathy was wearing a *My Hero Academia* shirt, and Jessica was dressed like Misty from *Pokémon*, with a yellow short-sleeved shirt and blue jean shorts paired with a *Pokémon* baseball hat. Suddenly, I felt self-conscious that I was wearing a sweater and jeans—regular clothes, and not even particularly cute ones at that.

". . . had a couple thousand students show up throughout the day. Not a bad turnout, overall," Jessica was saying to the vendor. She looked up and grinned when she saw us. "Oh, hey. You guys made it."

"Yeah. Sorry we're late," Chris said.

"Lost track of time," I offered, aware that it was a poor excuse.

If Jessica or Kathy suspected I was lying, they didn't let on. "You came just in time to catch one of the last panels." Kathy plucked a couple of flyers from the top of the stack beside her and handed one to each of us. "I'm going to see the one happening in five—'Contemporary Japan Through Anime and Manga'—if you wanna come. I'm heading over now, actually."

It wasn't like I knew what else to do, so I followed Kathy into an auditorium, with Chris trailing in our wake. There were a few people sitting in the front row. I recognized Robert and Cindy, the TAs for Sources of East Asian Civilizations.

"Wait, aren't those our—" said Chris, and Kathy giggled.

"Let's pretend we didn't see anything," Kathy said.

I nodded fervently, glad that we were all in agreement that we didn't want to have to see our teachers on a Saturday evening, and not at an anime convention of all places. It was always strange to see teachers outside of the classroom.

We took our seats in the middle of the auditorium, and within moments a young woman dressed like Misa from *Death Note* took to the stage, sweeping her blonde hair off her shoulders. She launched into a lecture about the quirky image of contemporary Japan and how it emerged out of the nation's identity crises between strong phases of nationalism, and as a way for Japan to define itself against Westernization. It was a better lecture than I would've expected from the school's anime convention. The only thing that bothered me was that the presenter wasn't Asian, but I'd seen enough of the Asian studies staff to understand that most of the visible roles went to non-Asian people.

Once the panel was over, we rushed to leave before Robert or Cindy spotted us. Outside, convention-goers continued to trickle out into the night, and I caught a distinct whiff of body odor in the air. I could see from the unpleasant expressions on Chris's and Kathy's faces that they'd noticed the same.

"Um, I'm probably gonna dip now," I said. "Lots of reading to get through this weekend." It was the truth, even though the reading I meant to do was mostly related to the Order of Alpha.

"Yeah, I'm gonna head out too," said Chris.

We said goodbye to Jessica and Kathy, and then left the building. As Chris and I headed toward West Tower, all my real-world problems came rushing back. I forced myself to think, focusing on tying together everything I knew so far.

There was this stranger, Jane, who may or may not be connected to the hate crimes at Sunny's Bakery and West Tower. But if that was the case, then that meant Jane was also involved with the Order of Alpha. Maybe even involved with the unsolved mystery of Melissa Hong's murder.

Maybe all of these pieces were related. Maybe they weren't related at all. I didn't know which thought was scarier.

I let my mind explore the possibility of Laura's involvement in the doll incident. I definitely wanted to think it was her. More than anyone else in the dorm, that was for sure. But there was no evidence. Nothing to trace the crimes back to her, besides the sense of discomfort I got from her. It wasn't like "bad vibes" was a valid reason for suspecting anyone, though.

"Still thinking about Laura?" Chris asked. "And the Order?"

I jolted. It was like he'd read my mind. "Am I that obvious?"

"A bit, yeah. Your expression says you'd like to punch someone in the throat. That's how you usually look when you're talking about Laura," he informed me.

Oops. I opened my mouth to reply but was interrupted by the buzzing sound of two phone notifications. It took me a moment to realize it was mine. I pulled it out of my pocket and checked my texts, where I'd received two new messages.

Kathy: H
Kathy: HELP

Chapter Twenty

I STOPPED IN MY TRACKS.

"What's wrong?" asked Chris.

"I—I don't know, but it—it's Kathy." I showed him my phone. My fingers were shaking.

"Kathy? We were just with her." Chris stared at the screen, eyes growing wider as he registered the words. Then he raised a horrified gaze toward me. We stared at each other for one confused second that lasted an eternity. "Text her back, and let's retrace our steps."

Without waiting for my response, Chris rushed off back the way we'd come. He took long, loping strides that forced me into a light jog just to keep up. I couldn't type a reply to Kathy fast enough, my hands were shaking so badly.

Anna: What's wrong?
Anna: R u hurt?
Anna: Kathy? Where r u?? At Mason Hall still?

There was no response. When I finally caught up to Chris, I looked into his tight expression. The horrible sinking feeling in my stomach intensified. "Kathy can't be far from here," I said breathlessly.

Chris muttered, "God, we were just with her. I should've insisted that we walk her—"

"If you can talk, save your breath for running there faster!"

We took a shortcut through an open field students called The Hill, the grass rustling beneath our own feet. A few stragglers returning from a long evening at the library were streaming into Mason Hall, but there was no sign of Kathy. I strained my eyes against the dark to catch a glimpse of the pink sweater and white backpack she'd been wearing earlier.

"Should we split up and look for her?" I suggested.

Chris replied, with a sharp intake of breath, "That won't be necessary."

I looked over to see that he was pointing to a streetlamp illuminating the bottom of a hill, a sidewalk across from ours.

As if in slow motion, I watched the scene unfold before me. Two figures locked in a struggle, with one person attempting to drag the other. When that failed, they pushed them instead. There was a cry, and then a pink-and-white blur tumbled down the hill, crashing into the streetlamp with a sickening thud. The other figure turned and sprinted away into the woods.

"What the hell are you doing?" Chris bellowed, giving chase.

I rushed over to the fallen figure on the sidewalk.

Kathy was sprawled on the concrete, groaning. I couldn't see any injuries on her aside from a streak of blood running down the right side of her head, but she was covered in grass and bits of debris. "Kathy? Can you hear me?"

She nodded slowly, her eyes closed.

"Chris, can you call campus security?" I turned around to see that Chris was already on the phone. He nodded at me.

"Who pushed you down the hill?" I asked Kathy. "Did you see?"

Wincing, Kathy shook her head. I had a million other questions I wanted to ask, but now wasn't the time. Campus security was rushing over, and besides, it was clear that Kathy was in no shape to answer any questions.

I grabbed Kathy's hand and squeezed it. "You'll be fine. Help is on the way."

"M . . . ," she murmured, and then grabbed my shirt. "Man. It was a man."

"You're sure?"

A nod. Well, that didn't give me that much to go on, but it was something, at least. As two members of campus security rushed over, I stood up and watched as they helped Kathy to her feet.

There was no proof, and yet my gut was certain that the same person behind the other attacks was behind this one, too.

After he'd gone into the woods after the culprit, Chris had come back out alone, unsuccessful. According to him, the figure had vanished into the dark—almost like a ghost. We'd been able to stay with Kathy just long enough to tell campus police what we'd seen and confirm that Kathy was fine, if shaken, with only minor injuries. Now Chris and I were back at West Tower in my room, having been shooed away from the scene by campus police.

"But when you think about it," I said, "so far every person who's been a victim is Asian." At first glance, what happened to Kathy seemed unconnected to the figure of "Jane" and the strange threats I'd been receiving. It seemed unconnected to the vandalization of Sunny's Bakery.

Chris's jaw clenched, and his eyes turned cold and hard. "Do you think there's one person behind this—attacking Kathy, going after you, even messing with Sunny's Bakery—and they're out to get Asians?"

My mind flashed back to the memory of being in Professor Wittman's office, the Asian studies professor telling me his theory that someone was using the Order of Alpha as a scapegoat for their crimes.

Before either of us could say anything, the door flung open. Laura rushed in. She looked entirely unlike her usually well-kept self. Her hair was a tangled mess, and her mascara had smeared and run down her face in tear tracks. She didn't even acknowledge Chris—or me, for that matter—before flinging herself onto her bed and dissolving into sobs.

An uncomfortable expression rose to Chris's face at the

sight of Laura crying, and he made for the door. I might have laughed if it didn't feel so inappropriate for the moment.

"Um, I'll, uh—I'll text you," stammered Chris, and then he fled the room. I couldn't blame him. I didn't want to be here right now, either.

I briefly considered saying something comforting to Laura but talked myself out of that idea within moments. She didn't even like talking to me when she was in a good mood. She'd probably just cry harder if I tried to ask her what was wrong.

I put in my headphones and tried my best to drown out Laura's crying with classical music. I had a paper dissecting *Pillow Book of Sei Shonagon* due in two days, and I hadn't even started on it yet thanks to everything that had been going on. Though the text itself, a collection of journals by a gentlewoman named Sei Shonagon in the 990s and 1000s, fascinated me, I kept getting distracted by theories about the potential connection between Sunny's Bakery being vandalized, Kathy getting attacked, Melissa Hong's unsolved murder—not to mention Jane's threats.

Or maybe I was overthinking. Maybe these were separate crimes, separate issues. Either way, I still had to keep my guard up. Who knew what Jane might do next?

Out of the corner of my eye, I spotted the glow of a notification on my phone screen, where I'd tossed it on my bed. Thinking it was a text from Chris, I reached for it.

It was an email, not a text. I opened the message. It was from what appeared to be a spam email account. All it said was:

NO ONE DESERVES YOUR FRIENDSHIP BUT ME.

KATHY WENT FIRST.

CHRIS WILL BE NEXT, IF YOU DON'T STAY AWAY FROM
HIM.

Chapter Twenty-One

IT WAS THURSDAY NIGHT. INSTEAD of going out to celebrate the weekend early like most other students, Jessica, Kathy, and I were sitting inside the nearly empty cafe on the second floor of the UgLi. I'd just finished powering through and somehow wrangling out a twenty-page essay for Great Books, and all that was keeping me awake now was coffee and the need to know what exactly had happened to Kathy.

I knew Jane could be watching me. Jane wanted me to stay away from my friends, wanted to isolate me fully—to do what, I didn't even want to think about. But I needed to take this risk, one last time, to hear from Kathy's mouth the details of what had happened to her.

Kathy shuddered and took a small sip of her matcha latte. "After you and Chris left, Jessica and I said goodbye right outside the Center for Chinese Studies."

Jessica nodded fervently, her eyes wide.

"I was walking toward The Hill. Next thing I knew, someone grabbed me from behind. I managed to text you, but then they started dragging me away—I think they meant to kidnap me, and they might have succeeded before you and Chris showed up. I didn't get a good look at who it was before they shoved me, but I'm certain it was a man. I lost my balance and tumbled down the hill." Kathy recounted these details very quickly, as though pulling off a Band-Aid. There was a glazed look in her eyes.

"So you never got a good look at who your attacker was?" Jessica whispered.

Kathy shook her head.

"Shit, Kathy. I'm so, so sorry." There was something different about Kathy. She'd changed. The normally shy, mousy girl had a sharp, hardened glint in her eye. "You're not injured, right?" I asked.

"I mean, it hurt being shoved down a hill, but I would've been in much worse shape if you and Chris and the campus police hadn't shown up when you did."

"I can't believe that happened to you." Jessica shuddered. Though it wasn't cold inside the library, she pulled her overcoat tighter around her, as though protecting herself against an invisible wind.

Kathy said quietly, "You know, once my parents heard what happened—and with Sunny's Bakery, too—they wanted me to leave school and go back home."

"My parents have been saying the same thing," I said. And I had a feeling that if one more horrific incident occurred on campus, Ma and Ba were going to show up in my dorm and force me to go back home with them.

A tense silence settled between us.

"What're the police doing about this?" Jessica demanded. "Don't tell me they're going to just sweep this under the rug. I mean, you could've been seriously hurt."

Kathy shrugged. "They said they were going to investigate, but I don't know if they'll manage to catch anyone."

I resisted the urge to roll my eyes. The police continued to say the same things, but nothing ever changed. We couldn't rely on them for protection. We had to protect ourselves and uncover who was behind this on our own.

"But this campus is so huge. It's so easy to just disappear. How're the police ever gonna pinpoint who's behind this?" asked Jessica.

Again, Kathy shrugged.

"That would require stationing officers on every street at every hour of the day," I pointed out. "Think of all the money and manpower it would take. Our school would rather pour their funding and resources into the football team. And I mean, there are things that are more important than football season, but I doubt the majority of the student body would think so."

I had a million other questions to ask Kathy, but I could tell that asking her was doing more harm than good. Her initial bravado had turned into weary reply after weary reply, and she'd hardly drank any of her matcha latte.

Plus, I was exhausted from the effort keeping up with my schoolwork and trying to stay on alert for the enemies that were coming out of the woodwork seemingly all at once. It was getting late, so we left the cafe.

As we stepped out into the evening air, Kathy let out a sigh

of frustration, kicking at a pebble on the path. She shivered in
the chilly air. "I should've been braver Saturday night. I should've
fought back, maybe held the attacker down, and—"

"You didn't even see them coming, though," I said. "There's
no way you could have won against them."

"But—"

"It's okay." I placed a hand on Kathy's trembling arm.

Kathy's eyes were bright and wet with the threat of tears, but
she nodded and took a deep, shuddering breath, steeling her
resolve. Her shoulders went tense. She raised her chin high.
Her eyes met mine again, and this time they were dry. Narrowed
in determination.

At the Quad, we parted ways, each headed off to our own
dorms. I headed into West Tower and made a beeline for the
dining hall, as it occurred to me that it was past dinnertime.
I hadn't eaten anything since breakfast, and coffee didn't really
count. Suddenly my hunger overwhelmed me.

I grabbed a burrito and a plate of chips, and then filled up a
cup with Pepsi at the drink station. Luckily the dining hall
wasn't too full tonight. I managed to snag an empty booth near
the back. When I pulled my phone out of my pocket to check
my social media, it became impossible to ignore the string of
texts Chris had sent me—that I hadn't answered. So instead I
replied to the messages from my worried parents, reassuring
them that I was safe.

There was no way I could tell my parents the truth—that
someone on campus was targeting me, stalking me, and even
hurting my friends. They'd immediately demand that I come

home. They'd pull me out of school. And as hard as college was, I'd grown to love it here. I couldn't go back to my hometown—especially not because someone seemed hell-bent on driving me out of Brookings.

Ever since I'd gotten that email from Jane, I'd kept a careful distance from Chris, even though I wanted more than anything to have him by my side to help face down this stalker. Every time we'd run into each other in the hall or in class, I'd quickly made up an excuse and practically sprinted in the other direction, ignoring his confused calls behind me. It killed me that I couldn't even tell Chris why I was ignoring him. But this was a problem I had to solve on my own—that I was determined to solve on my own, without risking the lives of my friends and acquaintances. Even if it turned me into the most lonely, isolated person in the world.

This person had made it clear who their true target was: me. I wouldn't risk anyone around me getting caught in the crossfire. I'd take them down, once and for all.

After I finished my burrito, I was still hungry, so I got up to fix myself a yogurt bowl at the self-serve station. I topped it off with granola and chocolate chips. When I sat back down at my booth, I hadn't eaten two spoonfuls of my yogurt before a shadow loomed over me.

"Um, excuse me?"

I looked up at a tall, red-headed girl who I'd seen around the dining hall a few times. "Hi?" I said uncertainly, the word turning up into a question.

"Did you come here with anyone?"

"No, I'm alone," I answered, still not seeing where this was going.

Her eyes widened with unmistakable horror. She glanced down at my Pepsi and raised a hand to cover her lips. "Don't touch that drink. I just saw someone—a man, I think, though I couldn't tell because the person was wearing this really baggy black cloak—come over here and put something into it."

I almost spat out my yogurt. "What?"

"I thought it was weird, so I wanted to tell you," the girl said.

"Are they still around?" Heart hammering, I scanned the dining hall for any suspicious figures, but everyone around me seemed to be too busy chatting or doing homework.

"No, they tailed it out of the hall. Again—it was really weird, and . . ." The girl gasped as though she'd come to a sudden realization. "Oh my God. Do you think they put drugs in your drink?" She stared at my drink as though it had developed fangs.

At those words, the last of my appetite deserted me. My pulse raced as I put together the pieces and reached a conclusion that my gut told me was correct. This wasn't a random incident of some creep wanting to drug just any girl in a dining hall. I knew exactly what was going on.

"Jane," I whispered.

"Jane?" The girl appeared alarmed.

I was right. I knew I was right. Jane had gone too far. This time I realized, with a dreadful, stomach-dropping certainty, that I was fighting against someone who I couldn't beat. If this person was bold enough to mess with me in public, bold enough to go after my friends, then it was only a matter of time before they succeeded. Enough was enough. This stalker couldn't keep getting away with this.

"Thank you," I told the girl. "I'm going to go report this."

"Yeah, I really think you should do that." Her mouth was slightly open as she gazed at me, like I was a train wreck she couldn't keep her eyes away from.

I grabbed the drink, even though just looking at it made me feel ill. I sniffed it. All I could smell was soda, but from what I recalled, drugs didn't usually have a strong taste or smell. If that girl hadn't warned me, I might have drunk this totally unsuspectingly. Now I really wanted to vomit, but I forced myself to keep it together as I quickly left the dining hall.

As I walked through the second floor, I saw that the door to my room had been flung wide open. Laura was back, evidently. When I waltzed into my room, it was to find my roommate in a rare state of being out of sorts. She sat on her bed, hugging her knees to her chest, leaning back against the pillow, a blank expression on her face. Her normally blown-out hair was limp and tangled. Makeupless, Laura looked like she'd put on ten years.

I raised the cup. "Was it you?"

I didn't expect a confession. Laura's eyes found mine, and the hollowness in them startled me. I didn't need to clarify my question. Laura bit her lip, her chin wobbling, and then burst into tears. She nodded.

I didn't let my shock show on my face. Instead I pressed, "You're Jane, aren't you?"

Another nod.

That was the confirmation I'd needed ever since I'd started suspecting my roommate. And yet, somehow, the whole situation seemed bizarre, had played out totally different from the scenario I'd imagined in my mind when I finally caught whoever was masquerading as Jane.

I'd been expecting to have to go through hell to unmask the mastermind behind all of this. I hadn't been expecting this. Hadn't expected Laura to reveal herself so easily. Maybe my roommate was finally experiencing a shred of remorse for what she'd done.

"You're coming with me to talk to the RAs," I said, barely able to contain my fury. Laura had tried to drug me just now, and was almost without a doubt the one who'd cut off a lock of my hair to threaten me. Now she had the audacity to cry, as though she were the victim here? My roommate wouldn't find sympathy from me.

Laura didn't try to fight me. She got up from her bed, tears still streaking down her cheeks, and followed me down the hall. Elise's door was closed, which was rare, but it meant that she was out. So I walked toward Patrick's instead.

Patrick's room was easily recognizable because of all the decorations that had been plastered over his door. Silly pictures with residents, cut-outs of cartoon characters, even a couple of early Christmas stickers. I knocked on the door that had been left slightly ajar, my other hand still holding the cup.

"Come in," came Patrick's voice.

Confusion flashed across the RA's face as I marched in with Laura right behind me, but he smoothed it over quickly.

"Tell Patrick what you did just now, and what you've been doing." My voice stayed remarkably steady considering how rapidly my heart was beating. I didn't look at Laura. I kept my gaze on Patrick, whose expression had frozen. Adrenaline pumped through my body. I'd never been good at standing up for myself—Ma and Ba had always encouraged me to simply hide, to ignore the problems—and I was almost certain Laura's family was powerful enough to retaliate in the future, but in the moment I didn't care. I'd had enough.

Laura let out a choked sob. Then, in a quiet, broken voice, she laid out everything she'd been involved in. I listened as though from a distance, as though Laura were recounting events that were totally unrelated to me. She confessed to posing as Jane in order to get closer to me. Taking my doll. Snipping off my hair. Keeping tabs on me, pushing Kathy down a hill. Her words came out robotically, almost rehearsed.

I should've been relieved that I'd finally caught my roommate and that she'd willingly confessed. I should've been furious that she'd been allowed to get so far. Instead I felt numb, as though the realization that it was over—it was over—hadn't set in yet.

Patrick's expression was full of shock and outrage. After my roommate finished speaking, he opened and closed his mouth, speechless. "Laura, this—this is beyond appalling. This—stalking, threatening—I—it's a serious crime."

A loud, frightened sob escaped Laura's mouth, but I had no sympathy for her, not when she'd been terrorizing me for weeks on end.

"Crying's not going to help you! How could you?" Patrick's voice grew angry and heartbroken. "I would have never believed it of one of my residents."

"I never even did anything to offend you," I said to Laura, still refusing to look at her. "Why the fuck did you have to do all that to me?"

Laura said nothing in response. Not that I'd expected her to. What could she possibly say? There wasn't any room for her left to make any kind of defense for herself.

"I'll report this to the dean immediately," Patrick said, his voice quieting down again, though no less angry-sounding. Every word was shaky, like it was costing him a great effort to form these sentences. "They'll expel you. Expel, Laura. And, by God, that'll be the least of your concerns." Muffled sobs in response. The sound of Patrick's voice—quieter, but no less harsh. "Why? Just answer me one question. Why'd you do this?"

"I . . ." Laura's voice trailed off, and then she buried her face in her hands.

Disgust overwhelmed me. Even after confessing that she'd been harassing and stalking and terrorizing my friends and me, Laura had the gall to cry and play the victim in this situation.

"I'm not even crying," I spat, finally unable to hold back the tide of fury inside me. "What the fuck are you crying for?"

That only made her sob harder. If Patrick weren't here, I probably would've thrown the contaminated drink at her.

"Did Professor Wittman put you up to this?" I demanded. Was Laura one of the students who'd gone to his office hours at some point, asking about the Order? My roommate didn't seem like the type to be interested in Asian studies, but this had to be the explanation.

Through her tears, she gave me a blank look. "Who's Professor Wittman?"

"Anna, please leave," said Patrick abruptly, before I could press my roommate further.

"But I—"

"I'll speak with you after I deal with her." The RA spat out "her" as though it were poison, and Laura visibly flinched.

Swallowing any protest back, I obeyed and left the room, closing the door behind me. Though the doors were pretty much soundproof, I could still catch some words thanks to Patrick's raised voice. It sounded like he was planning to take Laura straight to the dean and contact her parents as well.

After a few minutes, the door flew open. Laura stood there, wild-eyed. She let out a wail and sprinted back down the hall toward our room.

"I'm going to deal with her first." Patrick emerged, too, following Laura down the hall. "I'll be back soon. First thing we'll do when I get back is help you file a restraining order. Okay?"

I nodded, still shell-shocked. "She—She also put something into my drink earlier," I said, remembering the reason why I'd come up to the second floor in the first place. "I don't know what it is, but could you get it checked out?"

I held out the cup to Patrick, who took it gingerly, his eyebrows furrowing. "Jesus. She drugged your drink? You didn't drink any of it, did you?"

"No. A girl saw what happened and told me not to."

Patrick swore. "Are you okay?" he asked me in concern. He set the cup down gingerly on his desk, as though afraid it might bite him.

I didn't think I'd ever felt less okay in my life, but I gave a quick nod. All the noise had attracted attention, and students had poked their heads out of their rooms to check out what was going on—including Chris. They watched and whispered as Patrick headed down the hall toward the elevators.

"What the hell's going on?" Chris asked, eyes wide.

Even though I'd been ignoring Chris and basically acting like an asshole, suddenly, I wanted nothing more than to tell him everything that had happened. With Jane exposed now, that was okay.

"It's a long story," I said.

"Does it have to do with you ignoring my texts?"

"Oh, yeah. Sorry I haven't been replying. I, um—I couldn't talk to you."

Looking confused but thankfully not angry, Chris opened his door wide open. "Wanna come in and talk about it?"

I nodded. It wasn't like I could go back to my own room right now, not with Laura in there. I needed a moment to process what had just happened. A huge burden had just been lifted off my shoulders, but instead of leaving, part of it had settled in my gut. Laura wasn't the nicest person, and we had next to nothing in common, but I couldn't believe that she'd actually managed to commit those crimes and that she'd confessed. I'd expected her to deny my accusations until there was solid, undeniable proof against her.

After stepping into Chris's room, I realized I'd never been here before. I hadn't ever imagined his room, but even if I had, I knew my imagination would have been very different from the reality of his mancave. The floor was spotless. Everything was neat and tidy. Books stacked on the shelf above his desk. Textbooks arranged in one tall pile on his desk. There was even a shoe rack next to the bunk beds, where all the shoes had been stacked neatly in rows.

His roommate, Devon, surprisingly kept his side of the room tidy, too. The only thing that differentiated the two boys' sides of the room was the posters they'd chosen to decorate their walls with. Devon had a bunch of superheroes posted on his wall—the Hulk, Superman, Catwoman. Chris had a poster of *My Hero Academia* hanging over his bed.

"I didn't know you watched anime," I said.

"Huh? Oh, yeah. Well, I used to watch a lot of it, but school's kept me pretty busy."

I filed away that information for later. Right now wasn't the time.

"So do you want to explain what's been going on with you, or what?"

After taking a deep breath, I launched into an explanation of everything that had happened since we'd last spoken—from Jane's email telling me to stay away from Chris and anyone I cared about, to Laura's confession just now.

To his credit, Chris took the explanation with stride, not batting an eye, even though I was sure the story had to sound ludicrous from an outside standpoint. "Well, that does explain why you've been running away from me like you've just seen a ghost," he said when I'd finished. "The fact that someone was threatening your friends, too? And it turned out to be your own roommate?"

"Yeah . . . it's like something out of a thriller movie." I tried to smile but must have failed magnificently, because his expression turned more concerned.

Chris paced the length of his room while I sat down on his desk chair, numb. "So that's it, then. Laura's the one who's been threatening you. And pushed Kathy down a hill."

"I . . . I suppose." That explanation didn't quite add up, though. Now that I was thinking more clearly, I realized there were holes in Laura's explanation. Even though Jane was a fake person, the person behind the screen had felt very real. And very different from Laura. I mean, Jane and I had bonded over anime, and there was no way Laura was secretly an anime geek. "I don't see why she would confess if she wasn't involved with all this, but based on what I know about Laura, some of this just . . . doesn't make sense."

Chris shook his head, bewildered. "Maybe not, but what I do know is that Laura's always given me weird vibes."

"Tell me about it," I grumbled.

"Anyway, it looks like our work was finished for us. So . . . that's the end of that. Right?"

I shrugged. Would the crimes stop now? Would we get to feel comfortable in our own skin, comfortable being Asian in our own country, a country that had always viewed us as a foreign threat? "Right," I said, but I'd never felt less right about anything in my life.

⊷————⊷

That evening, Laura left the dorm. Her parents had come all the way to Brookings to pull her out of school for the rest of the semester. Nobody would give a clear reason why, but I knew what was going on—that Laura's parents, powerful as they were, had probably paid a good deal to keep matters hushed up as they dealt with their daughter's actions in private.

Or maybe Laura's parents wouldn't even deal with her. Maybe they just wanted to keep Laura at home and wait while the few of us who knew what Laura had done moved on from it all.

Of course I'd known that Laura was exactly the kind of person who could get away scot-free from anything in this country, but that didn't make the reality of seeing it unfold in real time sting any less. The unfairness of it made me want to scream.

I didn't even see Laura go back to our room. I'd spent the afternoon with Patrick at the local courthouse, where we filed a restraining order against Laura. When I got back, I couldn't stomach the thought of being in my room, where I'd shared a space with her, so I spent the evening in the study lounge.

As Laura walked by with her parents and all her belongings, I heard quiet voices, the soft scoldings of parents who were angry but didn't want to alert the entire dorm.

I watched Laura leave, though she didn't notice me peeking around the corner. She was with her parents. Her mother was an impossibly tall, beautiful blonde who could have been a model. Her father, the former senator Jason Dale, was shorter and had the softened physique of an office man who once was athletic but had grown too accustomed to sedentary life. He looked precisely like the man he was—a politician whose career had gone to seed.

The family glided through the halls in silence, almost gracefully, pushing a giant blue bin down the hall. At the end of it, they were met by two campus police officers who stood ramrod straight. Their expressions were inscrutable.

Laura looked the worse for wear. She wore sweats, her hair pulled up in a messy bun. This girl had fallen far from the confident girl I'd met in the first week of school. She'd toppled from her heavenly throne, right down to the dirt of the earth. Laura entered the elevator, her own worn features unreadable. The fresh lines creasing her forehead made it seem like she'd aged a decade in the month she'd been here.

I might've felt bad for her if I didn't hate her so much for everything that she'd done.

The last thing I saw was Laura's long dirty blonde hair swishing through the closing doors. And then she was gone.

Chapter Twenty-Two

WHEN I WENT DOWN TO breakfast in the dining hall the next morning, the whole place was buzzing with the news of Laura's sudden and unexplained departure. Patrick had sent me an email, all formal and everything, asking me not to name Laura as the culprit behind the recent string of crimes on campus— not unless there was official proof that could confirm her as the perpetrator, beyond a shadow of a doubt.

Still, it seemed word must've slipped out somehow, or maybe someone's wild speculations coincidentally had a grain of truth to them. Laura's name was being passed around the dining hall, and not in a good way.

"Knew there was something off about that girl," a girl was saying heatedly to her friends as I passed by their table. "Her father's a snake. And the apple doesn't fall far from the tree."

But even Laura's group of sophomore friends no longer stood by her.

"She's probably done something horrible and fled campus while she still can."

"I heard she's descended from a family of hardcore Ku Klux Klan members."

I didn't bother getting invested in the wild theories everyone was throwing out left and right. What really bothered me was the fact that Chris hadn't returned to the dorm the night before. I'd sent him a few texts, but he hadn't even responded.

"He's been spending all his free time studying for his huge orgo exam, right?" Kathy asked, digging into her eggs with a thoughtful look on her face. After learning that Laura had been caught as the culprit, some of the color had been restored to Kathy's cheeks, and her appetite had returned enough to eat hearty meals again.

"Right, but he could at least take twenty seconds to respond to me," I grumbled.

"If it makes you feel better, Chris hasn't messaged me back, either." Kathy shot me a sly look. "Though I'm not the one waiting night and day for my beloved to text me."

"Beloved? Who?" I spluttered, my cheeks heating up. That only succeeded in getting another cackle from Kathy.

"Seriously, though," Kathy said, her expression turning grim again, "I'm still reeling over what happened. Getting pushed down a hill, and then finding out this stuff about Laura . . ." She grimaced.

"Tell me about it. Laura was my roommate."

Kathy winced in sympathy. "At least you'll get the whole room to yourself now."

"True." Now that Laura had moved out, I could breathe somewhat more freely. "I wonder if they'll give me a new roommate."

"Whoever it is, they couldn't possibly be worse than Laura," Kathy said.

"You can say that again."

After breakfast, we found an area in the study lounge to finish up our homework for Sources of East Asian Civilizations. My mind kept drifting back to Laura, though. Something wasn't adding up. The way she'd stared at me in confusion when I'd brought up Professor Wittman's name didn't seem at all right. Unless there was someone else who wasn't connected with the professor, who'd helped Laura commit crimes under the name of the Order. But then, who?

My head throbbed. If this new theory was correct, it would mean that Professor Wittman had nothing to do with any of this, and that information about the Order was coming from a different source entirely. The longer I continued investigating this case, the less I knew.

Hours passed as I immersed myself in my class notes. I was startled out of my concentration when my phone buzzed with a text notification.

My initial thought was that it was Ma discovering a new set of stickers and sending them all to me in a wild string of spam. She'd been doing that a lot lately. Then I took a closer look and saw that the incoming message had been sent from Chris.

Chris: Laura wasn't the mastermind

Anna: Yeah I've been thinking this too tbh, but how do you know?

Chris: fjashfaoi233`8**7
Anna: ??????

"Kathy, look at this." I tilted my phone screen at her, and her eyes steadily widened as she took in the text.

"Not the mastermind?" Kathy croaked. "Why would Chris say that and then follow up with a line of gibberish?"

My mind raced as I waited for another reply, but nothing came. As the minutes stretched, my stomach sank. Something was very wrong. And I couldn't sit here and study when my thoughts were miles away.

"I'll be right back," I told Kathy, not waiting to hear her response. I dashed out of the quiet study room and into the lobby, where I could raise my voice without disturbing anyone else. I dialed Chris's number once, twice, three times. Each time, the phone went to voicemail. Finally, on the fourth call, I heard a click on the other end of the line.

Gripping the phone so hard that I thought it might crack under my hand, I demanded, "Chris? Hello? What's going on?"

Heavy breathing. Muffled noises in the background. Then a male voice, calm and icy cold. Definitely not Chris's. This voice was lower and more guttural, almost too much so, and I realized they were using a voice distorter. It sent shivers up my spine.

"Chris can't speak with you right now."

"Who is this?"

"I told you you can't just unfriend me, Anna. I warned you. You didn't listen."

My insides turned icy as my own words played back in my

mind. *It's likely that Laura had at least one accomplice.* And Chris's text just now. *Laura wasn't the mastermind.* "You . . ."

"Don't tell me you've already forgotten me. I left you those notes."

My heart hammered. "You—you're Jane?"

"So you didn't forget me."

"Laura has been caught. You—it's only a matter of time before the police get you, too." I tried to force authority in my voice, to sound much more confident than I felt.

"Laura's played her part well, and she won't give up my name. Because even though I was telling her what to do all this time, I never told her my real name."

As the man spoke, my mind raced. The person speaking on the other end was a man. The person who'd attacked Kathy was a man.

And Jane was a man. Jane was the man who'd been messing with my friends, messing with me.

Now the pieces were clicking into place at long last, forming the true story in my head. Laura wasn't the true mastermind after all, as I'd suspected even as she was leaving the dorm. No— if I was correct, this ran much further, deeper than that, as far back as seven years ago. Laura had been obeying this person's orders. And now the true criminal had Chris in his clutches.

"Put Chris on the line," I demanded. "Or I swear I'll find you and kick your sorry—"

"Well, that's not very nice of you to say, Anna. I thought Asian women were submissive. My exes were all like that. You must be the exception to the rule, eh?" The man's voice was no longer level, but rather shook with excitement.

I wanted to vomit. "You pervert," I spat. "Tell me where you are, or—"

"But of course. Your friend here is company . . . but I'd rather have yours. 104 Madison Street. Come alone within half an hour, and don't call the cops. Or this guy dies."

Click.

I stared at the blank screen on my phone. Jane—whoever this person was—had hung up. Nausea seized my insides and made my stomach buck, and bile snaked its way from the pits of my stomach into my throat so quickly that I had to lean against the nearest metal pole to avoid kneeling over in the wave that had washed over me.

Chris was trapped with this psycho who, judging from our phone conversation, thought he was starring as a villain in a comic book. But this was real. I knew that someone this sick could do dangerous and evil things.

I should call the campus police. Even though he had warned me not to, I didn't see any other option. I couldn't rescue Chris on my own.

Jane had told me not to call the cops, but . . . that didn't mean I couldn't call someone else for help. I wasn't about to try to rescue Chris without any kind of backup.

I bolted back up the staircase, nearly knocking several students down the stairs. The only thing that mattered was getting to Chris in time. I didn't stop running past study rooms until I found myself facing a stunned-looking Kathy. I grabbed my backpack and slung it over my shoulder in one fluid motion. "I gotta go somewhere."

"Um . . . is something wrong? You're acting funny." Kathy's eyebrows furrowed as she slowly packed up her things, and I imagined what I looked like to her—frazzled, frightened, wild-eyed.

"It's Chris. There's an emergency." I gave Kathy the rundown. Her eyes were as wide as golf balls once I'd finished relaying the events, and she nearly dropped a huge textbook onto her feet.

"That's just . . . wild," Kathy said with a little whimper. "And terrifying. You think the police actually got the wrong person, and this man is the culprit?"

"I don't know what to think. I just know that I need to get to Chris."

Kathy's eyes widened with fear. "I'm coming, too."

"No. I need you to stay here."

"But, Anna, it's dangerous—"

"Exactly. That's why you have to stay here. If I don't come back in fifteen minutes or so, then you come. 104 Madison Street. Got it? I'll share my location with you, too." I took my iPhone out of my pocket, opened my Find Me app, selected Share My Location, and entered Kathy's phone number.

Kathy stared down at her phone screen, and then back up at me. She bit her lip, looking like she wanted to protest, but then swallowed back her words and nodded. "Be careful."

"I will." I turned around and set down the path before I could lose my nerve.

One hundred four Madison Street wasn't too far from West Tower. It was early evening now, so there was still a good amount of light outside, but it wouldn't last for long. I needed to get this done quickly. I hurried past rows of cozy-looking college apartments and houses. Then I emerged onto frat row, with its huge Greek letters that loomed ever-ominous. I passed students and older couples out on runs or walking their dogs. It was amazing to me that none of them were aware of what was happening right in their quaint corner of campus.

I slowed my pace as I approached the address. I'd passed by this place before, but I'd never paid much attention to it before now. It was a small house painted light blue, with several wooden rocking chairs on the front porch. The house was silent. No sign of activity. No sign of students, or anyone else.

Now all that was left to do was enter.

"Let's go," I said quietly to myself. Then I ran up the steps to rescue Chris.

Chapter Twenty-Three

THERE WAS NO DOORBELL. ONLY a door knocker, which was painted red and shaped like a dragon. I'd only seen stuff like that in those old-timey Chinese dramas Ma loved to binge-watch. This boy took his interest in Chinese culture to the next level.

I knocked. Once, twice, three times. A minute passed. Three. No response. Then I rattled the doorknob, but I might as well have been trying to break into a vault for all the good it did.

What the hell was this creep up to? He'd told me to come here, and now he was nowhere to be found.

I stepped back from the door, eyes scanning the front of the house. Maybe he was in the basement. Like every horror movie ever. I couldn't suppress the shivers that ran through my body.

I double-checked the address. One hundred four Madison. This was definitely the right place. Well, if I couldn't get through the front door, maybe there was some other way in. There was a small window to the left, and I peered inside.

No sign of life in the neat and tidy room behind it. I pressed my ear against the window and heard nothing. The inside was quiet. Too quiet. I never would've guessed that a male graduate student lived here.

The brown coffee table in the living room was empty except for a pile of magazines stacked in the middle. Opposite the window, textbooks had been arranged into neat rows along the bookshelf. There were scrolls of calligraphy on the wall, and a katana had been framed and mounted to the wall, too.

I hopped over the railing of the front porch, landing on the grass. I skirted around the side of the house, heading around to the back. Bushes lined the walls, blocking off almost all possible routes leading to the inside. There was a back door, but one jiggle of the doorknob told me that was locked, too.

I turned to walk along the other side of the house, considering breaking and entering through that front window, when I heard a rustling noise behind me. I turned back just in time to see the shadow of a figure emerging from behind the house, raising something in its hand.

I opened my mouth to scream. Big hands clamped over my mouth, pressing a chemically, sweet-smelling cloth against my nose. For a few seconds, I summoned my sapping energy to struggle, causing my attacker to grunt in pain when I stomped on their feet. Then all went black.

◦⊩——⊩◦

"Anna. *Anna.*"

The voice came to me from far off. I blinked my eyelids, which felt heavier than usual. It took me another moment to realize I was lying on a cold, musty floor. I tried to move my limbs but found my arms were bound behind my back with thick rope. Gritting my teeth against the pain of rope digging into my wrists, I reached inside my jeans' waistband and was glad that my captor had missed the pocketknife stashed in the seam. My phone was gone, but I had a means of self-defense.

My heart was hammering. In the still dark, I could make out the shapes of a desk and storage bins stacked against the wall. It seemed like I was in a basement. But where, I had no clue. There was a window high on the wall above the storage bins, but no light came from it—it must have been hours later, and night had already fallen.

A figure lay on the floor a few feet away from me, his eyes meeting mine. It took me a moment to register who it was. To remember that I'd been trying to rescue him earlier. "Chris? Wh-Where are we?"

"I—I think it's the abandoned Sigma Chi house. We're in the basement."

So I was no longer at 104 Madison Street, then, and the address I'd given Kathy was useless.

Damn. My last hope was that wherever my phone was, that it hadn't died, and Kathy could still check my live location and track me to this place.

I'd seen enough horror movies to know that nothing good ever happened in basements. Especially not in the basements of abandoned frat houses. Straining against the rope, I pulled myself up to sit and flipped open the pocketknife, doing my best to ignore the pain of the rope burns on my skin.

"Chris—move closer to me," I whispered. "I can cut us out of these ropes."

Chris shifted his body toward me. I worked at the ropes that bound my own hands, mentally cursing at how long it was taking, and Chris sat and leaned his back against mine.

Footsteps thudded down a set of stairs. Then a large figure emerged at the bottom of the staircase.

I stopped cutting at the rope with my knife and held still.

A smell hit me first—the overpowering scent of cologne, but it couldn't quite mask the body odor. The person walked closer until they were standing just beyond one of the pillars in the basement. The little light that slanted in from the tiny window high above illuminated watery eyes and a dreamy expression on his face, a face marred by a huge, red welt on his right cheek from what appeared to be a fingernail scratch.

And that face. I knew that face. I'd seen it three times a week ever since the start of classes. I never expected to see him here now.

"Robert?"

The TA's mouth curled upward into a grim smile, illuminated eerily by the beam of light.

"Dude," said Chris. "What the fuck?"

"You were the one behind everything? You're Jane?" My mind raced a mile a minute as I tried to piece together everything I knew about Robert, figure out how he could have possibly been the one behind all that had happened.

Aside from him being our TA for Sources of East Asian Civilizations and his love of Asian literature and movies, Robert hadn't stood out in my mind—at all. I couldn't even remember being one-on-one with him before. My impression of him was that he was awkward and quiet.

But the longer I thought about it, the more it made sense. Professor Wittman and Robert were close. No doubt if Robert had asked about the Order, the professor would've answered without a second thought, trusting that his TA would never do anything dangerous with that information—like using the Order's symbol as a scapegoat to commit crimes.

"You understand what you're doing, right?" I said. "You know this is abduction? It's illegal?"

Robert gave me a condescending, pitying look, as though I were the one who'd let him down. "This didn't need to happen. I expected you to be obedient, Anna."

"Wh-What do you want with us?" I blurted out. I was still working at the ropes behind my back, trying to make as little movement as possible.

Robert spread his arms out as if to say, *I'm unarmed. So harmless.* "I thought you'd be happier that you finally get to meet Jane in person. You were so eager to meet on Friend Me."

"That was before I knew you were catfishing me," I snapped.

"Let us go," said Chris. "Now." He sounded like he was forcing as much authority into his voice as possible, but his voice still trembled. "You're a TA. You can't do this. You'll get kicked out of your grad program."

Robert's smile widened. Sharpened. Eyes glinting with a hint of madness inside them. "I'm afraid I've come a bit too far already to turn back now."

My mind whirred, trying to put all the pieces together, trying to recall everything I knew about this person. Robert was a new TA. This was his first year teaching here after taking a few years off to travel, but he'd done his undergrad here.

"Was it you? Were you the one who trashed Sunny's Bakery?" Chris demanded.

Robert's eyes flickered over to me. "Anna said she wanted to be rid of that bakery." The lack of emotion in his voice was astonishing. He sounded like a robot who'd obeyed orders.

My face heated as I realized Robert's implication—that *I'd* directed him to sabotage Sunny's Bakery. Maybe, in his messed-up brain, he actually believed that. Actually believed we'd had a relationship that ran deeper than online exchanges.

I could sense Chris stiffen behind me. "N-No, I didn't say that," I rushed to clarify. "I only said that I wished we could get some business back!"

"And I did what you wanted," Robert said.

"I didn't want that, you racist creep."

Robert flinched at the last two words, as though they'd wounded him. "I'm not like those horrible racists out there. I *love* Asians. You know that."

"You don't actually *like* Asians," I spat. "You fetishize us. There's a fucking difference."

"I've been protecting you, Anna. Because you're special."

"What about those incidents in West Tower?" I demanded. "Were you the one who told Laura to cut off part of my hair and steal my doll? And put something into my drink?"

"Laura was happy to obey me," said Robert. "Given how her

father's gambling problem has sunk almost her entire family fortune, and how I gave her more than enough money for her to keep living a lavish lifestyle. She didn't even press me for my real identity." He sneered. "I predicted, too, that she'd be caught and would fold under the first sign of questioning. That girl is weak, just like her father. I'm sure the police will find out that someone was giving her commands, but I've cut off all ties to myself. I'm not stupid."

Of course that was what it all came down to. The true reason behind Laura's involvement in all of this. Power. Influence. It didn't matter if it was a secret society or an open one, like the fraternities and sororities. These elite, exclusive circles only let in people who looked and acted the same as them, were on the same financial level.

"But, no, Laura didn't physically do anything besides take your doll," said Robert.

I'd finally dared to use my knife again to finish sawing at my ropes. They came free, but there was still the matter of freeing Chris. Shifting my hands as much as I dared, hoping the shadows would hide my movement, I reached out for Chris's hands and pressed the pocketknife into his palm. He grasped it immediately.

Keep Robert talking, keep Robert talking, I thought wildly. There was more to the story, so much more. Seven years ago, Melissa Hong had been murdered. Around the same time, Robert had been an undergrad, and Professor Wittman was still teaching.

"Laura isn't your only accomplice, though, is she?" I asked, my words tumbling out in a rush of realization. I was rambling.

Thinking through the whole situation aloud from Robert's perspective. "You've got a wide reach. You've had help from at least another person, if not more, over the years. Melissa Hong," I blurted out. "Does that name ring a bell?"

Robert's expression twisted, not in guilt, but in surprise. And though I had no proof—yet—I knew I had him.

"You killed Melissa," I accused. "Or you had someone do it, in the name of the Order."

Robert neither confirmed nor denied this, but I didn't need his input to know that what I was saying was true. All my snooping around had led me to this moment, I was sure of it. The moment of truth. I could get justice and closure for Melissa Hong, for everyone these sickos had attacked, as long as I made it out of here alive. But that was a tall order.

Robert took a threatening step forward, and I cowered on instinct. My heart leapt in my throat. Robert crouched down and spat on the floor. Then without warning, he brought his fist back and punched Chris in the nose.

I screamed. Chris fell sideways. There was a horrific *crack* as his head hit the concrete wall, and then he fell over limply. He was out cold.

"What the fuck did you do that for?" I shouted.

"Damn. His head is like a rock," Robert muttered under his breath. Then he turned his cold, beady eyes toward me, and a tremor of fear ran through me as I registered the wild, animalistic glint in them. "I had to do it. I had to protect you from him."

"Protect me from Chris?" The whole situation was so absurd that it would have been funny if it weren't horrifying. And the thought occurred to me—not for the first time, but certainly more strongly than before—that Robert's version of reality had been warped. That he wasn't sane.

"Now we can be together," Robert said. "Just like Melissa and I were supposed to be together, seven years ago."

"You're out of your goddamn mind."

"It's just like in *The Wolverine*," Robert said, and I didn't know who he was trying to explain this to, me or himself. "Logan saves Mariko from those perverted Japanese men, Nobu and Shingen. I'm saving you, Anna. And then we'll finally be able to be together. Or—have you seen *The World of Suzie Wong*? Another classic, one of my favorite films of all time."

There was no reasoning with him. Though my insides were heaving with disgust, I did register one important fact—that Robert was deluded by some twisted, gross infatuation with me that he'd made up all inside his head. He'd murdered. He'd attacked. He hadn't yet been caught, and he seemed bent on doing *something* to me.

My heart threatened to burst out of my chest. I'd never felt so alive than in this moment, when I was sure I'd never been closer to death.

Then the basement rang with the sound of a door opening, followed by someone coming down the stairs, and none too quietly.

"Robert? I'm here. Got held up by bus traffic," came a familiar voice, and for a moment, I forgot to breathe.

Another figure I knew. Another figure I never would've expected to see here. Illuminated by the dim lighting in the basement was Jessica. She stared down at Chris's unconscious form, and then turned toward me, a disdainful look on her face.

"You were part of this, too?" I asked incredulously.

Neither of them responded, though the answer was obvious. Of course Robert couldn't have done everything on his own. He couldn't get close to me, not as close as he needed to, without the help of more than one accomplice.

I was sickened. Sickened that I'd considered Jessica a friend, when all along she'd had a nasty ulterior motive for getting close to me. Robert was a gross older man, but Jessica was around my age and had seemed genuinely interested in friendship. That was the greatest betrayal of all, the pill that was hardest to swallow. I was as winded as though a giant had smashed their fist into my gut. The air had been stolen out of my lungs.

"You already took care of that one, huh?" Jessica nodded toward Chris.

"Yeah, we'll probably have to get rid of him." Robert spoke about Chris not as though he were a fellow human being, but rather as though he were an insect that he intended to squash with his feet.

Anger flared inside me. "You're not doing anything to Chris," I said as assertively as I could, though my voice quaked with fear. "For a pair of Asian studies nerds who obsess over East Asian cultures, you two sure don't seem to care about actual Asian people."

I could tell my words had struck them on some level, because Jessica winced, and Robert clenched his jaw.

"I'm not obsessed," snapped Jessica. "It's called appreciating different cultures."

My heart hammered in my chest. Provoking these two wasn't the smartest tactic, but in the moment all I could think to do was to keep them talking and buy time to get Chris and myself out of here. "So is the Asian studies department in on this?" The question was a leap, but also not an entirely unreasonable conclusion given what I'd witnessed so far.

"The Asian studies department has nothing to do with this," Robert said coldly. "Don't blame anyone there."

"Then what's the connection with you two?" I looked between Robert and Jessica with narrowed eyes, as though that would somehow reveal their intertwined intentions. As far as I knew, they were friendlier than the average TA and student, but that wasn't saying much considering how the average student hardly spoke to their TAs.

My senses were working in overdrive, hyperfixated on every movement in the room. My eyes tracked the way that Jessica's right hand flitted up toward her left arm, right below her bicep, where there was a fresh tattoo of a familiar symbol—a wolf's head, with its jaws open wide. That was the last bit of proof I needed to confirm my suspicions.

"The Order of Alpha," I breathed. "It does still exist. You're in it. You're both in it."

Robert's expression revealed nothing, but his hand twitched, and I was sure my hunch was spot on. "The Order doesn't officially exist any longer," he said slowly. "But that doesn't mean the old members' descendants aren't still well-connected."

"That's how you've been operating." My voice shook. "You've been able to get around and get away with everything thanks to the resources and protection that your families offer, or something. But if the university got wind of this—oh, you'd be in big trouble, wouldn't you? Trouble that even you can't snake your way out of. The university disbanded the Order decades ago. I'm sure the dean wouldn't be happy to know what you've been up to."

Robert didn't deny anything, nor did Jessica. For a long moment, the only sounds in the basement were that of our breathing.

"Don't threaten us, you stupid little bitch," snapped Jessica. "You don't understand anything."

"You're right. I don't understand why you're going around terrorizing people on campus," I retorted.

"I need to do this if—if I want a shot at my dream job. Robert promised me. It's nothing personal."

For the first time, fear and desperation flitted across Jessica's face. My stomach twisted. I had no sympathy for Jessica, but at the same time I could see how Robert had manipulated her into doing whatever he wanted. Not that it excused what she was doing.

"The Order doesn't exist in any official capacity," said Robert. "And you have no proof of our connection to it. It's your word against ours, and—well, do you really think the police would believe you over us?"

I gritted my teeth, but he was right. Robert and Jessica could pretend to be very innocent and charming when they wanted to.

There was the matter of Professor Wittman, too, who was highly respected as a tenured professor and no doubt would back them up if it came down to it. He hadn't even wanted to admit to Chris and me that he might've messed up, might've told the wrong student about the Order of Alpha. There was no way he'd admit it to law enforcement, not if it meant there might be real consequences.

"That's enough chatting," Robert said abruptly. He moved toward us slowly, as if stalking prey that might flee with any sudden movement. He slipped a hand into his back pocket a little too casually.

"Are you planning to keep me down here?" I demanded. "What's your plan?"

"I'll take good care of you here." Robert's smile sent my skin crawling.

I didn't know what that meant, but I could guess. Though the situation looked dire, I did still have one advantage—that Robert and Jessica didn't know I'd already managed to free myself from my ropes. Mentally I readied myself to jump out at Robert or Jessica as soon as they made a move. It was two on one, so the odds were stacked against me, but I had to try. I had to make a break for the stairs and call someone, anyone, for help to rescue Chris.

My breath hitched. In my muddled state of panic, I'd only thought to tell Kathy that I'd come out here. I should've told Patrick. Or Elise. Even if they went to the wrong address first, maybe together they would've been able to piece everything together and come to the abandoned Sigma Chi house.

Jessica stayed still, and I had the feeling that Robert had briefed her ahead of time to let him have this moment. Live out this fantasy with him as the savior and a pitiful Asian girl as his prize. Though it was much too late, I now realized why Robert's favorite movie was *The Wolverine*. He saw himself as the white hero, coming to save the poor, helpless Asian girl.

Robert's lecherous smile remained firmly in place as he reached into his back pocket and pulled something out. Held it up so that it glinted under the dim light. A sharp cutting knife. He examined it with wonder in his eyes, and then turned toward us, still smiling.

"What are you doing?" I demanded, proud that my voice came out firm and authoritative. "Don't you dare try anything. I—I can scream."

"No one will hear you here," Robert said softly. Then he turned the knife, not on me, but on Chris's unconscious form. "Now, watch closely, Anna. I'm going to get rid of Chris for you, just like you wanted."

"I never wanted that!"

"I'll save you. Then you and I can be together, just like you wanted."

I backed away, colliding with the solid basement wall. There was nowhere else to go. And Robert was still advancing on us, passing the knife from hand to hand, smiling easily. Like he was offering us candy instead of injury and pain.

Movement out of the corner of my eye, near the window. A flash of long, black hair. A face pressed against the window. I could've cried from relief.

Kathy. She'd found us.

I tore my gaze away from her and back to Robert, hoping he hadn't seen her. I had to stall for time. Keep talking about . . . something. Anything.

Robert's eyes were glittering with excitement as he fixed his gaze on Chris and me. Enjoyment knowing that he had us cornered.

"How many people besides me have you catfished on Friend Me?" I blurted out, desperate to keep Robert's attention away from the window.

Robert shrugged. "None. You're the only one I've actually wanted to meet with. There's just something about you that's very . . . exotic."

I wanted to puke. "So you decided you'd stalk me? Don't tell me you're one of those dudes with yellow fever?"

"Well, I certainly have a preference for Asian girls," Robert said unabashedly. "I don't like women of any other race, actually."

"So you have a fetish," I said in disgust.

"Some might call it a fetish. But I would say it's a preference. But especially after you brought up Melissa Hong—I knew I couldn't let you go." A shadow crossed Robert's face. Evidently my words had struck a nerve. He stroked the knife in his hand and took a deep breath, as though steeling himself to use it.

It was now or never. I flung off my ropes and kicked Robert in the crotch. He howled, stumbling backward. Jessica rushed at me, and I dove out of the way, toward Chris.

Then, before Robert or Jessica could recover, the basement echoed with the sound of feet crashing down the steps. A scream rang out. "GET AWAY FROM MY FRIENDS, FREAK!"

Robert and Jessica whirled around just in time to witness Kathy bursting in through the open door, wielding a baseball bat.

"You!" Robert accused, his tense shoulders going limp with shock for just a fraction of a second.

Jessica gasped, "Kathy, what are you—"

That tiny pause cost them both dearly. If Kathy was shocked by the sight of her friend Jessica, she didn't let it slow her for even an instant before swinging her bat into Jessica's gut.

I took advantage of the momentary chaos by lunging forward before Robert could slash at Kathy with his knife. I grabbed his right wrist and twisted it, forcing him to drop the weapon. When the knife clattered to the ground, I picked it up, quick as a flash, and drove it into Robert's left arm, then pulled it back out.

Robert howled in pain. Jessica had already crumbled to the floor. Kathy took advantage of the opening to bring her bat down on Robert's head. A nasty *crack*, and he was down. Robert crumpled to a heap on the floor. My hands trembled, and Robert's knife slipped out of my fingers onto the ground.

"Holy fuck." Kathy brushed a strand of sweaty black hair out of her eyes. "You guys all right? Oh my God—is Chris dead?"

"Robert knocked him out." I squatted next to Chris, checking his pulse, his breath. His eyes fluttered open, and I helped him sit up and untied his hands.

Kathy's concerned eyes swept over me, then at the bodies on the ground, and then at her own bat in shock, as though they couldn't believe what she'd done. She sank against the wall and closed her eyes. "Can you tell me what the fuck just happened here?"

Chapter Twenty-Four

THE CAMPUS POLICE ARRIVED WHILE Robert and Jessica were still down on the ground, out of commission. Only one officer came at first, but as soon as he glimpsed the scene, he went white-faced and called for backup.

Within minutes, a swarm of EMTs entered the basement, assessing Chris's head. They moved us all up out of the musty basement into the light, where officers stood before Chris, Kathy, and me, firing off question after question. When they had our statements, the campus police searched Robert's and Jessica's pockets. They found my phone and Chris's and returned them to us.

They took Robert and Jessica away separately. Chris, Kathy, and I were taken to the police station, where the city police officers questioned us about what had happened. Chris, who'd regained consciousness only an hour ago, sat through the whole thing with a groggy, stony expression on his face. Kathy was trembling worse than ever and, about three questions into the interrogation, buried her face in her hands, as if she were on the verge of breaking down.

We were all exhausted. It was midnight now, and all I wanted to do was be asleep in my bed.

"I'm Detective Scott," said one of the men, who showed us a badge with his name on it. "I know you're all shocked, but bear with me as best as you can, all right? Now—how did you end up in that basement?"

I explained everything from start to finish, from investigating Melissa Hong's murder case on my own, to befriending Jane on the Friend Me app, to Robert and Jessica's connection with the disbanded society called the Order of Alpha. When I finished, Detective Scott's eyebrows had risen so high they threatened to climb into his hairline, as though he were having trouble believing all of this.

"I'll be interrogating the suspects thoroughly," the detective reassured me. "If they're connected to all of these crimes— including the unsolved murder of Melissa Hong—they will be punished accordingly."

Just hearing those words was enough for me to let out a breath of relief. After seven long years, Melissa was about to get some justice at last. "Thank you."

Detective Scott finally broke his stony exterior, a sympathetic look crossing his face. "It's been a long and draining day for you three, hasn't it?" When we glanced at one another and then nodded, he reached into a basket beside his desk and pulled out a stack of business cards. "Trust me. It's been a long day for all of us." He rubbed his forehead and sighed. "First dealing with that hate crime culprit, then investigating another ethnic intimidation incident—"

"Another one?" Kathy whispered hollowly.

"—and now this." The detective shook his head and glanced from one wide-eyed student to the next, his eyes bloodshot. "I think the DA will want to talk to you about pressing charges. In this scenario, they'll likely be moving forward—though, of course, your wishes will be taken into account for the crimes against the three of you."

"I . . ." I gulped. My mind immediately flashed to Ma and Ba. They'd always wanted our family to keep a low profile, to never make any waves. Pressing charges against the people who'd attacked me was certainly the opposite of that. "Um . . . can I think about it?"

"In the state of Michigan, the prosecutor will have the final word on whether there's sufficient evidence to move forward with pressing charges," he explained. "It's not really up to you. I'm sorry. I'm going to take down your contact information, and then let the three of you go now, since I know you're tired. And I know the medics checked you over at the scene, but"—he looked at Chris—"you might want to follow up with a doc about that bump on your head." Detective Scott passed over three of his cards. "Be in touch if you think of any other relevant information."

⊷———⊶

The campus police must have contacted our parents about what happened, because my phone showed no less than eighteen missed calls from my parents. I texted Ma and Ba as soon as the police let us go back to our dorms, and then I finally went to sleep.

First thing the next morning, I went to the campus clinic, where my parents met me, looking frazzled and fearful.

I cracked a small smile. "Hi. I'm alive."

Ma immediately began sobbing, and Ba clasped my hand into his, as if making sure I was real.

"Oh, Anna," my mother sobbed. "The nurse told us you were kidnapped and attacked by a horrible man." She sniffed, dabbing at her eyes with the sleeves of her uniform. "Are you okay?"

I'd been trying not to recall what had happened, but at Ma's words, the blurry memories returned to me. One hundred four Madison Street. A darkening sky. Being knocked out, and then waking up in that disgusting frat house. And "Jane," aka Robert, revealing the extent of his stalking, manipulating Laura and Jessica to spread terror around campus.

I mentally paused before I could explore that particular memory further.

Ba grabbed hold of my other hand in a tight, viselike grip. "How did you get involved in this? How?"

"Ow. Ba, you're crushing me."

"I hope you see sense now. You need to get off of campus immediately," Ba said solemnly, frowning and causing the wrinkles lining his cheek to deepen. "Come home. Brookings is not safe."

"No. I'm not leaving."

Mom's eyes widened in confusion. "You could have been killed! How can you say—?"

"You're right. This campus isn't safe, and that's exactly why I need to stay."

"Anna, you are not making sense," Ba growled.

"No, Ba." My thoughts made more sense than they ever had in my entire life. Finally I was thinking clearly. Had a purpose. "If I drop out, it means the racists win." I had no idea what I was saying, but somehow the words tumbling out of my mouth were convincing even me that I was doing what I was meant to do. "As long as we don't fight back and defend ourselves, it'll never be safe. Remember what happened to Melissa Hong?" I looked at my parents pleadingly, from stricken face to stricken face. "She was killed for no reason at all."

My parents exchanged looks, the expressions on their faces torn. Ba was the one to break the extended, heavy silence with a long-suffering sigh. "What happened to Melissa was terrible."

"Yeah, and something similar might happen to other Asian girls on campus. Something similar almost happened to *me*. But the problem won't go away even if I leave Brookings. If I leave now, it just means the racists win. I have to stay. I promise I'll be more careful from now on, but I need to stay."

Ma shook her head. "All right, Anna. You're an adult now, and your Ba and I can't make you do anything you don't want to. Just make sure you check in with us more often."

"I promise."

"And be careful. No more wandering around campus at night on your own," Ma scolded.

"That was only this once. And I won't do anything like that." I had no intention. This experience would haunt me for a long time.

The clinic doctor entered the room then. "No major injuries, but Anna will need plenty of rest and recovery for the time being," the doctor told my parents. Then she turned to me with a warning look. "I'll expect you back next week for a check-in."

I nodded. "What about Chris and Kathy?"

"Your friends? They're shaken, too, but physically fine. You can see them in a few minutes."

Hearing those words, I could finally relax a little. My parents wanted to go back to West Tower with me, but I knew they'd already taken too much time off from work to look after me. I managed to shake them off with the one excuse that had always worked out in my favor—homework.

"You're sure you will be okay?" Ma asked, pulling a handkerchief from her back pocket and wiping her perpetually tearstained cheeks with it. I nodded. She flung her arms around me and kissed me on the cheek.

"Ow! Mom, I'm a college student already."

"To me, you are always my bǎobèi." Ma stepped away and examined me, a small, watery smile on her face. "You've grown so much, Anna."

"It's literally been three months."

"Still, you seem taller."

"You probably shrunk."

Ma frowned. "I was going to say more mature, too, but maybe not."

I smiled. "I'm just kidding."

Ba's farewell was much less affectionate, for which I was grateful. He stood there awkwardly, arms pressed to his sides, as if he wasn't quite sure what to do with them. "Stay out of trouble," he warned. "And no boys. Okay?"

"Where did that come from?" I spluttered. Did they think there was something between Chris and me? No, there was no way my parents could suspect that. I mean, there was nothing there to suspect. "You don't have to worry about that."

After reminding me that we'd see each other at Sweetea's reopening tomorrow, my parents left to head down the street. I stood at the edge of the Quad and watched them go. I wanted nothing more than to go to West Tower and take the longest nap of the century.

⊷———⊶

When I returned, the dorm was as I'd left it. Quiet and peaceful, filled with only the sound of pages turning in textbooks and the occasional student emerging from studying to do their laundry. It would be easy to believe that nothing had changed in the past twenty-four hours. For me, though, everything had changed.

Elise was pacing outside of my room. As soon as she caught sight of me, the RA let out a sigh of relief, and her cheeks flooded with color. Clearly she'd been waiting for me.

"Oh, hey," I said.

"Anna!" Elise hurried over to me and hugged me. "I heard everything. I—God, I'm so sorry about what that grad student did to you. How are you feeling? Better? Do you need anything?"

My head spun at the speed of Elise's questions. "I'm fine."

A guilty expression crossed Elise's face as she pulled back from me. "Look, I—I can't apologize enough."

"Apologize? What for?"

Her voice cracked, and her lower lip trembled. It was clear that Elise was barely holding back her tears. "I'm your RA. And I'm supposed to be looking out for all my residents, including you. I failed to protect you. I don't even deserve to be an RA anymore."

"Elise, it's okay," I reassured her. I was exhausted and didn't want to hold a grudge against her. Just the idea of that drained my energy. "It's not your fault. I went after this guy on my own."

Elise swallowed hard, blinking rapidly. "I wish you'd told me you were in danger. I could've gone with you as backup, or something."

"You probably would've ended up as another victim. Seriously, it's okay. I don't blame you." I patted my RA on the back awkwardly.

Elise wiped at her eyes and nodded. "What you did was very brave, Anna."

Brave? I didn't feel brave at all. On the contrary, I felt like the only one foolish enough to go after someone like Robert, someone who'd clearly been stalking me from the get-go, all because I'd given away too much personal information to a stranger on an app. Not that that justified any of Robert's crimes, but I wished more than anything that I hadn't been so trusting of strangers on Friend Me.

We were interrupted by the sound of my phone vibrating in my pocket. It was the perfect excuse to dip back into my room. Not that I had anything against Elise, but I really didn't want to be mothered by her—or anyone—right now.

"Gotta take this call," I said, raising my phone as I backed into my room.

"Let me know if you need anything!"

I waved, and then shut the door. A string of text notifications lit up my phone screen.

> *Chris:* Just got back to my room, you guys ok?
> *Kathy:* Yeah I'm in the dining hall
> *Chris:* Can I join you?
> *Kathy:* Ofc. We have a lot to talk about anyway lol
> *Chris:* Yeeee
> *Kathy:* Ok I'm behind the salad bar, at a table that's furthest in the back. Working on my hw rn and wanted to get away from everyone lmao
> *Anna:* I just got back too!! I'll come find you guys

I stuffed my backpack with textbooks, even though I had a feeling we wouldn't get studying done. Then I headed for the dining hall. Chris and Kathy occupied a table in the way back, like Kathy had said over text. I swiped my card to get in and immediately beelined for the pizza station. When I'd grabbed a slice of pepperoni pizza, I headed toward my friends and was relieved to see they appeared to be physically fine for the most part. Chris was sporting a bruise over his left eye and a cut lip, but Kathy wasn't showing any injuries.

"So," I said. "Um, how're you both holding up?"

"I just can't believe that happened." Kathy shook her head. "Like, it feels like it was all one big group nightmare."

"Tell me about it," Chris muttered as he dug into his ramen. "I heard Robert and Jessica are still being held at the police station," he added after some time had passed. "Apparently they're refusing to speak. Guess they're going to stay silent until they get some lawyers."

"Are you going to press charges, Anna?" Kathy stared at me, wide-eyed.

"I . . . I don't know yet. But it might not even be up to us," I said. "The prosecutor decides that."

"If it came down to it, though, would you be able to testify against Robert and his accomplices?"

I closed my eyes. The images I'd been trying to suppress swam before my eyes. That dank, dark basement. That brutal, almost inhuman way that Robert had gazed at me, not as a fellow human being, but as a piece of flesh. A shiver of horror ran down my spine. I knew it would be a long, long time for me to shake off the paralyzing memory of being in that basement—if I ever did.

"I don't know," I whispered.

Even if I did testify, even if Robert did get locked up, it wouldn't be enough. He'd been behind Melissa's murder, and he'd been behind some of the hate crimes, and he'd targeted me.

But there were so many other perpetrators on campus who'd gone unpunished. So many people who agreed with Robert's hateful stance. And the legal system couldn't even figure out all of their identities, much less throw them all in prison.

"The scariest part is that . . . I mean, Jessica was one of his accomplices. And we, like, were in the same classes as her," Kathy said. "We hung out with her sometimes. She was my friend, I thought. I—I let her into my *room* before." She closed her eyes and shuddered.

"And Laura, too," I added. "She was my freaking roommate."

Even if we hadn't exactly been best friends, Laura had been part of the West Tower honors program residents. She had eaten countless meals in the same dining hall as us, had partaken in the same Welcome Week activities. I'd shared a room with her for most of the semester. But all along, she hadn't had a problem helping Robert target me. She'd seen me—seen people who looked like me—as beneath her, as less than human.

That was the most sickening, hopeless feeling of all.

"So Sweetea's and Sunny's Bakery are having that joint grand reopening tomorrow," I said, changing the subject. "Kathy, you're going, right?"

Kathy nodded, though her eyes still had a faraway look to them that told me she, like I, had also been recounting what had happened at the abandoned Sigma Chi frat house, the memories looping over and over again like some kind of broken horror film.

"I hope the grand reopening goes well," Chris mumbled.

"It'd be a good way to show the racists that we aren't taking their BS."

I looked up into Chris's sad but determined eyes, wanting more than anything for Sunny's Bakery to come back bigger and better than before to restore some of the hope we'd been rapidly losing all semester.

"I—I can't sleep," Kathy blurted out in a squeaky voice. "I did for an hour in the morning, and then I had a nightmare that you both were back at Sigma Chi, but I didn't get to you guys in time. I really was almost late. It took me a little while longer than Robert because I was on foot. I—I'm sorry I didn't get there sooner." She burst into tears. I didn't know what to say, so I just put my arm around her. Chris followed suit.

"You did good, Kathy. If you hadn't come . . ." I shuddered.

"Yeah, you saved our lives," Chris said.

"I just hope we see real consequences," I said grimly. "I hope Robert and the others don't get away with this. You know how rich white people get away with anything." I bit into my pizza.

"They wouldn't just let him go like that," Chris said, though he didn't sound too convinced himself. "Would they?"

Kathy's mouth opened and closed. She leaned back in her chair and sighed. Then she reached for her white backpack, which had fallen to the floor. "Let's hope the police do the right thing."

A gloomy silence descended upon us.

"Well, no use moping around." Chris stood up, though his pizza was untouched. "I'm going to go back and shower."

I suddenly itched to shower, too. Had to get rid of all the creepy kidnapper germs on me.

"I've got to get to a calc study group," said Kathy miserably, pushing her plate aside with a queasy look on her face.

"You're going to a study group? Now?" I asked incredulously.

"Yeah, I don't exactly feel like it, but I promised I'd be there, so . . ."

"Just cancel," said Chris.

"It's okay. It'll get my mind off things." With a wave, she got up and dumped her pizza into the trash can. I watched her place her empty plate into the plate dispenser, and then she sped out of the dining hall.

Suddenly I was aware of the fact that Chris and I were alone for the first time since we'd been in the Sigma Chi basement. The silence between us was determined to suffocate me. I didn't know what exactly I felt toward him—or at least, I hadn't dared to name it yet—but I knew it wasn't the rivalry that I'd once felt. And holding eye contact with him now was like gazing directly into the sun.

"Um, I'm gonna go take a nap," I blurted out. "I'm still tired . . . and . . . yeah." Heat spread across my cheeks. Good job acting totally normal, Anna.

"Yeah, I'm pretty beat, too," said Chris. Thankfully he was as oblivious as ever.

We left the dining hall, and as Chris struck up a conversation about our latest reading for Sources of East Asian Civilizations, I tried not to focus on the fuzzy feeling in my chest from being around him.

"See you tomorrow for the grand reopening?" Chris said, pausing in front of his room.

"Yeah, I'll see you."

I went to bed with a small smile on my face and finally managed to fall asleep quickly.

Chapter Twenty-Five

THE NEXT DAY DAWNED WITH an email broadcasting Robert's and Jessica's arrests to the university. The email didn't name them, but given that the story was also broadcast over the news—which did name them—it wasn't hard to put the pieces together.

Swirls of fog and splashes of rain marked the outside world, reflecting my subdued outlook on life. Though the whole ordeal was over, whenever I closed my eyes, I could still picture Robert's sneering face. I could hear his threats, looping over and over in my head. In my empty room, I thought it was all too easy to spiral into a dark place.

So I was glad when Chris knocked on my door, even though it was at the ungodly hour of eight a.m. He was wearing a light blue dress shirt and running his fingers hastily through his hair. It was useless. There was just no way to tame that perpetual bedhead of his.

"Yo," he said. "You sleep at all last night?"

I shook my head.

"Me neither." There were dark circles under Chris's eyes that made him look about five years older. I didn't think I looked any better. All I really wanted to do was sleep in. The semester was winding down, but I couldn't let my guard down. I wanted to finish strong.

"All right, let's head over to the reopening," I said, suppressing a yawn. "I need carbs to fuel my studying later."

Chris and I met Kathy at the entrance of West Tower, and we walked over to State Street together. The student government even sent out an email about it on the morning of, urging the community to come out in support of Sunny's Bakery and Sweetea. By the time Chris, Kathy, and I arrived, I was astonished to see that a huge line was snaking from the doors and all the way down State Street.

"It's not even nine yet," Chris said, awestruck.

Kathy grabbed his arm and jumped up and down. "This is amazing!"

A huge grin stretched across my cheeks. *Thank God*, I thought. *Thank God people showed up to our joint reopening.* It was the first bit of happy news in what felt like ages.

We managed to shove our way inside Sweetea, where Ma and Ba were inside already. After checking in on them, we quickly headed over to Sunny's Bakery. Chris's parents were rushing around making last-minute preparations.

"We have customers!" Mr. Lu said excitedly. Beside him Mrs. Lu was wiping away tears on her flowered handkerchief.

As soon as it hit ten o'clock, customers who wanted goods from Sunny's Bakery and Sweetea swarmed the street. Though we offered to stay and help, Chris's and my parents shooed us off, telling us that it was much more important for us to be studying properly than being at the reopening.

"Typical parents," I said, snagging a red bean bun before leaving.

•⫶⸺⫶•

I spent the afternoon in the Thatcher Graduate Library going over my notes for Great Books and Astronomy 102, preparing for the two exams I had this week. By the time I was finished, my brain was thoroughly fried, and evening had fallen outside. My parents' reminders rang in my ears, and I packed up and rushed to get back to my dorm before it got dark.

Back at West Tower, to celebrate Sunny's Bakery's grand reopening, Elise and Patrick had bought a strawberry cake for all the residents down in the lounge. Or at least, they tried to. Apparently someone had dropped the strawberry cake on the way over, and though it was still edible, now it was more like strawberry crumble.

"Congrats to Chris for Sunny's Bakery's reopening!" Patrick shouted as soon as Chris walked into the lounge.

Chris turned beet red. "Oh, I didn't really do anything."

"Nonsense. You get the first slice of cake." Elise shoved a slice of pink cake at Chris, who obediently took it and sat down at the table, still blushing.

As the residents dug into the cake, I tried to ignore how the girls were swarming over Chris. They were just about tripping over themselves to fawn over him. I tried to convince myself that the sinking feeling in the pit of my stomach was due to eating too much sugar, though I had an inkling that wasn't really it.

"Has Chris always been this popular?" I muttered to Kathy.

"Of course. Now he's even more popular. Kind of a tragic figure who's finally getting a happy ending, that sort of thing."

"I'm a tragic figure, too." I bit into my cake with a vengeance. "Where's my fan club?"

A couple of times, I caught Chris's eye from the other end of the room, and he started in my direction, as if trying to come over to talk to me. But inevitably some girl would cut into his path and start babbling his ear off. Whatever.

One of the guys in Great Books class—Brent, if I remembered his name correctly—came up to me. I saw him coming out of the corner of my eye and tried to turn away, but he was too fast, and appeared at my shoulder.

"Hey, Anna. You enjoying the food?"

"Yeah, it's pretty—"

"The cake is too sweet for my taste," Brent interrupted. "Anyway, are you all caught up on our reading for Great Books?"

The last thing I wanted to do was talk about our homework, but I didn't know how to politely get away, so I played along for a bit. All I needed to do was nod and throw in a "oh, cool" or "how fascinating" every now and then when Brent paused.

"I don't feel like our professor really appreciated *The Iliad* to the lengths that I do," Brent was saying. He was attempting pretty obviously to impress me, without realizing that I was not at all taken by pretentious schoolboys whose personalities revolved around fawning over the classics. "I mean, in my research at Yale's accelerated high school program, I wrote my thesis on—"

"Hey, Anna. Mind if I have a word outside?"

Chris had inserted himself into the conversation, which Brent looked none too thrilled about. It reminded me of how he'd rescued me from that gross frat guy at Theta Pi what felt like eons ago.

"Sure," I said, glad to get away. I shoved the last bit of my cake into my mouth. "Let's walk. I'll see you around, Brent." I was only too eager to get away from him.

I followed Chris through the crowd. In silence, we walked out into the hall, and then outside West Tower. Chris's presence by my side was solid and reassuring.

"Thanks for helping me get rid of Brent back there," I said.

"You rescue me, I rescue you," he replied.

Fair enough.

It was an abnormally nice evening, the temperature not too hot and not too cold, and likely one of the last nice nights of the year. Chris and I made our way down the street, heading away from campus, toward the most woodsy side of Brookings. We turned onto a bike trail, entering a scenic route that went into the arboretum. The road meandered down to a serene nature spot along the river, where a lot of students went tubing in the summer. Now it was practically empty, though there was a small group of students strolling along the river in the opposite direction.

It was almost dark out now, the shadows creeping over the

garden in front of the small park. There were still a few joggers out, though. Everyone was taking advantage of the unexpectedly nice weather, even though it was growing chillier now that the sun had disappeared.

"This is where they found her," Chris said, breaking the silence. He was looking across the river, as though trying to see something on the opposite shore.

"Found who?" I asked, even though a second later I knew exactly who he was talking about.

"I read those articles, too, you know. I wasn't as gung ho as you were about solving the case of her murder, but I'd often find myself wondering about her."

I shivered against a chill. "Melissa Hong." Her name left my lips and traveled along the wind, into the trees themselves. If there were such a thing as ghosts hanging around this campus, I'd hope that the ghost of Melissa would finally be able to rest.

Chris stuffed his hands further into his jacket pockets and turned to me. "It's thanks to you that Melissa's family finally gets some peace."

"Oh, I . . . ," I murmured, my cheeks warming. "But you helped, too."

"I know," Chris said loftily. "But you're the one who's been hung up on Melissa's case all this time."

"I've kind of always had an unhealthy obsession with true crime, and I guess especially when it's connected to someone I knew." Clearing my throat, I was struck with the sudden urge to change the subject. Receiving compliments had never been my forte. Plus, being alone with Chris was giving me strange butterflies that I was doing my best to ignore. "Should we head back now?" Even though Chris was with me, I was getting nervous about the dark.

"Hold on. There's just one thing I want you to see," Chris said. "It's this little dock right off the river. I always go there when I feel like I need to get away from everything. Keeps me calm, you know?"

I nodded. "Yeah. I could definitely use some time away from everything." It was probably the understatement of the year.

Chris and I traipsed through the foot trail, dried leaves crunching under our feet. We were surrounded by trees and heading toward the river.

"Not much further in now," Chris reassured me. He pushed past a couple of low-hanging branches. "The view is worth it. I promise."

We emerged from the last patch of woods and stumbled into a clearing with a small dock overlooking clear blue waters. The waves lapped gently at the shore, but other than that and a bit of wind, there was no other movement in sight. The moonlight glinted off the water.

"Beautiful, isn't it?" Chris had closed his eyes. He took a deep breath, exhaling slowly, before letting his eyelids flutter open. "There should be more places like this in the world."

"Too bad humanity is a force of ugly destruction."

He choked, and then gave me an appreciative look.

I had a feeling that Chris was building up to something, but he sure was taking his sweet time. Maybe he needed some encouragement. I stepped closer to him, making sure to keep my eyes glued to his. "What did you want to talk about?" I asked quietly.

"Um . . ." His face was turning pink, and he broke our stare first. His gaze turned out toward the water, taking on a faraway look. "I know we haven't gotten along the best in the past."

"That was years ago. I think we've been through enough now to forget that," I said.

Chris grinned. "Yeah, probably. Anyway . . . well, you know, I've been thinking . . . you . . . um . . ."

I couldn't wait for him to spit it out, whatever it was that he meant to say. If I did, I had a feeling we'd be here forever, and I was ready to head back, since it was getting chilly. "Chris," I said.

"What?"

Impatiently, I grabbed his shirt and stared into his eyes, which were wide with surprise. Then I gave in to the feeling that had been slowly consuming me for weeks, answering the butterflies in my stomach. I pressed my lips to his.

It was electrifying. The feeling of his soft lips on mine. Feeling like I was finally realizing what had been building up inside me ever since we'd locked gazes at the Theta Pi party all those weeks ago.

Chris's lips froze beneath mine for a second, his breath hitching in surprise. Then his mouth molded to mine, his lips pressing against my lips, softly at first, then more firmly, urgently. He brought his hand around the back of my head and cupped it gently, and I brought my arms up to his neck, pulling closer.

After what felt like seconds and decades at the same time, we finally broke apart.

"Wow," Chris said.

I rolled my eyes. "Why did you really bring me all the way out here, Chris? I know it wasn't just to see this spot. It's dark anyway, you doofus."

He laughed as embarrassment colored his cheeks and his mouth spread in a smile. "I—okay, I wanted to tell you—properly—that—that I like you."

"I like you too."

Chris grinned at me, his perfectly imperfect, crooked little grin sending my heart into more palpitations. If I lived to see sophomore year without getting a heart attack, it'd be a miracle. "When did you start liking me?"

"When did you start liking me?"

"I asked you first."

"I take it back," I said, rolling my eyes. "I don't like you."

"Damn, you're cold."

We argued the rest of the way out of the woods and back to West Tower. But the whole time, as his hand held mine, I couldn't keep a smile off my face. Finally, it seemed, something was going right.

Chapter Twenty-Six

"YOU'RE SURE YOU'LL BE OKAY handling the catering for the student event today?"

"Ba," I sighed, trying not to let my father's super protective mode get on my nerves, "I've told you, I feel fine."

I'd come by to help deliver the Sweetea catering to campus for an interorg fundraiser dance event called Dancerush to be held in the Rickman Auditorium later that day. I was sweeping the floor, while Ba was refilling the napkins. "Okay. I just—I worry you're growing up too fast, Anna."

"I have to grow up some time, don't I?"

Ba sighed. "I guess you do. But please, let your mother and me help you when we can. Okay?"

I grinned. "Deal. I'll need help carrying all the food over, after all."

My father and I carefully brought the trays of food to the back of our family van. We were halfway to the Quad when my phone vibrated with an incoming phone call.

"Hello?" I asked, hating the slight nervous tremor in my

voice. It was Chris. Just Chris. Chris who was now my boyfriend, Chris who made the butterflies in my stomach flutter.
We'd only been dating for a few days, and the newness of it all
was still fresh and exciting. When I was in high school, my parents had forbidden me to date—not that I'd been interested in
anyone at my school, anyway—so this was my first real relationship. And I had absolutely no clue what I was doing.

"Hey." I heard a suppressed yawn on the other end.

"Did you just wake up?"

"It's Saturday," Chris mumbled.

"Lazy."

"Whatever. You wanna get breakfast?"

"I'm delivering the catering for Dancerush," I said. "I can
meet you as soon as I drop off the food, though."

"Cool. That gives me time to sleep."

I rolled my eyes. "I won't be that slow. I'll see you soon."

"Who was that you were talking to?" Ba asked after I'd hung
up. We pulled up to the side of the street, where the huge, color-
ful Dancerush sign was visible even from here. A huge sound
system was set up on the stage, and some of the organizers had
put up tables along the side.

"Just a friend," I said as casually as possible. No way could I
drop the boyfriend news on my overprotective father just yet,
especially given that Sweetea still had a friendly rivalry going on
with Sunny's Bakery. Chris had suffered enough lately.

I couldn't tell if my father believed me or not, but he didn't
press the issue, which was good enough for me.

At breakfast, Chris gave me the rundown of updates with

Robert and Jessica. After days of insisting he'd had nothing to do with Sunny's Bakery, Robert had finally confessed that he'd vandalized the property as a twisted way of trying to get more business to Sweetea. Jessica had confessed too, telling authorities that she and Laura had both been accomplices—contradicting Robert's claim that Jessica had been a coconspirator. They'd turned on each other, just like that. Then Robert had cracked under further investigation and revealed that he was the one who'd killed Melissa Hong—an accident, he'd claimed—seven years ago.

"Guess Robert thought the evidence was stacked against him?" I mused, picking at my pancakes.

"Maybe. It was only a matter of time given the evidence they found at his apartment. They found the hair of other Asian girls, stolen women's clothing, and pictures of what the police thought to be potential victims."

"God, that's disgusting. Did he really think he'd get away with all this?" I shuddered and suddenly realized that the missing sweater I'd never found was probably among the undergarments at Robert's apartment. Though being stalked had easily been the most frightening and traumatic experience of my life, there was one thing I was glad about—that it had ended with me, and no other Asian girls had to face what I had at Robert's hands.

"Robert probably did think he'd get away with it, just like how he avoided being caught for Melissa's murder for seven years. He's got the makings of a serial killer. On the news, it said that Robert was proud of what he did. He doesn't seem to regret it at all." A dark look crossed Chris's face. "People like that need to be locked up."

It was somewhat comforting to know that justice had been served. But I knew there were so many other instances where it wasn't.

"Let's not talk about this anymore," Chris said abruptly. "We're going to Dancerush. It'll be fun."

"Yeah. And I hear the food is amazing," I added. "It's from this great place called Sweetea."

Chris snorted. "Guess we'll have to find out for ourselves."

After breakfast, we headed back to West Tower and did our civic duty by harassing everyone on our floor to come out to the event. Almost every single one of my floor mates tagged along, led by Patrick and Elise.

We formed a sizable group the size of a small parade as we made our way across campus. At the Rickman Auditorium, the incredible sight of performers and audience members mingling everywhere greeted us.

There was no other way to put it. Dancerush was, well, a rush. Even in my listless state, I couldn't help but feel awestruck, overwhelmed, by the sheer number of attendees and performers.

Kathy came to meet us, a huge smile on her face. "Hey, you lovebirds," she said.

"Don't be gross," I groaned.

"Are you calling me gross?" Chris asked, pretending to be affronted.

"I am. What are you gonna do about it?"

Kathy laughed. "Glad to see that some things never change."

According to the paper programs we were handed, Dance-rush was the first time the university's dance teams had ever come together for a fundraiser in one single performance, and we soon figured out why. The event was a logistical nightmare. All the performing dance groups were called onstage to do a sound check, and it was chaos. Pure chaos. The event was so overwhelming that I almost managed to forget about the horrors of reality. Almost.

Every so often I noticed that people were stealing glances at my friends and me. They'd all heard the story by now.

"How many dance teams are part of this again?" Chris wondered, turning around to survey the scene before him, as if confirming that this was actually happening.

"Every single one on campus," Kathy said.

I shook my head. "Jesus, I knew our school was big, but this is huge."

Groups that I vaguely remembered seeing at Festifall were standing around in clusters. The Chinese Student Association's dance team were huddled in their red-and-gold gear as a unit. There was a Latinx-interest dance team, and there were also groups focused on ballet, hip-hop, and tap dancing. There was a team of girls in pink who had already strapped on their tap shoes, clicking their heels madly on the pavement. A Bollywood dance team was blasting Hindi music, the team members making up dance moves to go along to the beat. Right beside us was a group from Dance Sensasians, the university's Asian-interest dance team. A couple of the dancers closest to us were speaking excitedly in rapid-fire Japanese.

"Don't get so caught up in gawking at everyone else that you forget about the food," I said. "Speaking of—I gotta go help." Ba was alone at the food table, and I suddenly felt bad about leaving him on his own to meet my friends. "Save a spot for me inside, okay?"

Chris and Kathy left to go inside the auditorium. I headed over to Ba, but there wasn't much more to do besides make sure the food was properly on display and hand the customers their food when they came up for it. I spent half an hour manning the table, but then the crowd of hungry people thinned as everyone went inside to watch Dancerush.

"I can handle the rest. Go enjoy the show with your friends," Ba said, waving off my protests.

By the time I finally headed into the auditorium, sound check had ended for the dance groups. They were already running thirty minutes behind schedule.

Hundreds, maybe even thousands, of students sat in the auditorium, packed like sardines, almost every seat taken up. The only time I'd ever seen any area on campus so packed was during a football Saturday. Maybe the dining hall when they served up the ice cream sundae bar.

There was hardly room to maneuver through the crowd, and it took nearly a full ten minutes for me to push my way to the middle of the auditorium, where Chris and Kathy were sitting. I squeezed into the seat between them.

"I can't believe the turnout," I said, craning my neck to glance around the place. I'd never seen so many college students in one place.

"Should I join a dance team? Maybe I'll be popular then," Kathy joked.

A girl with short brown hair and dramatic winged eyeliner stepped up to the stage with the microphone to introduce the show. "Hi, everyone! Thanks for coming out tonight. I'm Michelle from Dance 'n' Beats."

"We love you, Michelle!" a girl screamed from the front row.

"Before we begin the first ever Dancerush, I wanted to take a moment to acknowledge some important folks, without whom this event would not have been possible." Michelle went off to list a bunch of official-sounding university departments and sponsors. When she mentioned Sweetea, Chris and Kathy both elbowed me, grinning. Pride swelled within me. When she was done, the girl tucked away the piece of paper from which she'd been reading. "I can see the incredible amount of love out there. Tonight we're going to show you just how much love the Brookings community has. All proceeds will be donated to Black Lives Matter, the Asian Student Union, and any other social justice organizations that you guys feel would be deserving." A thunderous round of applause nearly drowned out Michelle's voice so that she had to shout into the microphone. "With that, let's hear it for the first group of the night—Michigan Mirchi!"

The Bollywood dance team filed onto the stage to tumultuous applause. The girls were dressed in green-and-gold sari, the guys in matching gold-and-green outfits. A Bollywood song began blasting from the speakers set on opposite ends of the stage, and then the team launched into their dance. Spinning. Twirling. Having the time of their lives. As if they didn't have a care in the world, and the only thing that mattered was dancing.

Next up was Boys in Black, a group of guys who dressed as American B-boy as you could get. After that, a girl group took the stage. Then the group I'd wanted to see most—the Dance Sensasians.

Kathy was apparently friends with just about all the members thanks to her connections as Asian Student Union freshman rep. She screamed out their names as they took the stage. They danced to a K-pop song, BTS's "Not Today," and really got the crowd going. The song was so upbeat. It was angry. Defiant.

If the huge round of applause Dance Sensasians received at the end was any indication, the message of their dance got through to the crowd. Sweating, exhausted, but thoroughly exhilarated, the Dance Sensasians stood in a line, placed their arms around each other, and took a bow. Then they exited to thunderous applause and shouts for an encore.

"Anna, are you crying?" Kathy asked.

Startled by the question, I brushed my hand against my eyes—and was shocked to feel the wetness of tears. I sniffed and clung to my last shred of dignity by rapidly wiping them away. "I—I guess I was just . . . overwhelmed."

Kathy squealed and pinched my cheek.

"Ow!"

"Oh, you are so cute, I just can't. Chris, you'd better take good care of her."

"What, I—" Chris spluttered. I looked up to see his face turning bright red.

Then I started laughing through the tears. These tears, I knew, weren't just for the incredible feeling of accomplishment from hearing Sweetea acknowledged. They were also tears for this dance. For everyone coming together after a difficult semester, raising money toward causes that mattered.

At the end of the show, every dancer squeezed onstage to take final bows together. Dance groups got mixed up. People of all different shapes, sizes. Races, genders, sexualities. The audience stood up to give them all a standing ovation.

Chaos ensued as everyone trampled one another in their haste to get offstage. I was practically knocked over as people pushed and shoved around me, but Chris caught me and kept me steady.

"Are you okay?" Chris asked, his eyes searching mine frantically, his face etched with concern. I got the feeling he wasn't just talking about me being shoved.

I swallowed. "Not yet," I admitted, tears threatening to sting the backs of my eyes. "But—I think I will be. Eventually."

Chris's expression turned tender. He took my hand, pulled me in close, and pressed his lips to mine in a quick, gentle kiss. His lips felt like clouds.

We pulled away after less than probably five seconds, remembering that Kathy was right next to us. Sure enough, when I turned around, she quickly pretended to be looking at her phone.

"C'mon," I said, trying to cover my embarrassment. "Let's get out of here."

"Yeah," Chris agreed. His fingers curled tighter around

mine, and together, we were swept along with the crowd out of the auditorium.

Leaving the swarm of rowdy, cheerful dancers and audience members, we headed back to West Tower. Pretty soon—maybe even in a matter of hours—the rush of the event would leave us, and we'd have to worry about watching our backs, about protecting ourselves. But until then, we could celebrate these small moments of peace.

Kathy went to grab food with some of her other friends. Chris and I stopped in front of my room, our hands still entwined. I let go first, giving Chris a small smile. "I've got some stuff to take care of first, but wanna meet up for dinner in an hour?"

"Sounds perfect."

After organizing my desk as best as I could, I went down to the mail room to check my mail for the first time in weeks. On top of the pile of random ads, coupons, and misaddressed envelopes was a letter. An old-fashioned, handwritten one.

My heart thudded when I read the name on the envelope. The sender was Laura Dale.

Epilogue

Dear Anna Xu,

I know you probably hate me, but please don't tear up this letter. Not yet, at least. Please read what I have to say first.

I know you won't forgive me, and I don't expect your forgiveness. But believe me when I say I'm sorry. I wish I could take it all back—every terrible, hateful act I committed.

But even Robert couldn't have managed to do everything on his own. I'm writing to warn you because I think the number of people involved in these hate crimes is greater than anyone could imagine—beyond even the descendants of the Order of Alpha. I suspect there are people who may have been helping Robert or acting independent of him who are still out there, and there's a chance they'll never be caught. So I urge you and everyone else to be careful.

—Laura

"Not today. Today we fight . . ."

I played the BTS song over and over. Ever since the Dance Sensasian's performance, I hadn't been able to get the catchy tune out of my head.

Exams were over. Without constant studying to occupy my mind, I'd had lots of time on my hands. Too much time. Time to remember being stalked and terrorized. Time to remember Robert advancing on me in the dark. Over and over the memories played in my head, despite how desperately I tried to push them back into the dark recesses of my mind.

Several times I'd woken from nightmares in which I was tied up and trapped inside that damp, cold basement again. I was shouting for help, but Kathy never came, and Chris and I ended up dead at Robert's hands.

When the thoughts got really dark, I'd text Chris, and he'd come over to my room. We held hands for hours and hours and hours, listening to music, often not speaking at all. We lay there together for what felt like decades and centuries and millennia until it seemed like we were the last two people on Earth.

Eventually, I showed Chris Laura's letter. "Do you think she's actually sorry about her involvement with the Order of Alpha?" I asked. "Or is that something a counselor made her write?"

Chris gave the letter a long, hard look before handing it back to me. He closed his eyes. "Honestly, it's hard to say. But

I don't want to trust her. Not until her words are backed up by actions."

Strange as it might've sounded, I thought maybe, just maybe, Laura was sincere. The girl had gotten at least one thing right: we couldn't let down our guards. Robert and Jessica had been arrested, and Laura had been expelled, but they were just three amid a sea of nameless racists. The fact that the hate crimes had slowed for now didn't mean the true culprit was caught. That the hatred was gone.

We were telling lies, even to ourselves, if we said otherwise.

But there was still hope, no matter how tiny it seemed. There was still love. And that was something I needed to fight for.

"You ready for this university hearing?" Chris asked softly. He took my hand and squeezed it in his. He was looking handsome in a light blue button-down and black slacks. I was wearing a blue sweater dress with black tights. We were dressed in accordance with the business casual dress code that had been outlined in the email I'd received a week ago in advance of the hearing.

I squeezed his hand back, taking a deep breath. The nightmares hadn't stopped for me, and I didn't think they would even if the criminals were brought to justice. But I needed to attend this university hearing to testify against Robert and Jessica. I needed to do this much to stand up for myself, to stand up for all the Melissa Hongs who no longer could. "Let's go."

Together we stepped out of the room and headed down the hall toward the elevator.

One person couldn't fight centuries of hatred on their own. For a harmonious Brookings—a harmonious world—we had to work together to fight against the hate. None of us could win alone.

Now it was up to all of us to carry on the fight. A fight that had lasted hundreds of years and would last for many years more. We couldn't let the hate win.

Not today. Today we raise our voices, and we fight.

AUTHOR'S NOTE

It is an uncomfortable, frightening, and heartbreaking experience to be an Asian woman living in New York City at this moment in time—March 2022. Perhaps some of you have noticed the rise in hate crimes targeting Asians, especially the elderly and women, in the past two years. Perhaps, for the first time in the COVID era, it has been brought to your awareness that there is violence against Asian American women—and perhaps you believe this to be a new development. But this violence targeting Asian American women has festered for decades. Cruelly. Relentlessly. Asian American women are speaking up now because we have had enough.

I first drafted *The Lies We Tell* back in 2016, before public outcry against anti-Asian hate crimes became widespread. Back then, I was just a kid in college without the right vocabulary or knowledge to express this nagging fear that grew stronger with the establishment of a certain administration. Even then, I understood instinctively that people like me could never feel safe in this country—so long as the deep-rooted systems of misogyny and racism went unchallenged.

Today, I still remember it vividly. November 2016, fall in the air. A sleepless night broken by devastating news. The terrible dread felt by the women of color in my college dorm, the *moment* we knew which man had been elected into power. A man whose platform incited racism, sexism, and xenophobia. Many of us cried upon registering the election result, myself included. We knew what this would mean for at least the next four years. We knew that the illusion of safety and equality in the US had been shattered. And with each year since, our worst fears were confirmed with rising cases of hate crimes, with Asian women speaking up more and more about the dangers we have faced in this supposedly safe and free country, simply for daring to exist.

I am not an expert in Asian American history, but I am an expert on being an Asian American woman who has either experienced or observed despicable treatment at the hands of others, thanks to racist and misogynistic perceptions of Asian women. From experiencing fetishization on dating apps, to being told to "go back to my country," to reading about Asian women like Yingying Zhang and Christina Yuna Lee whose brutal murders had racist undertones. At every turn, against my will, I am reminded, again and again and again, that I could so easily become the next headline. That all it takes is being in the wrong place at the wrong time, and I could be the next victim of a racially charged crime, mourned for a moment, and then forgotten.

I wrote *The Lies We Tell* in the hope that these Asian American women, like the fictional Melissa Hong in the book, at least do not die in vain. That we can keep their stories alive.

When I conceived of this story, I never imagined—or perhaps I never dared to *hope*—that it would ever be picked up by a major publisher. In 2016, even many of my Asian colleagues did not believe that there was much, if any, racism against us; and that the racism that did exist was practically harmless. Back then, I did not know how to challenge this notion that racism could be "harmless," but now I can, though I wish we did not have so much evidence to show how anti-Asian racism devastates our community. Still, it gives me hope that there is much more widespread acknowledgment of anti-Asian racism and the devastation inflicted upon the Asian community. Change can only come if we first acknowledge that there is a problem.

Now that my publisher has graciously given me the opportunity to publish *The Lies We Tell*, I hope that the message behind this story helps put into perspective what Asian women mean when we say we *truly are not safe*. I hope that in these pages, I was able to convey, for even the most privileged American, a shred of the paranoia and anxiety faced by the less privileged, when we see people who look like us headlining the newspapers in gruesome manners.

And to my fellow Asian American women, I leave you with this message—uplift one another, hold each other close, and know that though this country does its very damnedest to erase us, we have a voice, we have allies on our side, and we are not alone.

ACKNOWLEDGMENTS

Thank you so much to my agent, Penny Moore, for being the best partner on my writing journey. There is truly no other person whom I can imagine keeping up with my many ideas, my unreasonable speed, and my undying passion for telling all kinds of Asian American stories.

Thank you to my editor, Sarah Shumway Liu, for pushing me to the best of my storytelling capabilities. I appreciate all your editorial insights from the first to final draft of this book, and I think we have created a truly memorable story here.

Thank you to all the hardworking staff who have worked on *The Lies We Tell*. To Kei Nakatsuka, Oona Patrick, Adam Mongaya, Jeff Curry, John Candell, Donna Mark, Nicholas Church, Mike Young, Erica Barmash, Lily Yengle, Phoebe Dyer, Faye Bi, Alexa Higbee, Ariana Abad, and Beth Eller, my deepest gratitude for your support of this book.

To all my writer friends, you know who you are—thank you for being the most uplifting cheerleaders. Thank you for putting up with me when I'm on a publishing-induced emotional rollercoaster ride (which is too often for any of our liking, I know). Thank you for being my first readers and my first fans. Without you, this writing journey wouldn't be half as fun.

Thank you to my non-writer friends as well, who keep me grounded by reminding me that there's so much more to life than publishing.

Thank you to my dear readers, whether you have found me through this book, or my young adult debut *How We Fall Apart*, or any of my middle grade titles (which, I might add, are much more fun and uplifting than anything else I write!). It is always for you that I write, and so long as I have at least one willing reader, I will never stop telling stories.

Last but not least, thank you to my family. Everything I am today, I owe to you. For ensuring that I had the means to chase my dreams. For instilling in me the belief that I can achieve anything I set my mind to, which, obnoxiously, I never questioned for a moment. I am eternally grateful.